Content warnings for this book,
and other titles by Alison Rhymes,
can be found on her website alionrhymes.com.

BROKEN PLAY

ALISON RHYMES

Line Editor: Emily Lawrence
Copy Editor: Zainab M. at Heart Full of Reads Editing Services
Cover Design: Kris Hack
Formatting: Sunshine Tucker

This book is dedicated to all the
readers who believe in
second chances, redeemable heroes,
and love that endures it all.

CHAPTER 1
Drew

Any man who tells you great head isn't as good as sex, has never had great head. I love sex as much as any man, too much probably, all things considered. There is a certain power that comes with a blowjob, a feeling unlike anything else when a beautiful woman will debase herself, drop to her knees, staring up at you in worship, all while you choke her with your cock.

Not a very romantic outlook, but there you have it. Somewhere, I'm sure there's a feminist manifesto that will dispute all my bullshit and tell me that women are the ones who hold all the power in this position. They may be right. But try telling that to the silver eyes that are glazing over with lust and a touch of tears as I roughly grip her head, keeping it where I want it.

The wet warmth encompassing me as I ease myself forward is one of the best feelings I've ever experienced. It doesn't matter how many times I've done this exact thing; the feeling never dulls. Her tongue flattens, then curves to cup my length as I slide slowly back and forth.

While it feels amazing, it's not enough to stop the memories that tease my mind back to the first time I looked upon my wife and knew I loved her. The day I knew I would want her to be my wife, take my name, grow old beside me.

We were so young then. I was just seventeen. She was two years younger; not old enough to drive a car, but she drove me crazy. June was always flitting around her house when I was hanging out there with Reed, her brother. He's my best friend, brother more like. June would storm into the room and suck up all my attention, all my oxygen, with her thick mane of mahogany hair and angelic face, always buried in a book.

A deep hum of pleasure makes my dick twitch and brings me back to the present. This happens often, nearly every time. My mind reminding me of all the reasons I fell in love with June, bombarding me with scenes while I fuck my way through them. I can't ever seem to block them out, no matter how I try.

Every push, I go deeper. She's good at this. She can take it. I move my hand to tangle it in the hair at the back of her head and guide her farther down my shaft, nose pressed to my groin, and I hold. Just a few long seconds, just a few stolen breaths, before I pull her back and set a faster pace.

The day I knew June was the one for me, I'd gone over to the Turners' after practice. I had been feeling under the weather for days, fighting through it. Both my father and my coach wouldn't care that I needed extra rest, not with the State Championship game coming up. Push through it, they'd say. Just push through it. At the Turners', I would have a chance at some peace, maybe a nap. I was asleep in Reed's room when she tiptoed in, wearing too short cutoff shorts and a thin white tank top, a pink bra strap falling off one shoulder. She carried a tray laden with soup, an enormous glass of water, and some vitamin C. I stared at her as she placed it down on the bedside table, then put her small hand on my forehead to check for fever.

I sensed the life flow to me from her cool hand. I know now that it was love. June was always giving everything she had to me or Reed, taking nothing in return. She was everything I dreamed of. Caring, smart, beautiful. Mine.

I stared up at her perfect face, sweet, rose-colored, heart-shaped lips. I knew it, even then. She's still perfect now, a dozen years later. Even with the scars she's collected over the years.

It was not the first time my eyes lingered longer than they should on my best friend's kid sister. Not by a long shot. I always tried to hide my longing for moments when no one else was likely to be paying attention. Including June. Me, being the idiot teenage boy that I was, it still didn't make me unaware of June's schoolgirl crush on me. I knew. Reed knew, and if he thought I reciprocated at all, he would take no pause in ham-fisting his way right through my skull.

I was a horny little shit, but I wasn't stupid. Defiling a young June wasn't a path I was going down for a multitude of reasons, Reed only being one of them. Besides, I wanted her pure, virginal. She was those things when I did, finally, allow my filthy hands to touch her, though she'd likely not claim to be pristine.

I had little good in my life at that point. Reed and June, their parents— they were my good. The only light in my dark world. I spent most of my free time at their house. Not that I had much of it between school, football practice, training, games. Mrs. Turner always fed me when I dropped in. She'd lecture me on homework and grades. She was the mother I needed before I knew I needed one.

Mr. Turner enforced the importance of reliability, being a man of your word, a standup guy, a gentleman.

I should have appreciated his efforts more, taken his words and actions to heart. If I had, maybe I'd be different now. Maybe I wouldn't be so full of chaos.

Slender fingers slide from where they've been gripping my hip, gradually traveling down to the inside of my thigh, then back until they reach my sack. They cradle softly, then begin a slow massage, around and around. Both of us know what comes next, and I widen my stance in preparation. Leaning my head back, I take in how the lights of the active city outside are playing on the ceiling of our darkened hotel room. Globes of pink filtering through the drapes trace across my vision, flashes of white too. I hear the thrum of a bus as it travels by, the honk of a car horn, so many voices adding to the constant noise in my head.

It all quiets as my abs constrict. Peace as I push the head back away from my cock and spill over the flushed cheeks and pretty, swollen lips. It's a gorgeous sight, one much needed after the hard game I played tonight and the even harder hits I took. Something like drunken double vision takes over, though I'm completely sober. One eye seeing the sight in front of me, one seeing the innocence of my wife the first time I had her in this position. A few hard blinks wash the sight away.

A soft tongue licks me clean, like it's her job. I guess it kind of is; she knows what I like, how to please me after all this time together. Once she's done, I run my hand down her head and cup her cheek. She stands and turns to walk into the bathroom. I watch with appreciation as her bare ass bounces away.

I hear the call of room service over the knock on the door. Pushing my legs into my boxer briefs and grabbing a few bills I set on the dresser, I go to let them in.

"Hey, can you just drop it on the table?" I ask and point to the other side of the room and drop the bills on the tray, turning my back to the young woman. She looks barely legal, and I wish I had thrown on a T-shirt and sweats before opening. Keeping my back to her and the door, I grab the remote and flip channels until I find the sports highlights.

I try not to watch these, knowing it's always better to wait for the official film review with Coach. He doesn't like his players to listen to commentary, and I don't like to hear it. I want to see what went wrong tonight, though.

They sacked me four times. Four fucking times. Bruised and battered is a feeling I'd like to avoid the next time we face this defense.

I've been a starting NFL quarterback for only a handful of seasons. If I have any more games like this, my career will be short. But not sweet. I'm young and I'm fit, sure. Even I can't take too many beatings like the one I took tonight. I never look at our offensive line as the first to blame. I'll always look at the other team first. Maybe they were just that much better. Tonight, I have my doubts; we were off. If there is a broken link on our team, I need to find it and repair it.

My goal has never been to be one of those quarterbacks who play well into their forties, but we've hoped for a solid decade of excellent play. This life is hard. Hard on my body, hard on my time, but hard on June, too. It's taken a heavy toll on her career and she has a hard time settling and making friends. Ballers' wives and girlfriends are a lot higher maintenance than June is used to. I've made promises to her for things to come, after the sacrifices she's made for the sake of my career. I want to keep them. Not just the promises I've voiced to her, but the ones I've made to her in my head, the ones I've left unsaid. I owe her all her dreams... and more.

Guilt knots in my stomach as a quiet voice says, "You're all set, sir." A moment later, the room door opens as she leaves.

"Dollface, dinner is here," I holler into the bathroom, its open door just to my right.

"I'm coming. You got cum in my hair, babe. That takes a minute to get out," she responds.

I give a little laugh. I know she hates that shit. "Sorry, next round, I'll save it all for that tight ass of yours. I know that's your favorite and I neglected it last time."

She walks out and wraps her lithe nakedness around me, then shoves her hand in my boxers, waking my dick back up.

"Mmm, yes, you did." She pouts.

It's the soft whimpering gasp that stops her hand. A gasp that sounds as loud as a bullet ricocheting several times off metal walls.

Right before it lodges in your heart.

A gasp that turns my blood cold.

I know that sound. I've heard it before.

It's the sound my wife makes when she's scared or hurt. The same sound she made two years ago when we received the call that her dad had perished in an auto accident. The sound she made just over five years ago when she woke up in a hospital bed, terrified, after being attacked by a man who had stalked her relentlessly. It's the sound that marks every horrific experience of June's life. The sound she made each time I had to wake her from her nightmares, for months. A sound that would have me rushing to her side, sliding my arms around her. Promising her everything will be okay and that I'll be by her side as we get her through whatever the problem is.

But everything will not be okay. Not now. It can't be. Maybe it never will be again.

Finding some strength inside me, some courage I didn't know I possessed, I remove the hand from my body. I set the naked woman, her icy blonde hair now curtaining her face, away from me, and turn around.

My wife stands in the doorway of my hotel room, silent tears streaming out of pain-filled eyes, washing away all my hopes and dreams with them.

"Junie," I whisper, but it echoes in the still silence occupying this tomb.

She turns and walks out, shutting the door with a careful snick behind her. Calm. So composed, apart from that one small whimper and noiseless tears. It's such a June-like reaction, always so restrained when there is an audience. She only ever let her temper fly in private with me or Reed.

"Fuck!" I'm raging as I rush to throw some clothes on. Why is she here?

Lorelai is quiet, unmoving. She's like a statue frozen in the middle of this hotel room. Pale, cold stone. A nude goddess with smooth, unblemished skin, ready to be worshiped by anyone who happens by. I don't have time to dwell on her or her panic, though. Not while my wife is running away from me with who knows what thoughts ravaging her mind.

Dressed, I shove my feet in some shoes, grab my room key, then dart down the hall to the bank of elevators.

This makes no sense. She shouldn't be here. She has never once in any of our time apart sprang a surprise visit on me. Never. She shouldn't fucking be here. The look in her eyes—so raw, so much pain. Worse than after her attack, even. Those brief seconds will haunt me forever. Fuck if I don't deserve that.

None of my rushing is of any use. By the time I've stepped out onto the lobby floor and almost taken out an elderly couple as I push outside to the street, June is closing the door of a cab and pulling away.

I grab my hair and yank at it while yelling her name.

She's left me behind without a word. Not a single damn word. I crave the quiet moments in my life. The few brief seconds when my guilt isn't plaguing me, or my hate isn't pushing me in directions I ought not to go. But June's silence is never a good thing. It's not something I look forward to or seek. When June is quiet, it's because she's internalizing, she's hurting, she's haunted. I never wanted to cause that, and this time it feels like the calm before my entire world implodes.

I'm not sure how long I've been standing on the sidewalk, staring at the fading taillights. They've blended into the traffic now, indistinguishable from the rest. I blink a few times, then move to head back into the hotel, only to notice several people with their cell phones out, all pointed at me.

My heart racing, I hang my head and make my way back inside.

Back to Lorelai.

Into the arms of a woman who is not my wife, but my relief.

A woman I don't love, but I cherish. A woman who has saved me in some ways, yet is also my greatest downfall.

CHAPTER 2
June

Nearly three hours on the flight back to Seattle, and my mind still feels like pebbles rattling around inside a tin can. There hasn't been a single second of mental quiet since the scene in Drew's hotel room. I'm moving on adrenaline alone. If I stop now, I'll pass right out.

I can't believe any of this is happening. We've seen so little of each other these past few weeks. I thought it would be a pleasant surprise to show up after his game. Stay with him until he'd be traveling home with the team tomorrow. I guess I now know why Drew has been having me travel with him less and less these past months.

The air I try to drag into my lungs feels stifling as tears well in my eyes. Damn it, I don't want to lose my shit in the middle of the airport. There's something horrifically tragic about a lone person breaking down in public. Pitied by all the passersby, choking on the awkwardness of it all.

Besides, people here will recognize me as the wife of their beloved home team quarterback. Drew has never kept me in the shadows. He often has me with him at public events, charity fundraisers, visits to the local children's hospital. They know me as a woman in love with her husband, proud of his accomplishments, supportive of every move he makes.

Right now, I don't feel proud at all.

What would they see if they looked at me now? A shattered woman with no hope for the future? Feeling it is one thing, allowing the world to see it is another. I've accomplished so much over the past five years and I can feel it all fluttering away, as if the rope I've been climbing is finally too much to hold on to.

How could he do this to me? To us? I've lost count of the number of times I've asked myself that, since fleeing his hotel. The other question I keep asking is, for how long has this been going on? I witnessed the familiarity with my own eyes. The ease with which they spoke, in how she touched him. My husband. My Drew.

Maybe that isn't what he is anymore. Mine. I can't help but wonder if he ever truly was.

My brain tells me it wouldn't be any different if I knew this was a one-time hookup. Cheating is cheating. This still feels like a much larger betrayal, though. A bigger hurt.

I'm so lost in my head that I don't notice the body stepping in front of me until it's too late. Strong arms engulf my small frame and I soak up the warmth and comfort only Reed's hugs give me. I texted him when I was back at LAX and had secured a seat on a flight home. Failing to tell him why I needed him to pick me up earlier than planned, I knew he'd be here, regardless. However, I'm surprised to see him waiting just outside of the security gate when he'd usually be waiting in the cellphone lot to pick me up on the curb.

Raising my head to look at him, I know he knows. The look in his over-wrought eyes says it all.

"Drew called you?"

I haven't turned my phone on since I landed back in SeaTac. After tex-ting Reed in Los Angeles, I immediately shut it off. Drew had called twice, which I ignored. He'd also sent several texts, which I also ignored. They still sit unread. He must have given up on me and called the one person he knew I'd run to.

Reed nods and squeezes me a little tighter.

"I'm going to fucking kill him, June. Forget about being a divorcée, you're going to be a widow." He doesn't mean it, of course. Reed's a rel-atively passive dude, even if his size would suggest otherwise. Standing at six-foot-four, he's a commanding presence. The broad shoulders, tattoos, and thick lumberjack beard don't help any. That's not to say he wouldn't physically cause some harm in the defense of me. He would, he likely will, but he loves Drew, too.

Reed moved with us to Seattle when Drew landed his contract here, and he's very much embraced the Pacific Northwest lifestyle. Flannel shirts and all. He's completely acclimated in the year we've been here. I wonder how he does it. I still feel like I'm floundering.

"You didn't know, then?" I ask, but I know the answer. I guess I just need the reassurance that he's on my side and not his best friend's.

Reed's eyes narrow and he holds me out at a small distance so he can see me better.

"Of course not. Do you honestly think I'd keep something like that from you? Or that I'd even allow Drew to carry on with fucking around? Jesus, Ju."

"No. I know you wouldn't. I'm just feeling wounded here, Reed. Did he tell you what happened?" A tear leaks out of my left eye and I shrug my shoulders in defeat.

"Not in so many words. Come on, let's get on the road where we can talk without extra ears around." Wrapping a protective arm around my shoulders, he leads the way. I snuggle into him, partly to lean on his strength, partly to help hide my shame from the rest of the travelers.

I shouldn't feel ashamed. Drew should. Yet, I do. His cheating makes me feel unworthy. As if I'm not good enough to be his wife. Or maybe I'm not enough to keep him satisfied sexually. That is an area that needs improvement.

That thought can lead me down too many paths I'm not ready to face yet. But one thing I can't help wondering is if this woman is the only one.

There could be many. There probably have been many. My stomach rolls, and bile rises, stinging my nostrils.

Drew didn't have girlfriends in high school or college, but he hooked up constantly. I never saw him with the same woman more than a few times before he replaced her with the next. As if there were some invisible expiration date only he knew about.

Questions bombard me. Maybe he never wanted to marry me at all. It was such an unexpected proposal. He'd never expressed an interest in dating me, much less marriage. Never kissed me until I woke up in that damned hospital bed and witnessed fear in his eyes. My family had been taking turns sitting with me. I woke up on his watch, and when my vision cleared, it was him I saw. It was Drew who held me tight in his arms as the memories of being attacked rushed through me. Drew who weathered that pain with me.

I finger the long, puckered scar at the base of my neck. It's an involuntary motion. A habit I have yet to break and a constant reminder of that night.

Drew has always been aware of my love for him, much to my utter mortification. I'd assumed for years that he loved me too but needed to sort that out in his head. Always believing he'd come around eventually, and he had. Hadn't he? It didn't bother me it was my near-death that finally woke him up to it. I clung to whatever he gave me. The reason for his affection wasn't an issue for me as long as it was there. Fragility and fear are not the best bedfellows when making major life decisions. I can admit that now, considering my marriage is in shambles and apparently nothing about Drew has changed.

ALISON RHYMES

Guessing for days wouldn't get me any closer to understanding how he could tear our marriage apart in such a way. Knowing his motives won't help. There is no justification for such cold-hearted infidelity.

Before I even realize we've made it to the car, Reed is loading me into his SUV. I must have completely zoned out because he's even buckling the seat belt on me like I'm a child. I feel like one, too. Weak, too small to care for my own self.

We're already on the freeway before either of us speaks. The smell of tension fills the air. Panic and confusion on my end, pure anger on his. Reed has always been the protective older brother. He had misgivings when Drew declared he wanted to marry me. Somehow, Drew convinced Reed that his intentions were honorable. Reed won't take pleasure in being right in his concern.

"Tell me what exactly happened, Baby Girl. Don't spare details to help him look better than he is, either."

"I missed him, you know? Thought it would be nice to surprise him, and I had some news to share. He'd texted me the hotel and room number like he always does, in case of emergencies or whatever. I decided to just show up. When I got there, room service was leaving. I entered just as she left."

Calming my heart rate that has picked up again, I watch as Reed's fingers tense on the steering wheel. His knuckles whiten from the force. My hands rub along my thighs in a nervous gesture. I don't want to see the replay in my mind again. Not ever.

"His back was to the door, and he called out to someone. Dollface... he called her Dollface, told her their dinner had arrived."

I recount the rest of the story through a sheet of tears, watching the blurry cars fly by. Wondering if any of the passengers have ever walked in on a spouse and their lover. Certainly, at least some of them have experienced betrayal, but it's hard not to feel alone right now.

"Fuck, Ju."

"Yeah. Fuck," I confirm, resigned to being a sad sack of depression and self-pity for the foreseeable future.

"I'm taking you back to my place. I'll go by your house tomorrow and grab whatever you need."

"No. Take me home. I'll pack a bag and find a hotel in the morning. I'm not sleeping on your couch. Or making you," I say.

"Why aren't you freaking out? I'd expect you to be hysterical. You're kind of scaring me."

Me too.

"I don't know, Reed. I'm not sure how I'm supposed to feel. Do you suppose there is a manual for this? A book that will tell me how to act when I catch my cheating cunt of a husband with his mistress?" I sigh, pressing my forehead to the window. It's cool and the raindrops running down outside feel calming. Cleansing, somehow. As if they can wash it all away. I wish they would.

Reed chuckles. "No, Ju. No manual. But I feel like I'm closer to histrionics here than you are. I don't like it. It makes me worry."

Of course it does. It was always my way—keeping things inside. After my attack and therapy, I made strides to stop that behavior. To express my feelings, my concerns more. It's difficult still, erasing a lifetime of habits. Unhealthy as they may be, it doesn't happen overnight. But I've made small progressions.

"Part of me wants to be hysterical. Part of me wants to curl up in a ball and cry for a month. Another part of me thinks I should have taken a steak knife off their room service tray and chopped off his dick. A bigger part of me doesn't want to become the pathetic wife who's made a fool of, time and time again by the philandering husband."

That much is true. Whatever way this all plays out, I will not be the villain in it. And, while I am the victim of Drew's duplicity, I will not act like one. I've been there and fought too hard to get out of it just to go back. Also, I'll be damned if the tabloids try to turn me into a prudish prig wife or a psycho.

"Yeah, okay. I get that. Just, you know, don't hide from me, okay?" There's a deep concern in his voice. I get it, I do. And I hate that my past is the reason it is there.

"I'm not that same person anymore, Reed. I'm not saying this will be easy, or that I'll breeze through it. We both know that would be a lie. But I am stronger than I used to be. I'll be okay. Somehow," I say with as much reassurance as I can muster and try my best to believe the words.

Truth is, I don't know if I'll be okay. Catching the love of your life with another woman has a way of making you question your entire existence.

I don't say much else for the rest of the drive to my house. It's not a home. Especially not after today. But it never felt like one to me, anyway. When Drew was traded from San Diego to here, he rushed to find us a house. Because of a motivated seller, we got a good deal and could move in right away. The plan always being that if things worked out with the team, we could take our time to find something we loved.

I don't love this house. In fact, I kind of hate it. Never more than I do right now as I unlock the front door and step in. It feels cold, lifeless, and sterile. Ultra-modern, not warm or inviting.

Real estate is a strange infatuation I have. I don't want to be a real estate agent or anything like that, but I've always dreamed of restoring some crazy old homes or haunted mansions. Something about bringing a home full of history back to life completely fascinates me. I'll spend hours looking at real estate listings online, imagining what I could do to the house and all its pre-established personality.

Some people deep dive into serial killer documentaries. My rabbit hole is historically interesting homes. I can spend endless hours searching real estate listings online. Drew teases me about it, but often, when I find a good one, he falls in love with it, too.

Which only made his quick purchase of this house even more annoying. Finding a house was a distraction he didn't want to deal with. I understood because we were going through such a big relocation, and he was going through a big career change.

Maybe what he really wanted was a place to hide the wife away so he could quickly get back to his fuckbuddy.

I had done little to nothing to this house. There wasn't anything about it that inspired me.

"You sure you're going to be okay, Ju?" Reed asks as he drops my small suitcase inside the door.

"No, Reed. I'm not sure of anything anymore. I love him and I hate him. I don't know if I'll ever be okay again."

The tide breaks when Reed wraps me in another one of his epic bear hugs, and I let it. The tears flood, sobs erupt from my chest, and my knees give out. Reed takes the burden, picks me up, and hauls me upstairs to my bedroom. He gently lowers me to the bed and pulls the blanket from the foot up and over me.

"I'm not leaving you. I'll crash in the guest room. If you need me, you come get me."

I nod.

"I'll be okay. I'll sleep for a few hours, then pack what I need. If you're not up by the time I'm ready to get the hell out of here, I'll wake you."

He leans over to kiss my forehead, then exits the room, closing the door softly on the screaming of my dying heart.

CHAPTER 3

June

Sleep doesn't come, no matter how hard I try. After a couple hours of staring at the ceiling, I give up. Instead of lying here longer, I decide to get on with packing some clothes. I grab two suitcases from the back of the closet and start filling them.

I won't stay in this house another night. Drew will be back at any time now, and while I could kick him out, that's not what I want. He bought this house; he can keep it. Besides, if I accept the job offer—the news I'd planned on sharing with Drew when I got to Los Angeles—I won't be staying in Seattle long. I can figure out my next steps when I finish this project.

Maybe this will be what jump-starts my career again. I'm a food and travel blogger, but the goal was always to do that professionally. Hosting a television series was my dream, one that combined my love of travel, food, and old, haunted places. I went to school for journalism and was working as a reporter for the local news station for a while when we lived in San Diego. I would probably be closer to my goal had I not quit for Drew.

Not that he held me back or asked me to quit, but his career is demanding, and it was hard on both of us to be traveling. It made more sense for me to be there to support him. We thought I could hold my career off for a time until he slowed down. I never regretted the decision until now. Honestly, I love supporting Drew. It's all I ever wanted while growing up. To be the girl he could always count on. He had so little in his early life, but he always had me. And my family.

He spent most of his free time with us from the age of eight. Drew was a constant fixture in my life. I knew early on that he had my heart, even if he didn't reciprocate. Quietly suffering in the background while he dated his way through the Phoenix Valley in high school was just how I rolled. I traveled from my college in Oregon to his in California for as many of his home games as I could, even if he left the stadium with some random co-ed on his arm. He never had to love me for me to love him.

Oh hell, when he did love me, my life was complete. Now I feel like a joke.

I zip up my luggage and decide to take a shower. I should have done that as soon as I got home. Maybe it would have helped to wash away the memories.

It doesn't work, of course. At least, I no longer feel like I have a layer of airport filth on me when I haul my luggage downstairs and set it next to the small case I never unpacked from LA.

Reed isn't awake yet, so I make a pot of coffee and take a cup to the only place in this house I like. The breakfast nook looks out onto a green-belt behind the house. The thick evergreens always made me smile. They reminded me of Drew's eyes. I could sit here and watch the rainfall for hours and not feel like I've missed anything important.

Deciding now is as good a time as any, I turn my phone on. Within a few seconds, it's practically vibrating itself off the table with all the notifications coming through. Texts, voicemails, missed calls, emails, social media—so many notifications coming from every source imaginable.

Shit.

I check Drew's texts first.

DREW:

Junie, please answer the phone.

It's not what you think, baby, please.

Jesus, do all cheaters say that same thing? I can't imagine it works with any woman.

The last text from him was from this morning.

DREW:

I'm on my way back. Can we talk then? Let me explain. I love you.

I ignore the voicemails and the social media notifications. There is a text from my best friend, Leighton. We were college roommates, and next to Reed, she's the person I trust most in the world.

LEIGHTON:

Check your email, Love. I'm sorry and I'm always here for you. Call me when you can.

I don't check my email or social media, not yet. I'd like to at least finish my damn cup of coffee first. Placing my phone face down, I stare up at the wall. There's a picture of our wedding there. We married only weeks after Drew proposed, at a cheesy Vegas chapel no less. The only photographer was the chapel staff and my family with their phones. But one picture was perfect.

I stand in a simple lace baby doll dress, all white except for the light blue shoestring bow at my neck, looking straight ahead at the camera. A wide, brilliant smile plastered on my face. Drew, towering over me by a foot at six-foot-five, is looking down at me with the softest expression I've ever seen him wear on his ridiculously handsome face. All his attention was on me, and I remember thinking... finally. Finally, he's mine, as I've always been his.

What a farce.

I'm rinsing out my coffee mug in the sink when I hear the security system chime as the front door opens. My stomach tightens and I focus on just breathing. I don't know how I'm going to survive this conversation.

Drew must see the kitchen light on because he heads straight here, straight for me. I don't turn around. I can't. Can't look at him, can't face him and what he's done. He crowds me, pressing up against my back, his hands settling on the countertop to either side of me. Locking me in place.

He's warm, so warm. The smell of his aftershave permeates my senses. A smell that just days ago was the smell of home.

Not anymore.

Damn him.

Damn you, Drew.

I drop my head, and he follows. He breathes me in.

"Junie." It's a whisper. An apology, maybe.

It's not enough. Not nearly.

"Why?" I ask.

"I'm sorry, Junie. So sorry. I'll make it right. I swear."

His words, so many with so little meaning. He keeps saying them as he turns me around. He spreads his empty promises across my temple, down my jawline, over my lips.

I don't know why I don't fight it, except he's so warm. I want to snuggle into it, let the heat take me away from this cold house.

Drew's lips are tentative at first, only until my lips part and my tongue meets his. It's a dance we know well. He loves to kiss. He loves to kiss me. He loves me?

This is my Drew. My Drew whose strong palms cup my face, my shoulders, my breasts, as the temperature of our kisses rise.

Somewhere in the back of my vacant mind, a question grows. Why am I not fighting him off?

But it's my Drew whose sweatpants my hands push down. It's my Drew I kneel before.

"June, no…" he says, trying to stop me, but my hand moves to his length.

Then he grows quiet, the space still and silent except for a soft ticking sound. Tick, tick, tick. The teal wall clock I hung to bring some sort of color to this large clinical kitchen mocks me from the other side of the room.

Tick, tick, tick. My entire world is crumbling, and I can't focus on anything but that sound. That stupid, innocuous sound.

His hands reach to still mine. I look up into those green eyes I love so much.

"Is this what she does for you?" I ask, managing to keep out the snide tone that I hear in my head.

Sucking him off is something I rarely perform. Not for lack of trying on my part. He never seems to want that. And now I realize that he never seems to want it from me.

Why would he, when he has her?

Tick, tick, tick.

Drew steps back, pulls up his pants, then turns from me.

"Fuck," he yells as he punches the refrigerator. It's his throwing hand. His career. His money.

I can't help but care, so I stand up. I pull an ice pack out of the freezer and press it to his hand as I check it for breaks. I glance at his face to see him staring at me like he doesn't know me.

The feeling is mutual, I want to tell him. I don't. I don't say anything.

"Say something, June," he pleads at the same time my phone rings. Call me a coward, but I use the opportunity to put space between us.

"Hi, Mom."

"Sweetheart, what's going on? It's all over the tabloids!" She's whisper-shouting, something she does when she speaks of something salacious or scandalous. The familiar behavior brings a smile to my face, despite everything.

"I'll call you in a bit and fill you in," I say.

"June. Are you all right?"

"I will be. I'll call you soon. Love you."

"Okay, okay. I love you, too," she tells me before I end the call and pull up one site sure to publicize the end of my marriage.

And there it sits, the top post, complete with pictures. Pictures of me fleeing the hotel and Drew trying to flag down my cab.

Those pictures aren't the ones that feel like a thousand needles pressing into my heart. The ones causing that pain are the ones that follow. Fresh shots from this morning of Drew hugging his girlfriend on the sidewalk. Another of him cupping her face as they stare into each other's eyes. One more of him kissing her forehead as he loads her into the back seat of a car.

Yesterday, all I had seen of the woman was naked skin and wild blonde waves. I didn't see her face.

Now I see her all too clearly. Lorelai.

Knowing who it is, knowing he stayed with her last night… shatters me. Frays every thread I had holding me together.

"How long, Drew?" The calmness of my voice shocks even me. I'm not calm. I'm pure rage. My hands shake, and my head pounds.

He doesn't answer.

"How fucking long?" I turn back to him as I demand an answer.

Drew swallows hard, so I know the answer is bad before the words even leave his mouth.

"About a year." It's a quiet answer, so quiet I almost don't hear the words that feel like a knife in my spine.

I rush to the sink to make it there before the bile rising expels out of me. A year.

Lorelai. He's been with her for a year.

Heaving and heaving, I empty myself of the coffee I just drank. I'm not even sure of the last time I ate, so there isn't much else to rid myself of. I feel Drew's hands move to gather my hair.

"Do not touch me," I choke out.

My head is now chanting Lorelai, Lorelai, Lorelai, in between the ticking of the damn wall clock. I rinse my mouth out with water and wipe my face with a hand towel before I face him again. He looks terrified. Pale skin, red-rimmed eyes show he got little sleep, if any. I would be concerned except... Lorelai, Lorelai, Lorelai. My fists clench, which only makes me aware of the wedding ring I so proudly wear. I gasp for breath, trying to stave off more dry heaves.

"Junie."

"Stop. Stop calling me that." My fingers go to the ring. It was Drew's mother's, who died when he was too young to remember her well. A ghost his father never got over, and haunted the halls of the house Drew grew up in. Not literally, of course, but her presence lingered all the same. I loved that he wanted me to have it. Now, it feels like a band of fire.

I wiggle it off. His eyes find the movement, and his entire body tenses, his fists clenching tight like mine.

"No. No, put it back." Panic surges in his voice as water wells in his eyes. "Put it back on, June," he commands.

I'm helpless to stop the tears from leaking out of my eyes. Helpless to so many things, so many emotions.

"One day, I'm going to want the truth and the details, down to exactly how she sucks your whore of a dick. And you will answer every damn thing," I say through my tears. "But not right now. Right now, I need to get away from you and your stupid, beautiful face. It's going to take time to not hate you with every fiber of my being, and you're going to give me that time."

I push the ring into his hands, but he fights me on it, trying to push it back on my finger.

"Put it back on, June. Put it back on!"

"What the hell is going on?" Reed yells to be heard above Drew's pleading as he enters the kitchen.

"She needs to put her wedding ring back on! Tell her, Reed. Tell her! She can't take it off, she can't." Drew drops my hands and the ring tings on the hardwood. He stares at it and pulls at his hair. I can see the tears welling in his own eyes, and I look away. I don't want to feel bad for him, to sympathize in any way.

Drew doesn't show that kind of emotion. Ever.

"Will you tell her, Reed?" he asks quietly.

"Dude. You cheated on her. What did you expect?" Reed says.

"With Lorelai," I add, "for the past year."

Reed completely loses his composure at my words. Face reddening, he pulls Drew up, backs him against the wall, and keeps him there with a forearm to his neck.

"Is that true, Drew?" Reed yells in his face, only inches away.

Drew doesn't answer, just averts his eyes.

"I trusted you! I trusted you with Ju…" Spittle from Reed yelling lands on Drew's face. "And you repay that by making Lorelai your fucking girlfriend? You dumb motherfucker!"

A sob escapes me, enough of a distraction for Reed's attention to focus on me. Stepping away from Drew, he moves toward me. Drew tries to follow, but Reed pushes him away, and I'm once again wrapped up in Reed's arms as he leads me out of the kitchen and toward the entryway of our house.

Drew pleads with us both as we pass. "She's not my girlfriend. It's not like that. Just stay, please stay. Let me explain. I can make it right." He sounds like a broken record, on constant repeat as he follows us.

I turn to him, letting all the anger, all my pain rush out.

"Did you fuck her after I left?" I demand as I push on his chest, shoving him away from me.

"No! No, June, no."

"Why not? You stayed with her. Or did my showing up because I had something important to talk to you about ruin it all?"

"What? What do you mean, what happened?" His eyes search mine.

"Oh, now you want to talk to me. Now that Lorelai isn't here, naked with a ready ass for you to fuck? You stayed with her! That moment in your hotel room ruined me. That would have been hard enough for me to survive"—my voice shakes—"but then you tucked her away into a car this morning. A sweet goodbye for the entire world to see. For me to see. You put my pain on display to be mocked by others. There isn't a way for you to make that right."

"No, no, this is on me. I'm sure I'll get a rash of shit, but this shouldn't land on you, June," he states naively.

Reed laughs. "Dude, we all know that's not how this works. June's right. Public opinion will eat her up just as much, if not more, than you."

"All due respect, Reed, but shut the fuck up. This is between me and June."

"Are you sure about that? Sounds like it's between you, June, and your fucking mistress, Lorelai Simmons."

As soon as the words hit the air, Drew lunges for Reed. Arms tangle as they push and pull, yelling obscenities at each other. I can't force myself to step in until Reed lands a full fist at Drew's jaw, drawing a small amount of blood at his lip as he staggers back, eventually dropping to his knees.

"Stop..." I sigh. "Just stop. Reed, can you take my bags to my car? Give us a minute?"

His eyes don't leave Drew, who isn't even attempting to rise to his feet. But he nods and does what I ask.

Never have I seen Drew look so weak. Sometimes, when we were very young, after an awful scene at home with his father, he'd show up at our house pale, sad, vulnerable—a child in need of some tender, loving care.

But there was always strength in his dark green eyes, a determination. It's not present now. He looks defeated, and it occurs to me he never realized completely how his actions would affect my life.

Drew always had self-obsessive tendencies in relationships. Oblivious to the pain he may have caused all the women who came before me. Selfish isn't a word I'd use to describe him. He's not that. He's a giver at heart. Drew is always overly generous when gift-giving. Two Christmases ago, he gave my mom a full, state-of-the-art kitchen remodel. She had made an off-hand comment about possibly needing to replace her aging oven, as it was baking hot. He could have replaced that one appliance and she would have considered it too large a gift. An entire kitchen had her in tears and arguing with him for twenty minutes about how she couldn't accept it. He didn't relent, telling her he'd do whatever it took to keep her homemade oatmeal raisin cookies coming. My favorite cookie. He hates them as he was always biting into one, thinking it was chocolate chip and then being disappointed.

He also gives a strict fifteen percent of all his salary to charities. Something he has done since his very first contract when he was drafted. He spreads it between various women's and children's nonprofit organizations. He visits the Seattle Children's Hospital twice a month and volunteers at the food bank a handful of times a year. Not a bit of it is for publicity.

I guess being unselfish with your money and time doesn't keep you from being a cheating asshole. Or from thinking everything you do comes without consequence. He will have to pay some now, but I can't help feeling that I, too, am in deep debt to them.

"I'm going to get a room at a hotel until... well, for a while. I need the space, Drew. You need to respect that," I say firmly.

His head stays bowed, staring at the cold granite tiles in front of him.

"She's not my mistress. It's not like that, June. I love you. You know that."

The hard truth is I do know. He shows me in so many ways. There isn't anything he wouldn't do for me or give me. He can't even be in the same room as me without being near me, usually touching me. I'm not sure he's even aware of how attentive he is to me.

"Do I? I'm sure it was your love for me that drove you to Lorelai's arms." My hand shakes as I bring it to my forehead, kneading, trying to ease the first waves of a headache.

"I don't know how to explain it. But I want to. I want a chance to make it right. Please don't shut me out, Junie. You're all"—he clears the tremor in his voice—"you and Reed are my family. I won't lose you."

That's what hurts the most. Drew has always been and will always be a part of my life. A part of my family. He's a second son to my mother and losing her connection to him would cause her immense pain. And Reed, well, he and Drew have a bond that is so strong. I don't want to be the reason it weakens.

"We'll always be family, Drew. Right now, I just don't know what that looks like."

He stands now and steps toward me until he's only a breath away.

"Promise me we'll talk. We can go to counseling, work on this, work on us. I'll go alone, too. Whatever it takes," he says, determined.

Sighing, I respond, "We'll talk. I'll let you know where I end up, but you need to give me time. When I'm ready, I'll tell you. I can't promise it will be soon." Tears spill from my eyes again. "This hurts, Drew. So much. I don't even know who you are."

All at once, I'm encompassed by his long arms. His warm body tightens around me. On one hand, I want to push him away, fight him off. On the other, I want the comfort he's always brought. I hate this confusion. It's like a civil war breaking out in my body. My head battling against my heart.

"I'm sorry, baby. I'm so sorry," Drew whispers against my temple.

I can't stand to hear it again. Finally, pushing away, I walk out on the love of my life.

CHAPTER 4
June

The October Seattle sky is gray the following day, like so many days here. It's not raining, but you can smell it in the air. Clean, that's what I've always believed. The Pacific Northwest agrees with me. Much more than Arizona did, where we grew up. Two years after Reed and Drew had left for college in California, Berkley, and USC, respectively, I began attending in Oregon. It didn't take long to know that moving back to the seventh layer of Hell with its dry heat and lack of water would not be something I'd do willingly. Heat I can handle, but I am one of those weirdos who likes sticky humidity.

I find the coffee shop I'm doing a write-up on—its name is Par la Main— and step into the lively space. It smells divine and there is French hip-hop music playing softly. The decor is a minimalist fashion but with warm tones that bring the outside in. It's not stark, uncomfortable, or cramped, nor is it filled with bulky items or a wall of merchandise. More like a café where you could sit and spend hours catching up with a friend than a place to stop off for a quick cup of joe. The owners have done well in making it hip yet inviting.

Seattle is a very contradictory city, I've found. Filled with earth-loving outdoorsy types married to hugely successful corporate mega-millionaires living in luxury McMansions. Someone once told me in college that the Pacific Northwest is full of 'pretentious hippies.' It didn't take me long to believe her. I love it, though. The yin and yang, the opposites that fit together so seamlessly. Looking around at this space and the customers in it, I see the city perfectly represented. Hard lines softened with touches of nature. A table with a woman wearing a business suit sharing a coffee with a man dressed in bicycling gear. None of it looks out of place. None of it clashes with itself.

The barista counter is round and in the center of the space, making it easy for customers to watch as they craft their coffee. The shop sits on a corner. Two full walls of floor-to-ceiling windows bring in a bunch of natural light. A bar lines each of those walls, allowing patrons to watch the people pass by on the street outside. I throw my coat over a seat, then go to order and watch the show.

Ordering both a cappuccino and an espresso shot, I observe the care and skill brought to each. The entire process takes some extra time. I'm here to see if it's worth the wait.

I've only savored a few sips of the cappuccino, which is worth the fuss when I tune into a conversation happening behind me.

"Oh, he's definitely having an affair. That's not a one-night stand," some woman says.

"Maybe. It sure looked like it from that video. Look at her, though. She's gorgeous. What kind of idiot cheats on that?" A man's hushed voice this time. I should feel flattered.

I don't.

"Drew McKenna, evidently. Can't say I blame whoever the other woman was. That man is perfection personified." The woman again.

"Yeah, yeah. I'm already aware of your love for the guy."

"He's so damn good-looking. I bet women drop their panties for him left and right. Poor June never stood a chance," she says.

My shoulders sag under the heavy words. Maybe she's right, and I never stood a chance with Drew. My hand shakes a little as I take another sip of my coffee.

I woke up this morning in my fancy hotel room, the view from the window full of the Puget Sound. It took me a moment to remember where I was and why I was there. Reed had laughed when I told him what hotel I planned on making my temporary home. It's not inexpensive or frugal. But if Drew can fly his fuckbuddy around the country, he can pay for me to stay in a small amount of comfortable luxury after I leave his ass.

The suite is altogether more room than I need, but the bed is ultra-comfortable, the bathroom spacious, and there is a private balcony that sits over the water. It will be a cozy place to lay my head at night, even if I get little sleep.

I'm not sure how much time I spent staring out at that view before I forced myself to shower and prepare for the day. The only thing I wanted to do was stay curled up in that bed, but I told myself hiding away from the world wouldn't make me feel any better about this situation.

I am second-guessing that mantra now.

Poor June.

That isn't who I am. I'm not someone to pity. I was that when I woke up in that hospital bed, beaten and battered. That's not who I am now, and I will never be that again. Poor June is a victim. I'm a motherfucking survivor. If I can survive near death, I can survive heartbreak, too.

I just wish I knew how.

It takes effort to tune out the customer chatter, but I do, and then finish my coffee, savoring the last few sips. It was a delicious cup and I'm happy to give them a favorable write-up for the local magazine I do freelance for regularly.

I'm heading out the door, ready to walk back down toward the waterfront and my temporary home, when my phone buzzes in my pocket.

DREW:

> Coach pulled some strings, got us an appointment with his counselor tomorrow at 4. Will you go with me? Please, Junie.

I stop walking, moving to the side of a building, away from the other foot traffic, so I'm not in the way as I stare at the message. We didn't even make it to the seven-year itch before we needed couples therapy. It's hard to have any faith in our future as man and wife. I'm still unsure if I even want to save our marriage. How can I ever trust him again? Can you have a marriage with no trust? I'm just not sure I see the point.

But it's Drew, and he's so tangled up in every part of my life that it isn't as easy as simply walking away.

I type a curt reply, telling him to text me the address and I'll meet him there. Before I can even stick my phone back in my pocket, he's responding.

DREW:

> You never told me where you went. I asked Reed, but he told me to fuck off. Please let me know, so I know you're safe. I love you.

I know I said I would tell him, but after I'd checked in and settled in my room... I just didn't want to deal with him. With any of it. I'd ordered a bottle of wine from room service, wrapped myself up in the duvet off the bed, and sat on the balcony, working my mind into a sort of numb stupor.

ME:

> I have a room at the Edgewater. I'm safe. I'll see you tomorrow.

I don't say I love him back. I do and he knows it, I'm sure. But I can't give him that. Not right now. Maybe never. And fuck if that doesn't just break my heart in a whole new way.

I'm back in my hotel room and working on my article when my phone rings again. This time, it's Leighton.

"Hey, Love," I greet, using the nickname we've called each other for years. If you believe in soul mates, Leighton is mine. I would bow down to any deity that was behind placing her as my roommate freshman year at Oregon State. We had an instant friendship, like finding like, or fate. Call it whatever you want. Our friendship was destiny. We have never fought with each other, not even a squabble or bicker. There has been no catty jealousy, just love and appreciation for each other. She's my person, one thousand percent.

"Hey back. You didn't call me yesterday, and I was trying to be all mature and show some patience, but you know that's just not me. Tell me what the fuck happened and where I can hide his body."

I bark out a genuine laugh, and it feels strange, unnatural. But I love that Leighton can pull it out of me. I don't want to, but I replay the horror story for her, and when I'm finished, we both sit there in complete silence for a beat or two.

"Damn him, June," she finally says. "I adore the man, but damn him for this."

"I know, Leighton. That's the hardest part because I can never hate him enough to not have him as a part of my world. But how? How do I do that? How do I leave him and move on? I know I can't ever watch him move on, bring some other woman or Lorelai to family dinners and holidays." Pain pours out in my voice, and I hate it, hate that he's reduced me to a gaping wound.

"Love, those are future hypothetical situations. Let's just focus on now. What do you want to do today or tomorrow?"

I haven't told her the news yet, the big deal I'd flown to Los Angeles to share with Drew and never had the chance to.

"I had a job offer from ESPN. They've asked me to come host some pre-Super Bowl programs. They want to run some specials about New Orleans in the weeks before the big game." I pause the information so she can squeal in excitement.

"Please tell me you're taking it?"

"Well, I haven't given them a definitive answer, but I'd planned on accepting. It seemed like a simple decision. I mean, it's football-related, and Drew would have gone for the game regardless of if the team made it that far or not. It would have worked well enough with his schedule and the bonus was that I would be near you for however long I was there."

Leighton has been in Louisiana for about the same time I've been in Washington. We attempt to visit each other every few months, but it hasn't been easy and I miss not having her near. Leighton loves her job there as a reporter, and she enjoys living in New Orleans. I can't fault her for that. It's always been one of my favorite cities, too.

"So, say yes and come hang out with me for a while. Maybe a change of scenery will be good for you," Leighton says, and I hear the hope in her voice.

"I will contact them, get the details hashed out. It makes even more sense to accept now. And maybe I can go down early. There isn't any reason to stay here in a hotel room."

"Yes! Want me to put some feelers out for a place for you?"

Leighton has the tiniest apartment known to mankind. It's adorable and in a historic building in the French Quarter with a view of the river, if you're brave enough to lean out over the ancient balcony to catch it. I love her place, but it's the size of my closet and has no kitchen. It works for her as she hates cooking, anyway. It is not conducive for a houseguest, though. I can handle snuggling up with her for a couple of nights on a girls' weekend, but long term? Not a chance.

"That would be great. I'd really appreciate it."

"You got it, June."

We chat for another twenty minutes, mostly Leighton regaling me with her latest dates and hookups. One more reason not to bunk with her for long. The lady lives freely, and I don't want to cramp her style. By the time we hang up, I'm feeling better, more settled in my decision.

I email Jared, my agent, and tell him I want to accept and proceed with contract negotiations. There shouldn't be much to barter over. They'd come to me because they wanted a woman with some expertise in travel and dining, and they loved how Drew connected me to football. Drew crash landing us onto every tabloid website in the country will only make them want me more.

Sensationalism, especially of this sort—as salacious as it is—is a bigger sell. Jared could probably ask for an increase in the offer, but that's not what's important to me right now.

I need the distraction, the change of pace. And Leighton's probably right about the change of scenery doing me good.

CHAPTER 5

June

The following morning is uneventful. I spend it reading my Kindle on my balcony, once again wrapped up in the duvet. The weather is dry today, but cold as October winds down. The book is enjoyable, but it's a love story and I keep finding myself drawing parallels to my real life. Eventually, I give up and head downstairs to the restaurant for a late lunch before I leave to meet Drew and our new therapist.

I had a hard time sleeping the night before and spent the time thinking about what I wanted out of these therapy sessions. Judging by Drew's reaction at the house, he won't be looking for the same outcome as me. But his wants and needs can't be my priority right now. Putting myself first is the priority, and there is only so much I can handle, so much I'm willing to handle.

When I get to the address Drew had texted me, I'm met with a woman who I'd guess to be in her mid-forties. She has a kind face, if there's such a thing. I'm not sure what I was expecting. Someone stern with a tight bun and tighter buttoned blazer, maybe. But that's not what she is. She's shorter than my five-foot-six and has a salt-and-pepper pixie cut. She's wrapped in a full, flowing, colorful skirt that should overwhelm her small stature. It doesn't in the slightest. She looks like she could set up shop as a fortune-teller in a rickety old wagon. I instantly like her.

"Mr. and Mrs. McKenna, hello," she calls in almost a singsong voice, giving more credence to my imagery. Drew was here before me, sitting in the waiting area when I arrived. Thankfully, Dr. Fillmore appeared as soon as I walked in, and there was no need for an awkward hello to my adulterer.

Drew shakes her hand, then I do. "Nice to meet you, Dr. Fillmore."

"Sit wherever is comfortable." She gestures with her hand. There are several places to pick from, a small sofa and various armchairs scattered throughout the room. There is even a flat chaise lounge on the far wall under the window.

Drew sits on the sofa. I'm sure he expects I'll sit next to him, but I choose a chair beside it instead. This is an incredibly uncomfortable situation for me, but somehow, sitting that close to Drew right now won't make it easier for me, only harder.

I don't miss his audible sigh. Neither does Dr. Fillmore as she sits in a chair opposite me, giving him a small, sympathetic smile.

"Let's start with you telling me what brought you here?" she asks, eyes flitting between the two of us.

Mine go to Drew, expecting him to answer. He looks uncomfortable, too. I guess he should be. He's the one in the hot seat.

"I was unfaithful," he says bluntly. Too bluntly. As if it's par for the course. I read once that about fifty percent of couples experience cheating. So, maybe he isn't wrong.

Jesus. I lean back in my chair, already feeling defeated.

"Was this a one-time incident?"

"No," I answer quickly.

"How long has it been happening?" she asks. She's looking at me.

Drew doesn't answer. His mouth is closed, jaw clenched tightly. He's already told me, so I don't understand why he's not answering her.

Unless... fuck. He told me he was with Lorelai for a year. It didn't occur to me to ask if there were others before her.

I'd been certain my heart couldn't break any more than it already had. I was so, so wrong. They don't call it that for no reason, I realize as one of my hands automatically begins rubbing a small circle at the spot where that particular organ begins to shrink up and hide farther inside my body. Or that's what it feels like, anyway.

After a moment, Dr. Fillmore takes the hint that Drew isn't ready to give up those details. "Okay, how about we back up? Why don't you tell me how you met, how long you've been together?"

"I've known her since she was six. I've been best friends with her brother nearly my whole life. We grew up together," Drew says, finding his voice again.

"You must know each other well. When did you begin to date?"

"Just over five years ago," he answers.

"No. That's not right," I counter.

"Yes, it is." Drew's staring at me like I'm on drugs, as if I've forgotten when we got together. But that isn't what she asked.

"No. That's when you asked me to marry you. We never actually dated," I say quietly while I watch his reaction.

"Please elaborate," Dr. Fillmore states.

"Well, as he said, we've known one another nearly our whole lives. I've been in love with him for as long as I can remember, but that wasn't a recip-rocated feeling. Until I ended up in the hospital my senior year of college.

Shortly after I recovered from that, Drew proposed. We went from friends to fiancés."

"Between the proposal and the marriage, what was your relationship like?"

I look from her to Drew. He still seems shell-shocked. It never dawned on him that our relationship didn't take a natural course. It's just now occurring to him. He didn't have to court me into falling in love with him; I was already there. I was a given. A sure thing. You don't have to play to win when you already own the trophy.

"Honestly? Not much different from how it had been before he proposed. Except that he made more appearances in my daily life. He kissed me hello and goodbye each time. It wasn't a huge period, though. We married in Las Vegas just weeks after he asked me." Now I'm uncomfortable because I'm just realizing how easily I made things for him. How simply I adapted my life to fit into his, taking any affection he gave me and never asking for more, never expecting more.

I lived for whatever attention he gave me. To be fair, he gave me plenty. Obviously, there was more to spread around.

"Did you have a sexual relationship with each other before you wed?" She directs the question to Drew.

He rubs his hands over his face and drags them back through his hair, leaving his curls in disarray.

"No. She was a virgin on our wedding night."

"How has your sexual relationship been since you've married?"

"It's great," he says.

At the same time, I say, "It could be better."

"Please elaborate."

Drew stands now. "Yes. Please elaborate."

I rub my hands along my thighs. I hate upsetting him. Not because I'm frightened of him, or even because I think he doesn't deserve it. He deserves to be upset, to feel pain and guilt. He's caused this mess, I remind myself again. But a lifetime of trying to soothe the hurt his father inflicted on him is a hard habit to break. It's who I am, the one who takes care of him. I've done it for so long. It's second nature.

"Mr. McKenna, let's try to stay calm. Honest conversation is key. While it can be quite difficult to hear, it can also be quite difficult to say. But that's why we're here, to break down those barriers."

He sits back down but drops his head into his hands, hiding his emotion.

I try my best to explain.

"I don't mean to say that our sex life is bad," I start.

"Gee, thanks," Drew mumbles.

I ignore it and continue, "We have a loving sex life. We make love. It starts and stops there."

He's staring at me again, dark green eyes boring into me like I'm a puzzle he's trying to figure out. Yeah… same, pal.

"What does that even mean, June?" Drew asks me.

How do I explain? I'm not sure I even know what's wrong with our sex life. It's difficult to know what else I might like because I've only experienced what Drew has taught me. I know there is more out there. I know he's done more. Just not with me.

"There isn't an easy way to answer that." I sigh. "Something is missing. Drew holds back in the bedroom, like he's a clenched fist. He handles me with kid gloves. Even when I attempt to change things up, he refuses it. Kindly, he's not a brute about it, but it's refusal all the same," I say. What I don't speak is the truth about how it feels like he's rejecting me. Every single time. "I know there is more to sex than what we have. I see it in movies. I read it in books. Hell, I heard him talk to his girlfriend about things we've never done. What we have is, I don't know, detached, maybe. Feelingless."

"She's not my girlfriend." His eyes roll, and my anger spikes high.

"She's not your fucking wife, either," I snap.

Drew flinches and his head drops back into his hands.

"I'll remind you both again that it's best to stay calm during these conversations. Let's move on to where we're at today. What is your current living situation?" the doctor asks, probably to diffuse the tension quickly filling the room.

"She left me. She'd rather stay at a hotel than be at home with me." He sounds like a dejected puppy.

"That house isn't my home. You were, and you moved in another woman. Or women. I don't even know how many women you screw."

"Jesus. She's never made a snide comment to me before all this. Ever. Now, that's all I get out of her."

"Well, can you blame me for doing it now? You've been sticking your dick in other women."

Drew raises his hands in exasperation.

"How did you find out about Drew's infidelity, June?" Dr. Fillmore asks after clearing her throat to get our attention.

Anxiety flutters in my chest, and my hands immediately start rubbing my thighs again. I feel like I've done nothing but relive the scene since it happened; I don't want to repeat the story. The movement is a coping mechanism I developed while in therapy. After the attack, I'd panic nearly to the point of blacking out. When I'd come down from the static, I often found deep nail marks carved into my palms from clenching my fists so hard. Small, bloody crescents that would take days to heal. Further reminding me of not only my attack, but of my struggle to heal from it. The stress led to the marred palms; the painful palms led to the rubbing of my thighs in hopes of saving my poor skin. It's a cycle I've yet to break. Before this, I had been doing so much better. The panic attacks are nearly non-existent now and I'm much better about recognizing the signs and avoiding the freefall into them. Years of hard work have paid off, but all of this feels like a giant step backward.

Drew is aware of this behavior, of course, and as soon as he sees it, he's kneeling in front of me and clasping my shaking hands in his large, strong ones.

"June came to Los Angeles to surprise me. She found another woman in my hotel room with me," he answers Dr. Fillmore curtly. "I'd rather she not tell the story again, so I'll tell you it was clear what was happening. June left immediately. When I arrived home the following day, she had already packed."

"You didn't return home at the same time?" It's a question, but she states it more as a fact. There is no accusation in her tone, as if she's just getting her facts straight.

"No, we travel as a team. The team came home the following morning." His grip on my hands tightens slightly as I try to sink back into the chair. He's too close. I want his comfort, but I need him away from me.

Finding my voice, I tell her about the tabloid reports in as few words as possible. It's humiliating even in a space that's supposed to be 'safe.'

"I'm sure the public pressure makes this even more difficult to navigate for you both. It would be beneficial for each of you to eliminate as much of it as possible. Broken trust and broken hearts are difficult enough to navigate without the added burden of anyone else's opinions." She takes a drink from her mug. It's a strong tea I can smell from feet away. Lemon and something else I can't identify. It's a pleasant smell and I try to focus on it, letting it seep into my shaky lungs.

"June, are you currently in treatment for your anxiety issues?"

"Yes. I started seeing a psychologist after my attack. I've continued to talk to her. Though, I don't speak to her regularly now, only when I feel I need it," I answer.

"Good, that's good. Is the attack something we need to be discussing? Does it pertain to your marital problems?"

"I don't think so," I say, but Drew's eyes won't meet mine and he says nothing. "Drew?"

"No."

"Okay. June, how did it make you feel? Finding Drew with someone else?"

My head falls back onto the chair. I stare at the ceiling, smooth and cold gray. There's a small rusty ring in the corner. Evidence of past water damage. A scar left there for all to see.

"Lost. As if I'd stepped into another world, where I was too small to be seen. Or another time, where I didn't exist at all. Like I was looking at something that wasn't my life. I think I was mostly functioning on autopilot until I woke up the next morning and saw that Drew had stayed with her."

Drew's head dropped to my lap during my answer. Our hands are now clammy under his warm breath.

"How have you been since then? Do you still feel you're on autopilot, or are you in control?"

"Some of both, I guess. I've mostly felt in control, except for the time I heard strangers talking about us at the coffee shop yesterday. That was a hard moment, but for the rest of the day, I was a little more myself. Today was better."

"What do you mean people were talking about us?" Drew asks.

"There was a couple at the coffee shop I'm doing a write-up for. They saw me there and had a brief discussion on how 'poor June' never stood a chance with you and how they couldn't blame your girlfriend because you're so hot." I'm telling this to the ceiling, to the water stain. As if it's my friend, a confidant, someone who'll never betray my trust. Perhaps I should name this little spot.

I can't look at Drew, not right now.

"Fuck me," he says, and he rises, returning to pacing by the window.

"That news upsets you, Drew?" Dr. Fillmore asks.

"It makes me angry. June shouldn't be taking the fallout for the decisions I make. I never wanted that."

"You don't believe that comes along with marriage, that you weather the storm of each other's choices?" Dr. Fillmore asks.

His pace stutters. He hadn't ever given attention to how much this would all impact me. Has he always walked so selfishly blind in the world? How had I never noticed?

"I… I believe it's a partnership, yes. But in this situation, no. She shouldn't have to deal with the bullshit gossip. This is on me. It's because of my decisions."

"Yes, but as a married couple, most decisions you make affect both of you. The same as with the decisions June makes. Do you think the decisions you've made would be different had you considered that June would be in this position now?"

I send a quick prayer that his answer will be a resounding yes. Of course he'll answer yes. Say yes, Drew. Say yes. Plead all I can, the words don't come.

"Probably not."

Probably not. He says it as if someone just asked him if his favorite baseball team will make it to the World Series this year. Probably not, he said with a shrug. Two such casual words, yet they ravage me in the most complex of ways.

My eyes sting. So, I close them. Close them down, shut it out. Shut him out. A wall heater stops running somewhere in the room, and there is a low tick, tick, tick from it as the coils inside cool and constrict. I sympathize, relating to the feeling of warmth seeping away as you shrivel. I wonder if I will grow smaller and smaller until there isn't anything left of me. A husk of nothing but memories that were all lies.

Probably, I mentally shrug.

Calloused fingers pry my fists apart. I open my eyes to mossy green worry.

"Junie," comes his pained whisper as he rubs his thumbs in circles over my palms.

Pulling my hands from his, I say, "I think I'm done for today. I'm sorry."

"It's okay, June, no need to apologize. I want to tell you both that many couples have been where you are now. You're not alone in this. Our work here is to find the right path to get you both to a healthy place, valid in your feelings, and accepting of the choices you've made. There is no easy fix, simple solution, or guarantees."

A profound sadness over the idea drowns her voice out. That I may not only lose Drew in this mess, but myself, too. With or without him, who will I be after it's all over? Can it ever really be over? I doubt it. Maybe there's a way for us to reconcile, maybe not. I won't ever forget, though. There might be forgiveness in the far-off future. There will never be a time when I can unsee the image of her naked body wrapped around my husband.

"Do you love your wife, Drew?"

"Yes," he answers immediately. No hesitation. No second-guessing.

"Do you love Drew, June?"

"I do. I always will."

Drew makes a sound, low in his throat, as if I've startled him with my answer, but he should know this already. He should know this about me. I've loved him through so much already.

"The fact that you both answered that so easily is a good start. It's a solid base to work from. Do you want to stay married?"

Again, Drew answers affirmatively and instantly. I don't. I hesitate.

"I don't know. I think... I think I'm here because Drew is family and I want to reconcile my friendship with him. Reconciling our marriage is something different. Does that make sense?" I ask her.

"Of course it does. I'd like to see you both as often as your schedules allow. Twice a week preferably, but I understand you have busy lives."

"I'll make it work. Until the season is over, can we keep the appointments flexible?" he asks her. I'm surprised he's willing to commit to that, honestly. It's going to be difficult for him to maintain any appointments and keep up with his training and game days.

"I can work with that as well." She hands him a card. "June, can you manage that?"

"I can, but I may need to video in. I'm in contract negotiations for a job that will take me out of town."

Drew says nothing, but I feel his eyes on me.

"That should be fine. In the meantime, I have some homework for each of you."

I sit forward, propping my arms on my knees. A movement that brings me closer to where Drew sits. He reaches out and laces his fingers with mine. It's both familiar and foreign. I stare at my delicate, pale hand encased in his powerful grip. How do we still fit together? I blink a few times and focus again on Dr. Fillmore.

"First task, I'd like you two to date. I realize we're going about things in an unconventional order. However, I find dating an important part of a relationship. It is the time when we learn the other's likes, dislikes, behaviors. You may both already know those from growing up together, so I'd like you to take the time to learn how to be June and Drew the couple. Not June and Drew, who immediately went from childhood friends to a married couple. Woo each other as if you haven't spent a lifetime together already." She looks at each of us for affirmation.

"Second, your sex life needs attention. However, I am not saying that you should be intimate if you are not ready. Drew, am I correct in assuming you were also not a virgin on your wedding night?"

"I was not." He uses his other hand to wipe his brow, obviously uncomfortable with the direction of questioning.

"June, I'd like you to explore your sexuality."

Drew stiffens, his back now ramrod straight. His hand tightens on mine.

"What?" I ask softly.

"You heard me. The next time we meet, I'd like to know what turns you on, what you fantasize about. You understand?"

I give her a small nod.

"Lastly, Drew, I'd like you to think about what June said about your sex life. It's fair to say she follows your lead in that regard. Therefore, I believe I'm correct in asking you why your sex life isn't as fulfilling as she believes it should be."

He swallows hard, the knot in his throat bobbing. He doesn't like his assignment, but he nods all the same.

"Good. Send me your schedule right away and I'll get your next appointments set up. Until then, take care of yourselves and each other." She stands and gives my shoulder a soft pat as she passes to open the door for us.

CHAPTER 6

June

"We need to talk, Junie."

Drew walked me to my car but now stands in front of my door, preventing me from running away from him and this conversation.

"Probably," I reply.

"How do you feel about your homework assignment?" he asks, and I struggle to read his emotions.

This is not the first thing I want to talk about. It's far down the list. Like, last on the list. It's embarrassing, even with my husband. Especially with my husband.

"I don't know. I feel naïve, abnormal. I'm twenty-seven, Drew. Shouldn't I know by now what turns me on without having to study up on it?" Heat rises to my cheeks.

"I don't think it's strange."

"Yeah, well, at this point, I don't believe that. I was a virgin bride who had barely ever masturbated, and I married a manwhore who doesn't even want to fuck me. That's awfully strange, I'd say." I try to nudge around him.

Drew's arms surround me, halting my progress as he drags me into his chest.

"June, I can't remember a day in all my life that I haven't wanted to fuck you." His fingers tangle in my hair, tipping my head up to look at him.

"But you don't. You fuck others."

"But I love you."

I shove him away. "Are you kidding me? That's your answer. Is that supposed to make it better? You want me to say, sure, babe, sleep with whoever you want as long as you only love me?!"

He flinches at the accusation. "That's not what I'm saying."

"Are you sure? It sounds like that's exactly what you're saying." Tears pool in my eyes. I can't keep up with these whirlwind emotions. Angry one minute, distraught the next. It's exhausting.

His firm hands land on my waist. I've always loved his hands, big, sure. They've made me feel safe and comforted so many times since we married. They've given me the only pleasure I've ever known.

Once, those hands owned me.

Not anymore.

"Listen to me," he whispers, lips just inches from me. A brief touch, mouth to mouth. I tremble. Both need and hurt shivering through me.

"I need you to hear me. I only love you. You're the only woman I have ever loved or wanted. There is nothing wrong with you. We married when you were only twenty-two, June. Inexperienced yes, but then you had me. And I have tried to keep you satisfied." Another touch, as short as the last. "I don't know how to explain everything, to make it make sense. It doesn't even make sense to me. But I promise you, June, I promise I'll make it right. I will."

"How?" The word is barely out of my mouth when his lips meet mine.

Warm, firm lips asking for permission. Or maybe forgiveness. There is a need between us that has never been there before. His tongue dips in, eliciting a moan from me. Encouraged, he deepens the kiss in response.

No. No, I don't want this.

I pull away and step back as far as I can with his hands still on me.

"Sorry," he says, contrite. "Want to tell me about this out-of-town assignment?"

"I wanted to tell you in LA." I sigh. Drew's hands leave my hips and tangle with my own. Again, I had been making fists and not even realizing it.

"I'm sorry for that, too." His eyes bounce between mine and he takes a deep breath. He's hedging. Wanting to say something but unsure how I'll react. We know each other so well. It's unnerving that he's questioning my reactions now.

"How about I take you out on a date tomorrow night and you can tell me then?"

I wake the next morning to my phone ringing with an incoming call from Leighton.

"Hey, Love," I answer.

"Hi, babe. How are you?" Leighton asks.

"Hell if I know, honestly. I'm okay one moment, imploding the next. I feel like Dorothy, spinning around in a tornado. I don't know where I'm going to land, you know?"

There's a beat of silence before she responds.

"You'll land on your feet, June. You always have before."

I have. She's correct. I had to battle my way there, though.

A man named Jonas Givins stalked me nearly my entire senior year of college. It started with him asking me out. I declined the invite. He took it badly and became more and more aggressive in his efforts. My constant rejections prompted him to become more volatile. He began yelling at me in public, calling me a prude one time, a whore the next. He'd leave gifts at my dorm room, colorful flowers, cards filled with the explicitly detailed things he wanted to do with me and to me. Then the flowers started arriving dead. It was disturbing, but I still felt he was mostly harmless. Leighton was the only one I spoke of it with. A few others in the dorm knew—his attention was hard to miss—but I didn't tell Reed or my parents.

Gradually, the gifts increased. In number and creepiness. I began finding small dead birds on my doorstep. Then, small piles of bones, vials of fluid that looked like blood, small animal intestines tied in 'love knots.' By that point, I had alerted campus security and filed a police report. I was in the middle of filing a restraining order when Jonas found me one night. Vulnerable and alone.

I had been careful up to that point, but one night, Leighton could not meet me after a class to walk back to the dorm with me. She had to meet her guidance counselor. And though she begged me to wait for her, I was confident that I could make the four-minute walk home without incident.

I was very wrong. A stupid decision and mere moments changed my life irrevocably. It took me months to get to a point where I wasn't constantly looking over my shoulder for threats, even though my attacker was dead.

Jonas had caught up to me that night with a knife in hand. He held it to the base of my throat as he held me down on the ground. The blade cut into me slowly, the harder he pressed. He mumbled as he struggled to undo my pants with his other hand.

"I've waited so long. How dare you tell me no? You're mine. Mine."

I struggled to get him off, which only made him press the knife in deeper. Despite my fight, he got my pants undone, pulled down. No matter how many times I've tried to block that night from my memory, that feeling of fear will stay with me forever.

Incapacitating fear. Gasping for every shallow breath as my mind raced through ways to survive. Just survive. Survive.

His hand moved to his pants, and my vision blurred through tears as I screamed and fought. Screaming helped. Because of that, his hand moved from his groin to hitting my face. Over and over.

Eventually, help arrived. Two girls and a guy came rushing to my aid. Jonas, so startled by the interruption, moved the knife from my neck and impaled it in my abdomen. He used it as leverage to lift himself up and off me before he fled. The knife left a long wound from my belly to my hip.

When Jonas returned to his dorm, he hung himself.

I'm grateful he's dead. Grateful I didn't have to face the torture of a trial. I'm not grateful that he left precious lifeblood seeping out of me onto the cold, rough ground.

If the knife at my throat had gone any deeper...

He left my jaw broken and one eye swollen shut, but the worst of it was the knife impaled in my belly. It's very unlikely I can ever carry children because of the damage he caused. The risks of miscarriage are high from the wounds he left behind.

"I know I will, eventually. But this is Drew, Leighton. The blow is bigger because I trusted him. I can't imagine him betraying me in any bigger way. Unless he fucked you, of course." I laugh at the idea. Leighton and Drew love each other like a brother and sister. It would be like me fucking Reed and... well, just no.

"Ewwwwwaaaa," she groans. "Gross, June. I'd never. Honestly, I never expected this from him. The guy can't be near you without laying his disgustingly gigantic hands all over you. I would have placed huge bets on the odds that he'd never cheat on you. I don't understand what happened. Did he give any kind of explanation at therapy?"

"No. He keeps saying I don't understand. Yet he doesn't even try to make me understand. What can he say, though? How can he explain falling into another woman's vagina? It's not like I withhold sex from him, or we don't get along. The only thing I can come up with is that he may love me, but he doesn't want me. Not in that way." The last few words come out more choked than I would've hoped. I don't want to sound like a weak and wounded little dove. Not with Leighton, especially. She blamed herself so much for my attack, and the distance between us has been hard for her. I don't want her to worry.

"He loves you. I know that like I know my name." She says it with all the confidence in the world. "Are you still talking to your psychologist?"

"I haven't for a few weeks, but I should probably set something up. Dr. Fillmore suggested Drew and I date. We're going on our first tonight. How bizarre is that?"

"I'd say that's weird as fuck, but I guess it makes sense. You jumped straight from BFF's little sister to wifey in like five minutes."

"Yeah, I guess we'll see how things go tonight."

"You can do this, June. Unless you don't want to. You don't owe him another chance. You know that, right?"

I know it. Deep down, I do. But somehow, I feel like I owe myself one. "I do. I know," I say determinedly.

"Anyway, that's not why I called. I mean, of course I called to check in on you, but I have news! I found you the most amazingly perfect condo, and it's yours for as long as you want it," Leighton says excitedly.

"Tell me everything," I say, letting her enthusiasm work its way into me.

"Okay, my friend, Nina—you remember her, she does the weather. Anyway, her parents have a condo in the French Quarter. It's on Conti, right by the courthouse, so you know... in the middle of everything. Small, but two bedrooms, courtyard, and private balcony. Nina's parents usually only use it a few times a year, but her dad has some health issues and they're choosing to stay in the Mediterranean while he recuperates." Leighton catches her breath. "The rent is reasonable, too. They're just happy to have someone looking over the place for them. Not that it matters. Charge it straight to Drew's accounts, the asshole. Plus, that's only a five-minute walk from me. It couldn't be more perfect!"

She's not wrong. It sounds amazing.

"How soon can I have it?"

"Now, Love. As soon as you want it and for as long as you need it," Leighton answers, and the salting of sympathy in her voice makes me cringe.

"I'll call Jared as soon as I'm awake and fed. Keep you posted?"

"Yeah, June, sounds good. Call me if you need anything. Love you."

"Love you, too."

I shower, dress, and walk to Pike Place Market for coffee and a raspberry bear claw from the bakery there. I don't rush it, taking my time walking through the market. Listening to the chatter of vendors and customers, admiring all the fresh bouquets that are now full of vibrant autumn colors. Even stopping to enjoy a couple of fish being thrown, a big tourist attraction unique to Seattle. A toddler girl, maybe three years old, pulls on her mom's hand, complaining about the smell, and the nearby crowd giggles with her mother.

The entire experience brings a smile to my face. Despite the crowd or the chilly, wet weather, this is always a lively place. I realize I want that. A lively life. Carefree. Which, I know, is not realistic. Who lives a completely carefree life? It can be fulfilling, though. I can make my life that, at least.

A few days ago, I would have told anyone that I had that glorious life. Being married to the love of my life, having my brother close, and my mom happy. I never needed more than that. I was utterly content. Now, though, I feel differently. Now it all feels like a lie. I need to pull myself up by my bootstraps and call my own shots for my best life.

Even if that doesn't include Drew.

With that in mind, I call Jared on my walk back to the Edgewater.

The day goes by quickly and I end up rushing to get ready before Drew gets here for our date, or whatever this is. I spend a ridiculous amount of time stressing over what to wear. The wardrobe in my hotel room is limited to the random items I threw into suitcases while in a haze of heartbreak. And I don't know what Drew has planned. Not to mention, I feel like I need to look my best and that's a whole different problem.

My heart keeps reminding me that Lorelai Simmons is supermodel beautiful. Long legs, perfect curves, gorgeous blonde waves of hair. Staring at myself in the mirror, I can't help but compare. I know I'm not ugly. I'd even say I'm pretty. But I'm tarnished by scars I try to hide. I wear clothes cut high at the neck, never baring my midriff—regardless of my fit stature, thanks to Drew's healthy diet and our active lives. I've always had curves. They've diminished some over the past few years, but I'll never be a size two. Not that I mind. I don't at all. I love my shape.

Doesn't mean I can help the comparison to the body my husband has been sharing his precious free time with.

I'm not ashamed of my scars. That isn't why I cover them. When Drew and I married, there was some media coverage that led to information about me being uncovered. Including my attack. The press went a little wild with it for a few days. It was a hard time for me already, heavily in therapy trying to process all that had happened. The attention made it more difficult. I don't like my emotions on display, let alone my entire life being splayed open for the world to see. So I hid it away as best as I could and hoped people would forget and move on to the next sensational celebrity story. And they did. If I don't remind them about it, the story stays dead.

While Lorelai and her porcelain skin can run around in the sexiest, skimpiest dress, I'm more buttoned up. Prim and proper. Up top, anyway. I never hid away my legs. I have great fucking legs. Somehow, that doesn't seem enough anymore and I gaze at my chosen outfit of a close-fitting black turtleneck on top of a slim pencil skirt in a muted print with a high slit. I finished it with high-heeled sleek booties so I don't look like a child next to Drew's height.

I look good; I don't look supermodel good. Try as I might, I don't feel sexy. Damn Drew for that, too.

A knock on the door pushes away the idea of dwelling on that horrible train of thought. I open the door and it's like another knife to my back. Drew is breathtaking, dressed in a charcoal suit—cut to perfection over his muscular frame—with a dark green tie to match his eyes. Drew is casual to a fault; sweatpants are his everyday outfit. He only dresses up when it's necessary. His current outfit is a low blow. He knows this is my favorite look of his. I let my gaze linger over his body, and when I reach his eyes, there is a look of accomplishment there.

Smug asshole.

"Hey, Junie," he says as he holds out a fresh bunch of daisies, my favorite flower. I don't know how he possibly found them this time of year.

Drew has always spoiled me with little gifts. He gives flowers with regularity, and he knows the kinds I like. The simple ones—wildflowers, daisies, lavender. My wedding bouquet was just an enormous bunch of baby's breath wrapped with a wide ribbon. He often picks up special items for me, too. My favorite dessert from a bakery on the other side of town, a eucalyptus lotion only sold at the market in downtown Seattle. Little things to show he's been thinking about me and he'll go out of his way for me. I'd always appreciated the extra effort, even with his busy schedule.

Does he do it because he's always fucking around with other women? Does he give them these gifts, too?

I don't respond as I turn to place them in my room.

"You look beautiful." Drew follows me in, letting the door shut behind him. The sound makes me jump a little. He notices and says, "It's okay, June, it's just me."

But who are you?

"Let me put these in water, then we can go." I grab the ice bucket and take it into the bathroom. While it fills with water, I take a few deep breaths, trying to calm my nerves. Why should I even be nervous? This is Drew. I've known him forever. But I guess that's the real question. Do I even know him at all?

When I come out of the bathroom, I find him on his phone, his fingers moving fast as he texts. I stand, watching him for a moment. He doesn't even notice I've returned. There is only one thing on repeat in my head: He's talking to her.

"We don't have to do this, you know?"

"What?" he asks, glancing up at me.

"We can reschedule. If she needs you."

"Stop, Junie," he says in a pained whisper.

"I don't know how to stop, Drew. I don't know how to do this. To pretend I'm not suspicious of everything you do. Every minute of every day. Do you know how many times I stopped to wonder if you were with her today? Or yesterday? I don't know how to not hate you for this." My emotions get the better of me and I turn to retreat to the bathroom.

"I'm giving you two minutes, then I'm coming in after you," he says to my back.

I slam the door because I'm a petulant child like that now. I dream of the day I get control of my emotions again. Feeling like I'm nothing more than a nervous product of everyone else's behavior is draining. More importantly, it's not me. It's not who I've worked so hard to become.

Reed and Drew have told me so many times that I worry too much about others. That I should take care of myself better, tell people how I feel more. I don't enjoy arguing; confrontation is something I dread. I don't like the hurt feelings that inevitably follow.

This is a subject that has come up multiple times during my counseling. Rebecca, my psychologist, has suggested that I open up more about how I feel in situations. Especially with Drew. But she validates how I feel more comfortable working through my feelings quietly. It's my system, and it's where I feel most safe. Chaos is not a happy place for me.

Drew is currently my chaos. Yet I can't deny that it makes me feel better to put him in his place regarding his infidelity.

My safe space needs a renovation. Starting with how I see myself and how I allow Drew to see me.

True to his word, at least this time, Drew opens the bathroom door and steps in when he's deemed my time up.

"You don't need to be nervous around me, baby. You weren't last week. You don't need to be now."

Last week feels so far away. Last week feels like a betrayal.

"I understand if you're not ready to do this. We can try it some other time," he says when I don't respond.

Put in the work. That's what Rebecca would tell me. Not for him, but for me.

"I have a question. You need to answer it and then I don't want to talk about your cheating for the rest of the night. I want you to be honest and then take me to dinner like I'm someone you want to spend all your time with. Even if that's a fucking lie." I stand up straight and look into his stupid, beautiful eyes.

"Okay," he says with a hard swallow.

"Have you been fucking other people our entire marriage?"

Drew looks at the ceiling, jaw clenched. He takes a large, gulping breath before he looks back at me with glassy eyes.

"No, not at first." His hands reach up to hold my face, a thumb brushing my lower lip. "Do you want me to explain that?"

God, yes!

"Not tonight. I don't... I don't know what we'll get out of this whole dating thing. But I'd like to believe that if I can never fall back in love with you, at least I can fall back in like with you. So, the dates need to be free of conversations that will only make me hate you," I answer in a trembling voice, close to breaking.

Drew's forehead settles against mine, his eyes closed tight.

"You're breaking my heart, Junie. I know I deserve it," he says as his eyes open back up and find mine. "I also know that I will make you fall in love with me again. It's my sole mission in life and I'm never giving it up. I'm never giving you up."

With that declaration, he takes my hand and leads me out of the bathroom. I grab my handbag and a jacket he says I won't need. I don't know what he has planned, but I'll take it with me, anyway.

Turns out, we aren't going far. He's had the hotel set up a small private tent for us on their outdoor balcony. String lights hang inside, casting a romantic glow. They've placed space heaters strategically around and added a lap blanket on my chair, though it's quite comfortable inside without it.

"There have been paparazzi following me. I didn't think you'd want an audience. But I also didn't want you to think I don't want to take you out," Drew explains, and I'm thankful for the forethought, even if I don't tell him so.

The chef has prepared a special tasting menu for us. If she hopes to win some bonus points with me, it's working. She started us off with Kusshi oysters, followed by a Caldo Verde soup. It isn't until the arrival of the main course of scallops served on a bed of butternut squash mash and a light arugula salad that Drew and I discuss items more important than the weather.

"Are you ready to tell me your news?"

I slowly finish chewing and swallowing the bite of scallop already taken. Drew's eyes are on my mouth the entire time.

"ESPN offered me a job co-hosting some segments in New Orleans leading up to the Super Bowl. Mostly about tourist attractions, special interest stories revolving around sports, and the local food scene, of course." I watch closely for his reaction and hate that I no longer know what to expect. Will he be angry that I want to leave while our marriage is in shambles? Or will he be thrilled for me? And if he is, will it be because this is a great opportunity for me or because it conveniently gets me out of the way for him to spend more time with Lorelai?

"That's amazing, June. It'll be great exposure and give you some extra time with Leighton." He gives me a soft smile. "Would they want you down there around the new year?"

I give a nod. "They asked if I could head down shortly after Christmas. They want segments to start up right before playoffs."

"Do you know who you'd be co-hosting with?"

"Um, yeah. Noah Anders."

"Are you fucking kidding me?" Drew drops his silverware, fists clenching.

Noah Anders was the quarterback at UCLA when Drew was at USC. The schools had an intense rivalry that bled out between the two QBs. Drew never said why, but I know the rift between them was because of more than simply an old rivalry between universities. Drew has more than a general dislike for the man.

Noah only played in the NFL for three years before he suffered a career-ending injury. This is an excellent opportunity for Noah as well. I've met him a handful of times and he's always been kind and rather charming. Despite Drew's distaste, I don't have any qualms about working with him.

Drew was a first-round draft pick, sixth overall. Noah was third that same year, drafted to San Francisco. But their bitterness started way before that. There were plenty of rumors flying about the women they both dated, how even their private lives were a competition. But why hold on to it so many years later?

"No, I'm not kidding. Unless you give me some reason I shouldn't work with him, him being the co-host isn't a factor in my decision at all," I state firmly, leaving the door open for Drew to reveal his feud.

He doesn't. He says nothing and doesn't pick up eating again.

"Does this have anything to do with Lorelai?"

Lorelai was a USC cheerleader. While I never heard of her and Drew ever hooking up, she was a constant for the four years he was there. She was always on the periphery. I can hardly remember a time I went to watch Drew play where Lorelai didn't make an appearance. It would have been easy to assume Drew had a stalker of his own, except he was never wary of her. They had a friendship. She wasn't as vapid and annoying as many other women who hung all over him and she took an interest in his course work, not just his football. I liked her, too.

Look where that got me.

"We're not talking about Lorelai tonight," he barks, and I lose my appetite all at once.

"Fine. It doesn't matter, anyway. I've already accepted, and Jared is working on contracts now."

"You accepted without talking to me first." It's not a question. It feels like an accusation.

"Seems like we both make decisions independently of each other these days," I say with a shrug. He can't possibly expect me to consult him anymore, not after what happened when I first tried to tell him about the offer.

"I guess that's fair," he says.

"Nothing about this is fair, Drew. Not to me, anyway."

He's quiet for a long while, just watching me while I down the rest of my still nearly full glass of wine.

"I just want a chance, Junie. A chance to make this better."

"And I'm giving it to you. I'm here, aren't I? I've committed to counseling, even. But if you think I'll make it easy for you, you don't know me at all. And I've told you, stop calling me that."

Drew sighs. "I don't expect it to be easy. I want you to make it hard for me. That's the only way I'll ever be able to prove you can trust me."

Conversation wanes after that. What's there to say? I don't know if I'll ever be able to trust him again, but that's not great 'date' talk. Neither is Lorelai, even if we'd both shut that topic down tonight.

My career news doesn't seem like something he wanted to discuss anymore, either. I had a tingling sense that his problem with Noah stemmed from something to do with Lorelai. If that was the case, that was not information I could handle very well right now, anyway.

I hadn't even had the chance to tell him I planned on leaving much sooner than the producers asked. Probably for the best. His temper was on the edge. Mine wasn't far behind.

By the time we finished dessert, I was mentally drained and utterly defeated. Our date had started well enough, but it took little for it to career off the rails.

Drew walked me back up to my room in silence, not saying anything until I had my door open.

"I'll see you tomorrow at Fillmore's office," he says before pressing a quick kiss on the top of my head. "I love you."

He walks off while I stare at his back, wondering why the hell I wish he'd stay.

CHAPTER 7
June

After our date, I had decided it was time to do my 'homework.' That project kept me up later than I had planned, feeling like a naïve twenty-seven-year-old who'd never watched pornography before. Which was exactly what I was.

I spent hours scrolling Pornhub, trying every video that sounded appealing. Starting soft with clips that catered to women and quickly realizing they weren't much different from the sexual relationship Drew and I had. Sweet... satisfying enough, but nothing exciting. Not one of those videos prompted me to touch myself.

So deeper down the pornish black hole I went.

Anal videos caught my attention, but every time I tried one, I ended up imagining it was Drew and Lorelai. That only made me angry, and then I started clicking on rougher stuff. I ended up in a loop of light BDSM. The only video I watched in its entirety was of a nude woman bound to a bed by her wrists and ankles while a man pleasured her. A full twenty minutes passed before he pulled off his own clothes. It was all about her, giving her what she needed, what she craved. Bringing her to orgasm time and time again with his fingers, his mouth, his tongue. He worshipped her completely.

After her third climax, she performed oral on him while he kept one hand on her head, directing her, and the other hand stretching over her throat. My hand mimicked his, applying a little pressure, playing at the idea. Jonas's image flashed in my mind, but only briefly. My therapist and I covered the topic of sex regarding my attack, at length. I had to remind myself I was alone and okay, but then I found I liked the feel of the pressure I applied, intrigued by the pleasure this woman found with her partner's dominance.

Then he fucked her. Hard. He didn't stop until he was fully flaccid and falling out of her.

I'm not ashamed to say I watched the last part twice and brought myself to a bursting orgasm along with theirs before I continued to browse through other videos.

Needless to say, I'm still slightly groggy by the time I meet Reed at his favorite Mexican restaurant in the Capitol Hill neighborhood for lunch. It's the first time I've seen him since what I am now referring to as 'The Morning After.' I hate that there is so much worry on his face, so I paste on a smile that I know won't fool him but hopefully will wash away the doom and gloom I've been wearing for days.

"Hey, Ju," he greets me with a big hug that lasts a beat longer than a normal hello.

"Hi, big brother."

We're seated and we've placed our orders before Reed prompts any meaningful conversation.

"How are you doing?" he asks, his voice hushed.

"I'm overwhelmed, but I'm doing okay. I have some news."

"Fill me in."

"ESPN offered me a job co-hosting some pre-Super Bowl programming with Noah Anders. I'd need to be in New Orleans around the first of the year, but Leighton has found me a condo that's available right away."

Reed whistles. "Damn, June. That's amazing and the perfect news to piss Drew off."

"Yeah, well, my acceptance has nothing to do with Drew, and working with Noah is the least of the issues currently spilling off my plate."

Reed eyes me skeptically. "It has nothing to do with Drew, huh?"

"No, it doesn't. I planned to accept before I flew to Los Angeles. At the time, I didn't even know Noah was who I would work with."

"So, when do you leave?"

"I'm not sure. Maybe next week, but I think they want me in Dallas for the Thanksgiving Day game. I might wait and go straight from there, though I don't love the idea of living out of a hotel room for a few more weeks," I answer with a sigh.

"Does you leaving early have nothing to do with Drew, either?"

"That has everything to do with Drew." I laugh a little because I can't deny it. Of course I'm leaving early because of Drew's cheating. I don't feel guilty about it, either. And damn if I don't deserve some humor in my life.

"Good for you, June."

"Aren't you on his side even a little?"

"Fuck no. I love him, he's my best friend, but I would never take the side of anyone who hurt you," he says with all seriousness. "I do know he loves you and I know he's hurting from hurting you. That doesn't mean he hasn't broken my trust completely. He's got atoning to do with both of us."

I wish I could believe that Drew is hurting, too. My heart wants to believe it. Everything in me wants to believe it. Because if it were true, maybe I'd be able to forgive him. Maybe we'd still have a future together.

"You've spoken to him?" I ask.

"He calls every day. Mostly he asks about you. Couldn't care less about me or my life, the asshole. What a shit-ass best friend." He's smiling like a fool, but it might be as false as mine.

"Yeah? Try being married to the dickhead," I say, grinning again. Reed has always made me laugh, even in the worst of situations. I want to reassure him as much as he wants to do the same for me.

"Disgusting, Ju. It'd be like fucking... well, you." He shudders. We've always been very alike, very close. Reed is my forever BFF.

"Promise you'll come to visit me in New Orleans. Leighton would love to see you." I give him a wink. He's terrified of Leighton. Although, I think it's because he knows how good they'd be together. Leighton tries to bed him every time she sees him. At first, I believed it was because she saw how uncomfortable it made him and she found it entertaining. But it's grown from there. I'm positive they're both harboring some serious feelings for each other and are just too cowardly to act on them.

"Leighton on her best behavior at Sunday church is an experience I would barely survive. Put her on Bourbon Street after she's had a few drinks, and I am a dead man. Are you inviting me to an early grave, dear sister?"

"Oh, come on. She's a riot, but she's not lethal."

Reed cocks a brow at me. And, yeah, okay... she's more than just a riot, but that's what makes her so much fun.

Leighton is a sweetheart and kinder than most humans I've met so far. She'd also be the first one to accept the challenge of streaking through campus in our college days. She once jumped on stage at a strip club and joined the exotic dancers, baring herself down to just some skimpy panties. The lady has few limits and is a consummate exhibitionist. I've never known her to decline a dare, though she has tamed down since landing her current job.

She's the perfect fit for New Orleans. Business by day and ready to live it up every night. She's had a full life already in her twenty-seven years. While I'm a little jealous of that, I'm also abundantly happy for her and can't wait to see what she does in the next twenty-seven years. And honestly, I'm excited to experience her contagious enthusiasm for a while.

I want to live my life to the fullest, as she has. Sadly, I believed I had been, and that's something I genuinely should be analyzing. Because why is my happiness so wrapped up in Drew? He can't be the only thing that makes the difference between a mediocre existence and true happiness.

Grief is a strange thing, like an echo following you with horrible consistency. I'm terrified I'll always hear it. The rest of my life could be plagued by this tiny voice in the back of my head regularly reminding me that I wasn't good enough to keep my husband.

Worse, that I'll never learn to love again. Or that I'll never evolve to being comfortably alone. That no matter what I try, I'll always be chasing mere contentment.

"Where did you go, Ju?" Reed asks, shaking me from my brain fog.

"Can I ask you something, and you give me an honest answer, regardless of how brutal it may be?"

"Of course," he answers, albeit skeptically.

"Was I happy before Drew asked me to marry him? I mean, have I let my entire life revolve around him?" Tears sting my eyes, which only makes me hurt more. This is not who I am. It's not who I want to be. A simpering, emotionally unstable woman crying constantly over a man.

There are a few bloated silent moments before Reed responds. "I think before Drew proposed, you were waiting for your happiness to start. It was like you knew something was coming and you were holding your breath for it to arrive, constantly watching for it. Instead of enjoying life and letting whatever it was find you. Does that make sense?"

I give a shaky nod, taking a healthy gulp of my margarita, as he continues.

"When you and Drew married, it was like it had finally happened. It had arrived, that mysterious thing you'd been holding out for, which turned out to be Drew. And, fuck, Ju, I was thrilled. Seeing you light up as you did, I loved Drew even more for that. You'd come out of your shell, emerging into the world with such brightness despite what you'd gone through." He wipes a tear from his eye, and I reach over to grab his hand.

"I want to hurt him for taking that away from you. For taking it away from me. If the only way for you to find that again is without him, so be it."

"Are you saying you don't want us to get back together?"

"No, that's not what I'm saying. Whether you two stay together or don't, it is between you two. What I want is for you to figure out how to get that sunshine back on your own. Do you understand, Baby Girl?"

God, when he calls me that. He only ever does it when he's feeling uber emotional. It's equally endearing and heartbreaking.

"I get it, Reed, I do. I'm just now understanding that I've been hanging all my hopes and dreams on him. Stupid, huh?"

"Not stupid. Romantic. In a wholly unhealthy way and all that." Reed gives me a wink, lightening the mood.

"Thanks, asshole."

"Anytime."

Walking into the hotel, I glance at my phone to check the time. I have roughly an hour before I need to be at Fillmore's office for another therapy session with Drew. Enough time to close my eyes for a few minutes, ruminate on my conversation with Reed, and still have time to freshen up before heading back out. That stupid voice inside me still tells me I need to look my best whenever I see my cheating husband. I wish I could muzzle myself. Choke that bitch right out.

I'm almost to the elevator when I'm waylaid by someone calling my name. I turn to see who and freeze, my blood running cold.

Lorelai fucking Simmons is striding toward me on her long, gazelle-like legs. Her stupidly perfect ice-blonde hair flowing behind her. Even with oversized sunglasses on, she's not inconspicuous in the least.

"Are you fucking kidding me?" I hiss when she's near enough to hear me.

"June, please, I just want a minute of your time." The gall of this woman is truly baffling.

"You have had so many minutes of my time, Lorelai."

She flinches as if I've physically slapped her. Something I probably should have done.

"Please," she pleads. I look away from her, noticing several people, staff and guests alike, taking an interest in our conversation.

"Not here." I seethe. "Follow me."

As calmly as I can, I press the button to call the elevator and wait for the doors to open. Why is she here? What could she possibly hope to accomplish?

We step into the empty elevator, and I press the button for my floor. When the doors close, she offers a quiet, "Thank you."

"Fuck all the way off."

Lorelai shuts her mouth tightly until we're inside my room.

"What do you want?" I ask the bane of my existence.

She wrings her hands together. I find a grim satisfaction in making her nervous. This beautiful, perfect creature brought to anxiety by little old poor June.

Well done, me.

"I was hoping to explain, maybe. Try to help." The nerve of this woman, the absolute audacity of her not only showing up at my hotel, but to claim she wants to help… she's lost her addled brain.

"Don't you think you've helped enough?" I grit out.

"I'm so sorry, June. I don't know what to say, but it's not what it looks like."

"It's not? Because what it looks like is you've been having an affair with my husband. Sexual relations, to be clear. Not just the emotional kind. Though, maybe it's been that, too. Perhaps you could fill me in. Do you want to tell me all the ways you fill your time together? Breakfast in bed, accompanied by deep conversation while cuddling, maybe? Only after a long night of him fucking you in the ass, of course."

Lorelai pales. Her hands stop wringing, and I notice the slight shake in them. Whatever she expected out of me, it probably wasn't this. Maybe she hoped she'd get the polite June who never says the wrong thing, who charms everyone when she's on Drew's arm at public functions. It's the only me she's ever met before. That June is not in the room right now. She's buried deep in the cold ground, under six feet of pain and anger.

Or maybe she believed she'd find me broken, drowning in my own tears, unable to function at all. I bet she hoped for that version of me. Then she could have lorded her accomplishment over me, the trophy that is my fucking husband. The award for being the one who gets to fuck my husband.

"What do you want me to say, June?"

"You came here, Lorelai. What do you want to say? Leave off the verbal traffic, just get to the damn point. If it's not what I think, tell me what it is."

"I just meant that there isn't any love there. Drew does not love me. That's not what this is."

"Did you two rehearse that bullshit?"

She sighs. "No, it's the truth, June. I know it doesn't make it better, what we've done. But you should still know it. He loves you so much, and this is killing him. He's so upset that he's hurt you."

"Yeah? Did he tell you that?" I miraculously keep the anger out of my voice when I ask, but I can picture them snuggled up together, spent after a long fuck, discussing how sad they are that they hurt me.

Give me a break.

"Yes, all the time. He's distraught. He misses you so much."

"All the time, huh?"

Lorelai nods and her mouth opens to say something else before she realizes what she's alluded to. They talk. All the time. About me.

Fucking glorious.

"God, I'm making it worse, aren't I?" She pauses for a response. All I give her is a raised eyebrow. "Drew and I are friends. We have been for such a long time. This was a situation to help each other out, is all. It was never meant to be more than that."

Lorelai's head drops for a moment. When she looks back up, there is something new in her eyes. It's replaced the nervousness that was there before. Pain, or sadness, but I can't be sure it's for me and not for herself—a reaction due to Drew not immediately dumping me for her, maybe.

"Don't ask me to sympathize with you, Lorelai. I've been friends with him for longer, and if he needed help, he should have come to me. If you needed it, you should have found a single man. It's not like you didn't know he has a wife."

"I know. God, I know," she says, tears pooling in her eyes. "I never set out to be the other woman. I hate what I've done, what I've become. What I am. It's an awful feeling."

"Well, look at it this way. If I divorce Drew, maybe you'll get the chance to be his wife and you can feel how awful that side of it is, too."

"Is that what you want?" she asks, and that same emotion flashes on her face again. "Drew doesn't want that. He'll only ever love you."

"Oh, honey, I know he'll only ever love me. But this is no longer about what Drew wants. And for the record, this isn't what love looks like. Maybe you can learn that lesson before you help ruin another marriage," I tell her as I go to the door, holding it open for her to walk out.

CHAPTER 8
Drew

I'm a fucking idiot.

Complete damned moron. I know it. June knows it. By the way Lorelai just played this, she knows it, too.

I did not mean to let the name of June's hotel slip while talking to her. Hell, I didn't even want to be talking to Lorelai at all. I'm done with her. She doesn't believe that yet, but I am.

After about her fiftieth phone call, I answered, disgruntled... but I answered. I need her to lay off, to give the fuck up. Determined to convince her, I took the call.

Lorelai isn't who she seems to most people. I'm one of the few who knows that. She's all hard as nails exterior, but inside, she's still a fragile thing who's terrified of the real world. One night, before June and I were a couple, she laid out her secrets. I've always been sympathetic to them, even to the point of helping the situation financially.

After today, my sympathy is near nonexistent. She cried to me about how she hates being branded as a homewrecker, my sidepiece, a whore. About how awful she feels because she genuinely likes June. She even quit her job because her boss saw the tabloid stories and thought he could take from her the same things I do.

Did.

Then today, she confronts my wife and makes the situation worse.

While she was lamenting about her life, I, too, was lamenting mine, and in a depressive stupor, I let slip that my wife would rather stay at the Edgewater than with me.

Lorelai took that information and ran with it. Now she's texting me about how pissed June is.

More pissed, anyway; she's been plenty angry since that evening in Los Angeles.

I'm furiously texting back, telling her to stay the fuck out of my life. And to never say another word to June, let alone look at her, when the door to Dr. Fillmore's lobby opens. I know it's June by the scent of her. It's always the same. Sage and something like fresh rain and clean air. Earthy and calming.

Calm is not a word I'd use to describe her right now.

"June, I'm so sorry."

"Stop it. We'll only talk inside," she says, gesturing to Dr. Fillmore's office. I try to argue, but the doctor opens the door to call us in. She immediately steps in and takes a seat set away from all others. Effectively, making it so I have no choice but to keep a distance.

"How is everyone today?" Dr. Fillmore asks when we're all settled.

"I'm okay," I reply with caution.

"Just fucking peachy," June says, her words laced with sarcasm and a wince on her pretty, irate face.

"Well, isn't that interesting? Please elaborate, June." Dr. Fillmore settles into her seat, waiting for June to continue.

"Okay, well, today I woke up late because I spent hours watching porn as my homework. Which was interesting but exhausting. I had lunch with my brother and got to see firsthand how this is breaking his heart as well. Then, I was running late getting here because Drew's girlfriend dropped by my hotel to tell me she's so sorry and it's okay because they don't love each other. So, I should just forgive him so we can get on with our picture-perfect bullshit lie of a marriage. And to top it off, I've accepted a job that requires me to move to New Orleans and I'll probably be leaving next week." The word vomit rolls right out. It probably makes her feel better. It makes me feel like complete scum.

Which… yeah, I guess is true. No time for that, though, because what the fuck did she just say?

"A, she is not my girlfriend. B, what do you mean you're leaving next week?"

June rolls her eyes at me.

"That's a lot to unpack. If you don't mind, I'd like to start with your homework assignment," Fillmore says.

"Can we circle back to that in just a second?" June asks. "I'd like Drew to answer one question first."

"By all means," she replies.

Fuck my life.

"How did Lorelai know I was staying at the Edgewater?"

My leg bounces now that I'm in the hot seat. I could tell the truth. I should tell the truth. Except when I open my mouth to explain, all the right words don't come out.

"I told her."

"Why did you tell her how to find your wife, Drew?"

"Lore wanted to apologize, maybe try to make the situation better. At this point, I'm willing to try anything."

Not a lie, not the entire truth, either. I'd like it to look like I had some control of the situation rather than being a victim of Lorelai's games. But, again, I'm a fucking idiot.

"Lore?" June sneers at me.

I grimace. It looks bad, but it's what everyone always called her. It's not some pet name I gave her. Though, I did give her one of those. I don't know where to begin digging myself out of that grave.

"Do you understand how that action could make June feel you prioritize Lorelai's needs, or even your needs, over her own?" Dr. Fillmore asks.

"I do now."

"Isn't it interesting you were not aware of that before this moment, Drew? Perhaps that is an issue that you could work on, yes? Evaluating the angles of June's feelings before you complete an action that affects her." She takes a sip of her strongly scented tea.

I clear my throat before I answer. "I can do that, yes."

"Is that acceptable to you, June?"

"I'd like to say yes. But my faith in him right now is thin. It's not even the only thing that makes me feel secondary to her. They talk. About his feelings. About me." She sighs. "All he says to me is the same regurgitated bullshit every cheater says. He's sorry, it's not what I think, he only loves me, blah, blah, blah. If he is as in love with me as he says, why is he having those conversations with her?"

"I do not think you're secondary, Junie. Not at all."

She won't look at me as I plead with her.

"Why don't you talk to June, Drew? Tell her the things you tell your friend."

June scoffs at that.

"I don't know how," I say honestly. I don't know how to explain why I need what I do. And while June is under the impression that Lorelai and I have had some deep conversations about the subject, that's not the truth. I don't discuss my relationship with June. Nothing more than surface deep anyway.

"You speak the words. Why don't we try it? June, ask him something specific."

"Why do you have sex with her?"

The blood drains from my face, along with any ego or masculinity I had when I walked in here today.

"Straight to the point. I think that's fair," Dr. Fillmore says with pride. June practically preens under the praise.

Meanwhile, I sit here with shriveled balls.

"Shit, I don't know how to start. Um, for a long time I've had certain sexual proclivities, I guess," I say, running a hand through my thick hair, leaving it a mess. Much like my marriage.

"Can you not satisfy these proclivities with your wife?" she asks me.

"No, I don't think I can," I say, feeling like I just stabbed a knife into my wife's heart.

By her reaction, she feels the same. Her hand goes to her chest, rubbing at the acute sting of it all. Her breathing is heavier, more erratic. I recognize it as the start of a panic attack. I know the signs well since I've had so much experience witnessing them these past five years.

I've hated every single one. June's kindhearted, empathic, sweeter than anyone I've ever known. Nobody deserves what Jonas has done to her, but least of all someone like her.

I can't say I'm a much better person than him at this point. Because she isn't having this attack because of Jonas; it's because of me. And that's the exact thing I've tried so hard to avoid.

I move to kneel in front of June as Dr. Fillmore asks her to count to twenty, taking a deep breath with each number. Her hands look so small as I gather them into my own, trying to warm them with gentle kisses.

I didn't think I could hate myself any more than I did, but every day proves that's not the case.

When she gets to twenty, June opens those whiskey eyes. "I'm okay. I'm okay."

She tries to catch the attacks before they spiral out of control. At first, she always failed. My baby is a fighter, though, and now, often, she is able to get control of them before they get control of her. It helps when someone is close and can help distract her from them. I worry about her being alone through all of this.

Only have myself to blame for that.

"I need you to continue," she says.

"No, Junie. No. I can't keep hurting you like this."

"We're past that now. I need to know," she says in barely a whisper.

Fillmore takes her seat once again. "For the moment, I think it's important we trust June to know what she can handle and trust her to tell us when she's at her limit. Let's try to continue, Drew."

I'm quiet for a long time until she pulls her hands from mine and I finally look up at her. Then quickly away. I'm about to make this worse. She knows it. I know it. I also know I don't have a choice. It's why we're here.

"You've been hurt so much, baby. I just couldn't be someone who hurt you, too," I say.

"Then stop doing it." She looks confused and I shake my head.

"Do you mean you don't want to hurt her during sex, Drew?"

I nod, keeping eye contact with June in a desperate attempt for her to see that I hate myself for putting us here.

"Are you saying you are a sadist?" Fillmore asks.

"No. It's not that extreme. I don't crave giving pain. It's the control I need and sometimes that comes with an edge of discomfort."

June shakes her head, still trying to understand everything I'm saying.

"What type of discomfort? Elaborate, please?" Dr. Fillmore asks.

"Binding, spankings, that sort of thing. Occasionally light breath play," I say, my eyes involuntarily drawing to her neck. To the long and jagged scar that sits there, a forever reminder of the worst night of her life.

"Is this a joke?" Her hand reaches to the puckered skin as she tries to hide what little of it shows above her collar.

I shake my head, indicating it's not at all a jest.

"You can't fuck me the way you like because of my scar?"

"No! That's not it at all. I don't care about your scars. I never have. I care about triggering you. It scares me to death that you'll see Jonas when my hands are on you." A tear falls from my eye and I'm surprised to find hers are dry.

"Who is Jonas?" Dr. Fillmore asks.

"The man who attacked me in college," June answers, still dazed by the direction of the conversation.

"I thought that was something we didn't need to discuss here," Dr. Fillmore states.

"I thought so, too," June says.

"We don't. I mean, the attack isn't the issue exactly," I answer.

"But the attack is the catalyst for the issue we now face, yes?" she asks me.

I don't answer. Not because I don't want to. The words don't come.

"You said Jonas couldn't take anything else from me." The tears have come now, and she angrily swipes at them. "After we found out all the damage he had done to my body. After we learned he had killed himself. You said, he can't take anything else from you, Junie. Those were your words."

"He can't, baby, he can't."

"He has, Drew! He's taken you. And you let him do it."

No denying that accusation.

"Drew, did you ever attempt any of these sexual acts with June?"

"No, he never did," June answers for me. "Had he ever tried to talk to me about it, he'd know I would've been responsive."

"Are you certain of that?"

"Yes," she answers with so much certainty. "Returning to my homework assignment, the only videos I watched last night that held my interest were of women being controlled. Being bound, restrained, held down, spanked, choked."

My eyes widen with terror at her admission.

"I was more turned on than I'd ever been in my life and when I brought myself to pleasure, it was harder than any other time."

"June," I scream out my despair, except it comes out as only a whisper.

"Isn't that the rub? Our marriage thrown away for a reason that didn't even exist. You chose not to discuss it with me and instead lie and sneak around with other women. You chose betrayal instead of communication."

"I understand this is a volatile situation, June, but let's try to refrain from accusations and concentrate on what you're feeling."

Let her accuse. Let her blame me. Let her flay me alive and dissect me piece by rotten piece.

"Fine, fine," she says, resigned. "I feel more betrayed by Drew now than I did by Jonas after he attacked me." Brutal fucking honesty. She's over sparing me any feelings. She's been doing it her whole life. I'm proud of her, even if I'm the one on the receiving end. "I feel like this is the most bullshit reason to have cheated on me. It would have been one thing for him to approach me and get a rejection, but to not even try... hurts like fucking hell. Once again, it makes me feel like he wanted to choose her over me. Like he didn't even try to pick me. And all that makes me think is that it can't be just about sex. There must be emotions attached."

"Drew, how do you feel about what June has said?"

My throat is restricted, and I don't feel my fingers at all, since I'm clenching them so tightly. It takes several tries for me to swallow down my own panic before I can speak.

"There isn't a word for how horrible I feel. I can't believe I've put us here, that I fucked up so badly, no matter that I deluded myself into thinking I was doing it for some noble reason. I feel like she'll never forgive me for this."

She lets that hang in the air between us, giving me no indication of her current frame of mind.

Dr. Fillmore is the one to end the silence. "Forgiveness never comes quickly. It can't be rushed. There is grace in granting forgiveness, but that same grace must happen while waiting for forgiveness. You must give it time. Now, why did you think you couldn't speak to June about this subject specifically?"

"Our first time"—I pause to clear my throat—"on our wedding night, I knew it was her first time and I took extra care because of that. I figured we could work up to the things I like in bed after she had some time and experience. I didn't want to overwhelm her. But I didn't know about the nightmares. God, they were awful. I'd wake up to her screaming, fighting him off. Repeatedly. They lasted for so long, years, and I thought she'd hate me if she knew what gets me off. If she needed to fight me off like she was still doing to him, it would devastate us both."

My stare is on June, but that's not what I see. I picture her in those days. When she couldn't make it through the day without a panic attack, or a night without a nightmare. Even after I'd get her calm, awake in my arms, the sheer agony on her face wouldn't fade until she was back asleep.

It was hell. More so for her, of course. Though, Jonas made victims of all of us who love June, in varying degrees.

Asking her if I could tie her up and restrict her air while I fucked the shit out of her was out of the fucking question. And, yeah, I'm a bastard for not being able to restrain myself from finding that with other women. I'm not debating that. Only that some coping mechanisms are fucking hard to break and I didn't try hard enough.

"June, how do you feel about what Drew's saying?"

"I feel like I should get some time to process it all, if I'm being honest. Something inside me is saying I understand why he couldn't broach the subject with me back then. But that didn't give him the right to do this to us. To me. I worked so hard, so fucking hard, to get past those nightmares and to heal. Inside and out. And here I am, splayed back open because he didn't put the work in on his end."

Fuck.

"Do you still have these nightmares?"

"No, not for a long while now. At least a couple of years."

"Good, good. Would you like to give us some more details on the videos you enjoyed? Perhaps it would help Drew know what, exactly, you liked about them?"

Her cheeks lighten from the angry red they've been to a shade closer to pink as she moves from pissed off to thoroughly embarrassed.

"The man tortured her with pleasure for the longest time. He took all the control but gave her all the sensation by bringing her to orgasm several times before he even bared himself. When he did, he was forceful but never brutal. Though you could see she wasn't always comfortable in the positions he put her in, you could also tell how much she craved it, and more, how much she craved him." She pauses for a moment to compose herself. She's affected by the retelling. My dick tells me it is too, the stupid fuck. "I wanted to feel what she felt. It was so honest and real. So many other videos were obviously women paid to be doing what they were doing. Just going through the motions. This woman wanted it and the man wanted to give it to her, but in his way."

"Did any of his actions frighten you?"

"No. The woman had complete trust in him, so I did, too. Even when he was choking her, there was nothing but excitement in her eyes. I knew he wouldn't take it too far. I even tried to choke myself a little, to see if I'd like it."

"And did you?" she asks.

"I did. Well, as much as you can enjoy the things you do to yourself, I suppose. It's not quite like the real thing, is it?"

"No, I suppose it's not," Dr. Fillmore replies. "Perhaps now, if the time comes where you two could be intimate again, this topic won't be so taboo. Yes, Drew?"

June finally looks at me again. Hard as I try, I can't keep the heated hunger off my face. For years I've dreamed of similar scenarios with June.

"I'd love nothing more than to discuss this further," I say, my voice rough with desire.

June narrows her gaze on me, unimpressed by me being turned on by her homework lesson.

The subject changes to our date, and I explain how it went. June gives minimal feedback and only when prompted. Otherwise, she's sort of checked out of this therapy session. Pain clutches my stomach from the stress of it all, the rollercoaster of emotion I've put her through.

We wrap it up with her letting Dr. Fillmore know that she'll keep her updated on her schedule and move, and promising to keep appointments even if she has to video call in. These sessions are important. We need them. I only wish they didn't tax her so much.

I follow June out to the parking lot. She doesn't notice, too involved with her phone, until we've made it all the way to her car.

"Are you actually leaving next week?"

She sighs and turns around to face me. "I haven't decided. Jared just told me they want me in Dallas for Thanksgiving. I might go straight from there instead."

"I'm glad you'll be at my game," I tell her, a small smile on my lips.

"I'm not going for you. You didn't even invite me," she says pointedly. "Work did."

"I expected you were going with me," I say sheepishly, because yeah… I hadn't clearly expressed that I wanted her to go. It's Thanksgiving. I assumed she'd want to be with me for the holiday.

"That's news to me."

"Junie, please. Can we try to have a conversation without all this attitude?"

"No, and for fuck's sake, stop calling me that," she says flatly. "My whole life, you've tried to get me to stand up for myself. Well, here I am. Don't like it now? You can fuck off. Right along with your girlfriend. Or is it plural?"

"It's not even singular. She's not my girlfriend," I say, frustrated by this whole girlfriend bullshit.

"Drew, give it up. She is. What else do you call the woman you fuck, travel with, discuss your feelings with? When she's not your wife, anyway."

"She's a friend. That's it. And yes, occasionally I confide in her how fucked up I'm feeling because of the unique situation we're all in."

She laughs then, and it quickly becomes one of those hysterical types that takes over uncontrollably. It takes her a minute before she wipes away the delirious tears and speaks again. All I can do is watch the shit show I created.

"You are not in a unique situation. Men have been doing this type of bullshit forever. I'm the lady wife that the gentleman husband can't 'fuck' because that's always reserved for the mistress. Wives are for homemaking, baby-making, and lovemaking in a safe, passionless missionary position, right? The mistresses get all the dark and seedy goods. You're nothing but an antiquated cliché, Drew."

"Damn, you got mean," I mumble while looking down at my feet. "I thought we made progress today, but I guess not."

"Oh, we made progress. At least now I know my husband didn't trust me enough to talk to me about his sexual desires. Even when I tried to bring up the idea that we needed to change things. And now I know that you have zero faith in the progress I've made since my attack. You still think I'm that same scared, fragile girl."

"That's a lie, June. I have so much faith in you. I'm nothing but proud of what you've accomplished. You're the strongest person I know."

Her not believing that I see who she is, what she's accomplished is my biggest regret yet. Nothing hurts like that does. She came back from the brink of death. Torn, bloody, bruised, and broken. She fought through it all to be here. Every day since her attack she's grown stronger and braver. How could she think I don't see that?

"More than anything, I want to believe that. But your actions don't back up those words. You went to someone else for what you needed from me, Drew. She got what should have been mine. You've been looking at her the way you looked at me in there today. With desire the likes you've never shown me. It fucking gutted me."

I can't take any more. I wrap her up in my arms that feel enormous around her smaller frame. She snuggles in and even I know she hates herself for repeating the habit. I tighten my hold so she can't escape. I'm an asshole like that, but I also know she's falling apart and it's my job to keep that from happening.

Again, anyway.

"I hear what you're saying, baby. I do," I say, ruffling her hair where I've buried my face. "But what you don't understand is that I didn't do any of this because of anything you've done. It's because I'm a fucking coward, June. I want you to remember that. Hold on tight to it. Hold on to that hate for me. I deserve every bit of it." I press a long kiss on the top of her head. She tries to look up at me, but I don't release my hold.

"I fucking love you, June," I say, injecting as much feeling into the words as I can. And then I leave her. I leave her be. I give her space. Determined to give her the time she needs without me constantly in her face reminding her of what an asshole I am. She deserves that, and I'll use it to figure my shit out.

Even as I die a little more with each step.

CHAPTER 9

June

Drew contacts me very little after that day. In the following week, he cancels our session with Dr. Fillmore and only shoots me brief texts to check in on me and ask if I know when I'm leaving for New Orleans.

After discussing it all with Jared, the owners of the condo, Leighton, Reed, and my mother—all of whom had varying opinions on my current situation—I decide to head to 'The Big Easy' as soon as possible. It wasn't a tough move. I took what I had with me at the Edgewater and boarded a plane.

When I'd spoken to Leighton last, she'd promised me an epic shopping spree when I arrived in town. I would be holding her to it since most of what was currently weighing down the luggage I hauled off the baggage claim carousel was Pacific Northwest fall wear and would kill me here in the southern heat and humidity.

I'm grabbing the third, and last, suitcase when I hear a squeal behind me. A smile takes over my face, knowing that noise can only come from one person.

Turning, I find Leighton running toward me on six-inch, studded, black stilettos, and a dress just on the safe side of indecently short.

"You look amazing," I say, just as she lunges at me. I wrap my arms around her, too. "You're a sight for sore eyes, Love."

"I can't believe you're here," she says excitedly, placing a hand on each side of my face and giving me a loud, smacking kiss right on my lips. It's such a Leighton thing to do, and it makes me laugh every time.

She grabs one of my bags and leads me toward the parking.

"Why did you park? You could have just grabbed me curbside."

"Lady, please. I've been waiting in the parking lot for nearly an hour, waiting and hoping your flight would land early. I was too excited. Plus, I wore my chauffeur outfit. If I picked you up curbside, who would have seen it?" Her dress is a black, fitted, plunging dress that does not scream 'chauffeur,' but I play along.

"True, we can't deny all these jet-lagged travelers the adrenaline rush of almost seeing your lady bits as you bend over to grab my bag."

"Right," she agrees excitedly. "I've got today and tomorrow off, so I planned out our days. I'm going to take you to your place first. We have a couple of hours to get settled in, then I'm taking you for dinner and drinks at one of my favorite places. Tomorrow, we shop and my stylist friend is coming by for mini-makeovers."

Leighton babbles about anything and everything on our drive to the French Quarter, pointing out this or that. The best spot for manicures, the bar that makes the most amazing hurricane drinks, the spot to go for beignets outside of the French Quarter, etc. She'd settled into her life here and it made me so happy.

Leighton didn't have family outside of a single dad who raised her from the time she was four years old. Her mother fell off the face of the Earth due to drug addiction. Her dad, Larry, is the sweetest man, but he'd already been in his forties when Leighton had come along. He hadn't been able to keep up with Leighton and her wild personality in her teen years. Or beyond them. He was a military man, and they'd moved around a lot. It was hard for her to make friends. Until me, that is.

Her dad is currently enjoying his twilight years at a retirement community in Palm Springs, loving his life, but doesn't get out to see Leighton as much as he would like, and her schedule doesn't make it easy for her to go visit him either.

Leighton parks her car in front of a small, three-story brick building. I'm instantly giddy at its charm and floor-to-ceiling windows.

"Love, is this it?"

"It is. It's so fucking perfect. You're going to love it," she answers. "The entire third floor is yours, and it's fabulous. I met Nina here this morning to grab the keys and drop off some basics for you—coffee, wine, bacon." I laugh at that while we grab my luggage and head into the small entry space of the building. It houses a stairwell, three wall mailboxes, and not much else.

"Door code is 49275. There is a call box in your unit to buzz someone in." She takes the stairs in her heels like she'd been born wearing them. I follow, taking in the old-world feel of the building.

When she opens the door to my unit, I gasp at how perfectly gorgeous it is. High, white ceilings with dark, worn beams. Plastered walls that expose original brick in places. The furniture is all buttery leather, with woven blankets draped here and there. And the natural light shining in from all the windows gives it an inviting feel.

There is a larger main bedroom that just barely fits the king-sized bed and has an en-suite bathroom complete with a claw-foot soaker tub. A teeny second bedroom sits next to it, with a twin bed and a desk that will be a great workspace for me. The kitchen isn't very large either, but the appliances are all top of the line. Not that I'd be using them much, anyway. Art eclectically covers the walls, all with the same old world, almost gothic feeling much of the city exudes. But the best part is the wrought-iron balcony complete with a bistro table set that looks out over the building courtyard. I already know I'll be there every morning with my coffee.

I fucking love it.

"Leighton, it's perfection."

"I know! It's so weirdly you, like it was fate or some shit like that. Go unpack. I'll pour some wine."

The closets are every bit as small as to be expected. The spare room is where I ended up storing all my heavier items to save room for the upcoming shopping spree. Leighton comes in carrying two glasses ridiculously full of red wine as I am hanging the last few items.

"Damn, Love, you trying to get me sloshed?"

"Yes," she answered, sitting down on the bed to watch me work. "How are you doing?"

"I'm a depressing mess. My moods swing from sullen to psycho bitch in about two seconds flat. Like PTSD type shit. The smallest thing sets me off unexpectedly. And I think maybe I've never known honest happiness. Besides all that, I'm on top of the world." I sigh.

"Oh, honey. You've known happiness. I know how you felt when you married Drew. I could see it. Anyone could. Don't sell that short, despite what's happened since."

"I'm trying. It's just… I feel like maybe I put all my eggs in his basket. Only to find out there was a hole in the bottom."

"June, stop. You put nothing but your trust in Drew. And yes, he broke that in such a horrifying way that I want to string him up and gut him slowly for it. But there is absolutely no shame in falling in love and doing whatever it takes to build a life with that person. That's what you did, and it's okay. It hasn't worked out the way you expected, but you have this tremendous opportunity now and the chance to take it without guilt."

She stands and hands me my glass. I take it and down a large gulp of the strong wine.

"No guilt, huh?" I ask.

"Nope, none. You made sacrifices with your career because you wanted to be supportive and close to the man you love. If you think I wouldn't do the same if I ever loved a man the way you do Drew, you're wrong. Most women would, even highly career motivated ones. He fucked that up and now you get to make whatever decisions you want without that as a factor. Unless you want it to still be a factor, because that's your call, too."

"I'm not so sure anymore. I haven't spoken to him in eight days, Leighton. He texts occasionally, but that's it. What if he's made his own decision?" I turn back to my task, knowing that if I see her look at me with anything like sympathy, I'll break down.

"Ah, babe, I don't believe for a second he's decided on anything but giving you some space. He has plenty of soul-searching to do himself. But that man fucking worships you."

"He has a warped way of showing it."

"Amen to that shit," she says as my phone rings.

It's a number I don't have stored in my cell. Deciding it could be someone from the network, I answer, "Hello?"

"June," a male voice I don't recognize responds.

"Yes?"

"Hey, it's Noah Anders."

"Noah, hi," I say, watching Leighton's eyes widen at his name.

"Hey. Sally from the production team mentioned you'd be arriving in town today. I was just calling to see that you made it all right."

"That's sweet of you. I did. I'm currently settling into the condo I've rented. Sally told me you're living here in New Orleans these days." I knew he'd landed some sort of job with the Saints, but I didn't know the details of it.

"Yes, I've been here for a couple of years now. Listen, are you available tomorrow night? I'd like it if we could get dinner and chat. Maybe get a little familiar with each other before they put a camera in our faces and ask us to perform."

"Tomorrow night?" I ask. Leighton nods and mouths, Yes, yes, yes. "Yeah, that should be fine. I've got plans with my friend most of the day. Could we make it later? Maybe eight-ish?"

"Perfect. What part of the city are you staying in?"

"French Quarter, on Conti just off Decatur."

"Seriously?" he asks.

"Yeah. Why?"

"I'm just on the other side of the courthouse. On the corner of St. Louis and Bourbon."

"Why am I not surprised to find a handsome bachelor living on Bourbon Street?" I tease. Leighton winks at me like she's proud of me. She probably thinks I'm flirting, but I'm not. Am I?

"Yeah, yeah. It's temporary while I wait for my dream house to fall into my lap. Figured one of the few things I hadn't done in this city was a Bourbon Street balcony at Mardi Gras. Besides, when you see it, you'll understand." Noah laughs. He says it as if it's a given I'll see his apartment, making my stomach tighten with too many feelings. The guilt I'm not supposed to be feeling being one of them. "There's a place called Brennan's right around the corner from both of us. Great food. I'll text you the address. Meet you there tomorrow at eight-ish?"

"I'm familiar with Brennan's. That sounds great, Noah. I look forward to it."

"Me too, June. See you then."

I end the call and Leighton squeals again.

"You've been here five minutes and you already have a date. Lucky bitch."

"It's not a date," I say, placing a hand on my unsettled stomach. "It's work."

"Sure. Work with the hottest, most eligible bachelor in the city."

I ignore her and continue with my task. She takes the hint and changes the subject, telling me about the current stories she's working on. It's a pleasant distraction, somebody else's life. I jump in with everything, asking her many questions and giving her different angles to look at.

We were always good at that, bouncing ideas off each other. It helped a lot in college when we had papers to write. We ended up getting stellar grades on anything we worked on together.

Before long, her stomach lets us know it's time to eat and we walk to a cute little restaurant called Kingfish.

"Order the Pimm's Cup. You won't be sorry," she demands. We both do and several more during our dinner of crawfish and steak.

Damn, I've missed this city's food.

We're a little tipsy by the time we're finished and take a leisurely walk back to my place. There is no other city in the US like New Orleans. Others are as rich, or more so, with history, sure. The life and exuberance here are on a field of their own, though. While late-night Bourbon Street isn't everyone's cup of tea, including mine. You can go a block in any direction and find something that is.

We come across a group of teenagers playing their horns on a street corner and stop to watch the makeshift concert. It's another reminder of how special this city is, how alive it feels no matter the day or time. Culture still means something here, and the folks who live here make time to enjoy it regularly.

A not so small crowd of onlookers gathers quickly and soon the street corner becomes a dance hall. We end up dancing with a group of men who must be in their eighties, dressed to the nines. Until a pair of young boys, who can't be older than about eight, cut in and take the places of our elderly partners.

It's a blast and by the time we walk back into my condo, my cheeks hurt from smiling.

What a difference a day makes.

"Are you sure, Leighton?" I ask her in the dressing room the following day. She's taken me to this adorable little upscale boutique, and between her and the sales associate, I have about fifteen new dresses to try on. Each one shows more skin than I normally do.

It isn't Leighton who answers. It's Troy, the associate.

"Babe, yes. You are a beautiful woman. Why hide any of that?" He gestures toward me with a waving hand.

The dress I currently have on is a wheat-colored body-con, one-shoulder dress. It's short, but not indecently or even unprofessionally short. I could wear it on camera. The color looks great on my skin and next to my auburn hair. It's the missing shoulder that frames the scar on my neck that causes me to pause.

"Troy's right, June. It looks fantastic on you. I'm getting it in that cornflower blue, and I won't look half as sexy as your tight ass."

"Whatever," I say. Leighton has a perfect body. Any woman would die to look like her. She's tall, too. At five-foot-ten, she could have been a model, even with her big boobs.

"Hey," she says seriously, looking directly into my eyes. "Don't be ashamed of who you are or what's happened to you. You're a survivor and you're the strongest person I know."

Drew said the same thing. Most days, I believe in my own strength. Others, not so much. She's right, though; I am a survivor and I need to be done hiding that away.

I nod and reach for another dress to try on. "Hope you're ready for a large commission today, Troy."

"Lord, yes!" he calls as he heads out to the sales floor, presumably to find me more things to try on.

I end up buying eight dresses, four pairs of heels, and three handbags from the fabulous Troy, who tenderly packages them up for me. It's a lot in one haul, but we aren't far from Leighton's apartment, so we make a pit stop to drop them off before grabbing a coffee and beignet and getting back at it. She's made up an entire list of items she claims I 'must have.' It's all amazing dresses for work, swimsuits for the warmer days when we might enjoy her rooftop pool—she's insane, it's November—and sexy lingerie that she insists is for me to feel good in, even if nobody else sees it.

By three in the afternoon, she's satisfied with our haul and we're back at her place to meet with Briana, her stylist, who is making a special house call for us. It's sweet that Leighton took such good care of me today. I tell her so with a big hug.

"Anything for you, Love, you know that," she tells me.

Briana turns out to be the biggest of firecracker personalities in the tiniest package. She can't stand over five-foot-nothing when she walks in, carrying her tool bag and a step stool. She's a damned wizard, though. Two hours later, she has my skin flawlessly glowing, my eyes highlighted in a golden smokey look. And my hair—wow, pure magic. I'd let it grow the past couple of years and it had fallen nearly to my waist. When Briana had asked me what I wanted to do with it, I gave her free rein.

She cut off nearly a foot. It now falls just past my shoulders. With light layering, it looks fuller and has a sophisticated sexiness to it.

Staring at myself in the mirror of Leighton's bathroom, I feel like a different woman. Again, wondering if I'd become too complacent in my life. All too content with how things were that I didn't even bother to freshen up my look or style. I shouldn't beat myself up over it. Being comfortable with your life isn't a bad thing. It's a wonderful thing. Just not when the love of your life isn't comfortable at your side.

Determined not to fall into another melancholy moment, especially after such a fun day, I push the thoughts aside.

Briana is packed up when I exit the bathroom. I hug her, thank her, and tell her I'm interested in hiring her as my stylist for as long as I'm in New Orleans. Leighton and I load up her car with all my new purchases and head back to my place. The plan was for her to help me get ready for 'my date.' Her words, not mine. But it does sort of feel like I am preparing for just that. And it's not lost on me that I'm primping to look good out in public with a man who is not Drew. Even when I casually dated in college, I never took it seriously enough to pamper myself beforehand. I knew none of those guys were my end game. Now, I don't have an endgame. My future isn't clear; it's so much fog.

"I think you should wear the A.C.L. dress," Leighton calls from my now overflowing closet.

"Really?"

"Yes," she answers definitively. That dress is an oxblood faux leather with a plunging neckline, short cap sleeves, and a cutout midsection and back. It will not only leave the scar on my neck fully visible, but the scar on my side will peak through, as well. "I know you're tentative to put it all out there, but you've got this, June. Go out there and show the rest of the world what I already know."

"And what's that, exactly?"

"Men don't break you. They can try, but they will always fail. You're a motherfucking diamond, June. The more they pressure you, the stronger you become."

"Have I ever told you I fucking love you?" I wave my hands in front of my eyes as they well up. A technique all women use even if we know it doesn't work.

"Of course you love me. I'm amazing. Who wouldn't?"

CHAPTER 10

June

I walk to Brennan's with tentative confidence. I know I look great. But I am having dinner with somewhat of a local celebrity, at a very public place. People will notice us and there is no guarantee that a picture won't be sold to the tabloids and, overnight, I'll have even more scrutiny layered on me. I'm not living in that fear, but I'm not oblivious to the consequences, either.

Noah and I arrive at Brennan's simultaneously. He walks from the opposite direction and our eyes meet, my heart stuttering at the fire I see in his. It's not my intention to attract his attention, especially as we enter a working relationship and my precarious marital status. That doesn't mean I'm not flattered by the obvious appreciation he's showing me as his gaze takes me in from head to toe and back again.

Noah Anders is a very handsome man. Rivaling even Drew in what I like in a man. Tall, broad shoulders above a trim waist. He's wearing a sleek black suit perfectly cut to his potent form. White shirt, no tie. A simple ensemble that looks anything but that on him. His dark blond hair is styled away from his brow, but that, too, looks natural. He exudes an easy, simple confidence. I'm a little jealous of it and make a note to hold on to that. To work for it.

Because it's sexy as hell.

"June, it's good to see you again," Noah says as he steps up to me. One hand settles on my bare waist and he presses a brief kiss on my cheek. It's more familiar than he's ever been with me previously. But I'd always been with Drew when we swirled in the same circles as Noah. "How are you settling into my city?"

"Oh, it's yours, is it?" I ask, and he grins. "All settled. My best friend lives here and was an enormous help."

"That's great," Noah says, leading me into Brennan's, his hand slipping to the small of my back. It's warm and firm on my exposed skin.

"Good evening, Mr. Anders," the hostess says as we enter. "We have your table ready. Right this way, please."

We're led to a half-circle corner booth in the Audubon room, its pink walls decorated with mini portraits. The table is larger than we need for only the two of us. I appreciate the location, however, being tucked away in a corner by itself.

"How were you able to get such a great table on such short notice?" I ask after I've taken a seat on the bench seat, with Noah opting to sit next to me instead of the chair across from me.

"I may have name-dropped a certain food critic would accompany me. Plus, I come here a lot since it's so close to home. They're quite accommodating as long as I continue to tip well."

"Ah, buying your way in, eh?" I tease.

"I know what I like and how to get it." The way he says it, I'm certain he isn't talking about food.

I turn my attention to the menu and order myself The Widow's Delight when our server asks what we'd like to drink.

"A whiskey girl after my own heart," Noah says and orders himself a whiskey sour.

"The chef is preparing a special tasting menu if that's agreeable with you, Mrs. McKenna?"

"Of course, thank you so much," I answer our server.

"Okay," Noah begins once the server walks away. "Let's address the elephant in the room. Are you and Drew separated?"

"Awfully direct," I say through slightly gritted teeth.

"Look, June. I know it's nobody's business. I'm all too familiar with the court of public opinion and how it's complete bullshit eighty-five percent of the time. That being said, we'll be working closely together for a couple of months. Not only do I want us to be friends, but I also want to help you in any way I can. If there are topics I can navigate people away from, for you, I'm happy to help. I'd also like to know what I'm getting myself into." He pauses as the server drops our drinks. "Your husband already hates me, after all. I'm not a bad guy, despite what Drew might have told you. I'm a gentleman. Usually, anyway."

He seems sincere. Or he's a damn excellent actor.

"Why don't we start with that elephant? Why do you and Drew hate each other?"

He takes a sip of his drink while he studies me for a beat.

"He never told you." It's not a question, more a confirmation. "You wouldn't believe that it was just your standard run-of-the-mill quarterback rivalry?"

"Not a chance." I laugh.

"Smart woman. It was never that. It was, as cliché as it sounds, about a woman." He's not looking at me now, the first time since we met on the sidewalk outside.

"Lorelai."

He nods, looking uncomfortable.

"You can tell me, Noah. I won't fall to pieces. I think I'm beyond that now and in whatever stage of recovery requires answers. All the answers."

"Upsetting you is only part of the issue. It's not the easiest subject for me, either. What happened with Drew, happened during a dark time in my life." Noah downs the rest of his drink and raises his empty glass to the server that's making her way over to our table.

"I'll be right back with that, Mr. Anders. In the meantime, the chef has sent out turtle soup and oysters j'aime. Enjoy."

"Thank you," I tell her before turning back to Noah. "I'll listen without judgment if you can promise to do the same."

"Deal," he says after a pause. "I dated Lorelai. Was even a little in love with her. After several months together, she asked if we could talk about something she wanted to try. Of course I said yes. When she told me what she wanted, I didn't know how to respond. Honestly, she shocked me. I asked her for time to let me think about it."

Noah's features sadden as he tells me his tale, and I know it's a lie that he was only 'a little' in love with her.

"And did she give it to you?"

He laughs. "In her way. The following weekend, she made sure I knew she was out partying with Drew and a couple of other guys from their team. Drew, specifically, though. The information prompted me to agree to what she wanted, as she knew I would. Jealousy is a bitch at that age."

"What did she want?"

"For me to spank her. Whip her. Tie her up. You get the picture, I'm sure. It didn't go well. At all. I didn't know what I was doing. She didn't either. She kept asking for more." He clears his throat. "I was apprehensive but also a young, henpecked idiot. I took it too far with the crop she had brought for me to use."

"Jesus," I breathe.

"Eat your soup, June. We can come back to this before you lose your appetite altogether."

I bring a spoonful to my mouth and moan.

"Right? In this day and age, it should probably disgust us, but damn it's delicious." He takes a bite, too.

We talk about other things while we eat, mostly much more pleasant things. He tells about life before college football. He'd grown up in Lafayette, which makes more sense as to why he's living here now. There are several tales of him and his younger brother's troublemaking ways, and I laugh more than I'd expected. Noah is funny and charming, and I'm having a great time getting to know him for myself.

In return, I tell him of my early life in Arizona. Of Reed and Drew, of losing my dad. I skip my college years, my attack, my scars. If he notices my omissions, he doesn't let it show.

He's easy to talk to and our comfortable camaraderie should carry well on camera. He's a flirt, which will also carry over well. Noah is right. He is a good guy. The way he talks about his mother, father, and brother— Connor—makes it even more obvious.

We talk more about his house hunting, and I tell him he should find one that is haunted.

"I'd think they would be plentiful in New Orleans. I'll go look at them with you. It'd be fun."

"Fuck no, woman. I'm terrified of anything I can't see," he says, and I laugh again.

"Big, tough Noah Anders fears a few ghosts?"

"With certainty," he answers.

Turns out, all the food is amazing. After appetizers, they serve us tastings of redfish, scallops, and a bacon-wrapped tenderloin that will go straight to my thighs but is oh-so-worth it as it melts in my mouth.

It's not until we're served our table side bananas foster that the subject turns serious again.

"Are you ready for the rest of the story?"

I nod.

"I hurt her," he says bluntly but contritely. "I didn't draw blood, but the welts I left looked awful. Painful. I apologized over and over. I was frantic about it. She kept telling me it was fine, that she was fine. When she left the next morning, I believed we were on good terms. We'd discussed never trying that again since I clearly didn't know what I was doing."

He's playing with his food more than eating it, pushing the banana around in the sauce. I'm almost annoyed with it because it's so good and I've nearly finished mine while he's been speaking. Reaching my fork over to his plate, I steal a bite.

His eyes snap to mine.

"You'll pay for that, Mrs. McKenna."

I shrug and steal a second piece, ignoring the way he's studying my mouth with hunger in his eyes.

I'm so not ready to go there.

"How does Drew play into this story?"

"Lorelai told him. She exaggerated the situation. Made him believe that I took pleasure in hurting her that badly. He confronted me, I denied it, we threw a few punches. The rest, as they say, is history."

I drop my fork; my appetite vanished.

"Who am I dealing with here, Noah?"

He studies me again, not answering right away.

"Are you trying to reconcile?"

"I... I don't know. His affair was a complete surprise to me. I had no idea that Drew was even capable of ever cheating on me. I'm still struggling with that loss of trust. Whether I want to reconcile isn't a decision I've had any time to make. I still don't fully understand what's been happening." I down the rest of my drink, then pick up his and finish it, too.

Other than a raised eyebrow, he says nothing about me thieving away his order.

"I'll say this. Lorelai is a force. Determination is engrained in her DNA. If she wants Drew, she'll find a way."

"She told me it wasn't like that. That he doesn't love her. He says the same."

"If only it was just about love. I'm sorry," he says, looking unconvinced.

"Why are you sorry? You didn't break my fucking heart. You don't even know me."

"I'd like to. Know you, not break your heart." He laughs. "I know I had nothing to do with it, but I'm still sorry you're going through it. That they hurt you. You seem like a sweet person, June. Kind, smart, insanely beautiful. You don't deserve this. He should have treated you better. I would have."

"Aren't you the charmer?"

"Just putting it out there. I've had a great time tonight. I think you have as well. I understand what you're wading through, and that you're not ready for any kind of relationship. But I won't lie. You want a rebound to piss off your husband, I'm your guy." He grins like a little boy who just got away with sneaking a second serving of dessert.

"How magnanimous of you to offer yourself up for some no-strings sex with a side of revenge." I laugh.

"I aim to please. Especially when I know how well I do it."

Noah may be a nice guy, but he's definitely a dangerous one. To me, to my vagina, and to my marriage.

CHAPTER 11

June

I wake early the following morning to my phone ringing much too close to my head. Reaching for it on the nightstand, I see it's Drew calling at 5:00 a.m. Much earlier for him still on the West Coast.

"Hello?" My voice is groggy from too little sleep.

"What are you doing?" Drew sounds off, angry. My indignation rises. If anyone in this relationship should be angry, it's me.

"I'm sleeping, Drew. It's early."

"That's not what I fucking mean and you know it."

"I know nothing of the sort. What are you asking me? Be specific."

"Did you fuck him?" He seethes.

I sit up and turn on the bedside light, suddenly fully awake.

"Noah?"

"Were some other man's hands all over you last night?"

"If you have something to say, say it. I haven't had coffee. Or sleep. I'm too tired for this."

I realize what I've just said when the line goes deathly silent. I can almost hear the gears in Drew's head turning across the line. Someone must have taken photos last night. They could be from Noah greeting me on the sidewalk in front of Brennan's. Or, from him walking me to my condo and, again, kissing me on the cheek. Either way, I did nothing wrong or shameful and I'm not about to be judged by my manwhore husband.

"Did you fuck him, June?" He carefully enunciates each word, making them clear to me, but they also sound like they're causing him physical pain to say.

"Does it matter?" I'll admit, I'm being petty, letting my bitterness get the better of me. It's not my most mature moment. Sue me.

"You are my wife, so yes. It damn well matters."

"Save it, Drew." I laugh. "You have a girlfriend, and I'm pretty certain she hasn't been the only one." I head to the kitchen to start the coffeepot. Intravenous caffeine needs to be invented for days like these.

There is a bunch of noise on the other side of the line and I can only hope whatever he's breaking isn't something of mine that I'd eventually like to have back. I may not be in love with our house in Seattle, but I do treasure a few items inside it. Drew is a cheating asshole, but he's not vindictive. I remind myself of that and push aside visions of him destroying my grandmother's china.

"She is not my girlfriend, and you are not me."

"I notice you avoided admitting that there are other women, you know?" I roll my eyes.

"Goddammit, June. Answer my question. Did you fuck him?"

"No! I did not have sexual relations with that man," I yell at him. "If I decide to, it won't be your fucking business, Drew."

His heavy breathing fills the line, but it's his turn to talk. I continue to make my much-needed pot of coffee.

"When do you fly to Dallas?" His sudden subject change makes my eyes blur and my temples throb. Today is Monday. Jared emailed me my itinerary yesterday. ESPN has booked a flight for Noah and me tomorrow afternoon. We'll be in Dallas until Friday morning and they'll be announcing the plans for our show during the pregame show on Thursday. I'm nervously excited about it all.

Not only the show, or having more attention on me than I'm used to. I'm also anxious about seeing Drew outside of the controlled setting of our couples' therapy sessions. The pit of my stomach gets heavy every time I think about it. Whatever plays out will be in full view of other athletes and fans alike.

"Tomorrow."

"Perfect. We can have a date on Wednesday after I arrive," he says.

"Are you on drugs?"

"Of course not."

"You woke me up by being an accusatory prick and you expect me to go on a date with you?"

"Yes, I do. You committed to therapy and the work that implies. Dating is part of it. With you in New Orleans, that's going to be difficult. I'm taking what I can get," he tells me. "I'm sorry I woke you up, but I didn't like the pictures I saw of you and him out together. It pissed me off."

"I could tell." I snort. "It was a work dinner. We're just trying to get to know each other before we're expected to be on camera together."

"I don't believe Noah took you out for work, June."

I don't reply because that may have been the main reason for Noah inviting me out, but I agree it wasn't the only one. Noah showed enough interest for me to know he had a few ulterior motives. Even if he hadn't bluntly admitted them to me, I'd have guessed them.

"I don't like you spending time alone with him, even if I've lost all say in your life. You don't know him like I do. Besides, the world doesn't know you're working together. It looked like a date."

"Dinner dates are so boring next to hotel hookups with your mistress, though, right? Besides, maybe you don't know him at all," I say. Contractually, we're not allowed to discuss our working relationship until after the network makes the announcement.

"What did he tell you?" he asks.

"Things I should have heard from you. If you want to know my conversation with Noah, you're going to have to answer my questions first, Drew. You don't make the rules here, not anymore."

"We'll see about that Wednesday night. Text me your hotel information when you get checked in. I'll meet you at your room Wednesday night at six. Be ready, Junie."

I stare at my phone when he ends the call. Drew hasn't even attempted to call me for well over a week now and this is how he breaks his silence? By accusing me of having sex with a man I barely know.

His anger is making him stupid. If he'd taken half a second to think about it, he'd know I wouldn't do that. Even if I wasn't still married. Virgin brides that held out for the love of their life don't turn into ho-hos overnight. That's not how we're built.

Unfortunately for my vagina. Too bad Leighton didn't have 'big fat dildo' on her June's must-have list.

I shoot her a text.

ME:

I need a vibrator.

LOVE:

The sex toy stores are asleep right now. Go back to bed, you psycho.

ME:

Can't. Wide awake.

LOVE:

Thoughts of Noah keeping you awake and horny?

ME:

Drew called. Must have seen paparazzi pics online.

He asked if I fucked Noah.

LOVE:

Tell him what you put in your twat isn't his business.

ME:

I did. But my twat is lonely. See above.

LOVE:

Use your fingers or a pillow for now. I'll have you one by the end of the day so you can pack it with you to Dallas.

ME:

Have I ever told you I fucking love you?

LOVE:

Doubtful. Tell me when I'm awake.

I take my cup of coffee and grab a throw blanket off the sofa before heading out to the balcony. The city is still mostly quiet and dark. I take the time to just be still with it. The past few weeks have gone by like a hurricane ravaging my life. Not that it's all been bad, of course. I'm loving the work opportunity, and even more so spending time with Leighton. The bad, though, has been apocalyptic. The small respite of a calm cup of coffee is more therapeutic than it should be.

Clinging to the quiet moments for dear life is just plain sad. It's not as if they're even enjoyable, anyway, since I spend them in constant question about the lie I've been living. That's exactly what it feels like. Fake, false, an untruth.

My day stays a lazy one. I go get a manicure and pedicure and meet Leighton back at my place for dinner. As promised, she's got a new boyfriend in a bag. A few, actually.

"You need options," she claims.

She also brought takeout, and we eat while I pack for Dallas. We call it an early night since I was so rudely awakened this morning.

Noah tightens the rope above my head, effectively attaching my wrists to the bedpost, as Drew inserts another finger into me. My back bows off the bed as his tongue joins the action.

"Oh, God. More," I moan.

"Say please," Noah demands, his naked form moving back into my line of sight. Dewy sweat beads on his rippled abdomen.

"Please, please," I whisper.

"I think she's ready," Drew announces from between my thighs. Noah sends him a wide grin as he steps closer to my head, placing his long, hard dick mere inches from my mouth, his hand reaching to draw my chin down, parting my lips. Drew rises to his knees and spreads my legs to accommodate his size.

Simultaneously, they enter me.

I wake up, gasping for breath and horny as hell.

Fuck my life.

Having sex dreams about my new coworker is bad enough. Having my husband there to join the fun... well, that's a whole other can of worms that I never want to open. I immediately grab my phone to text Leighton.

ME:

I just had a sex dream about Drew. And Noah.

LOVE:

YES, GIRL, YES!

ME:

NO!! How am I supposed to face Noah after that?

LOVE:

How dirty was it? What are we working with here? Details, I want the details. Where on your body, EXACTLY, did they finish off?

ME:

You are the literal worst. There was no finish. Just the start of some DP.

LOVE:

Yummy! But why worry? Grab that new
Hitachi, finish yourself off, and move on.
Do you think that man didn't go home after
dinner the other night and handle himself in
the shower with thoughts of taking you from
behind? Because he did. I guarantee it.

ME:

Goodbye, Leighton.

LOVE:

Happy to help, love ya!

Leighton changed the direction of my fantasies with just a few short text messages, and when I grab one of my new toys she dropped at my doorstep earlier today, the image in my head is Drew fucking me while Noah directs the scene from the corner.

Again, fuck my life.

On my way to the airport, Noah texts me to meet him in the airline lounge. As I approach the door, my heart rate speeds up. It feels dirty and disrespectful to masturbate to your coworker. It's shameful. I am ashamed. The sex dream isn't my fault. You have no control over what you dream of. But I added him to my fantasy willingly. Is that a betrayal of trust? I don't know. I'm so confused over it, and it makes me even angrier at Drew because I shouldn't even be in the position where I am dreaming of sexual interactions with Noah Anders.

Shit, how am I going to face him?

Spotting Noah at a table far off in a corner, I grab a coffee on my way over, sit, and mumble a hello without making eye contact. I can feel his gaze on me, even though he says nothing.

Being the coward that I am, I pretend to be involved with something important on my phone.

"What's up with you today, June?"

Nothing, I mouth around another sip of coffee.

"June. One thing you should know about me. I don't lie. Ever. I expect the same from you." He says it with authority. Something he doesn't have over me. So why does the idea of it excite me?

I know that answer and I blush with the knowledge.

Sighing, I turn to him. "Fine. I'm off my game today. I had a hard day yesterday and didn't sleep as well as I'd like."

The truth. With huge omissions, of course.

"Drew?"

"Mmm," I confirm. "He showed me his possessive side."

"Ah, I assume he saw the photos. But I can't blame the man. I'd be a jealous husband, too. I'd imagine you'd be used to it by now."

"Well, that's the thing. He's never shown it to me before."

"You're kidding me?" he asks, astonished.

"Did we not just establish a no-lies rule?"

"We did. I guess I'm having a hard time reconciling the Drew I know with the one you do."

"I, too, am having a hard time reconciling the Drew I knew with the one he actually is. He's always been protective and sticks close to me when we're around other people. But he's never acted like he did yesterday."

We're both quiet for a while. Maybe he's letting me ruminate over the turn my life has taken. Maybe he doesn't want to speak the words, the truth. I married a man I've known most of my life, and also not at all.

"Can I ask you something, Noah?"

"By all means."

"Are you happy?"

"Generally, yes. Are you asking if I'm happy in a specific part of my life?"

"You worked at a goal for the better part of your life, right? To be an NFL quarterback. You made that dream come true only for it to be stolen away from you shortly after obtaining it. In a split second, the most important thing in your life, for so long, disappears. Or drastically changes, at least."

"You're asking how I moved forward," he says, and I nod. "In the spirit of truth, I'll tell you it was the hardest time in my life, and I spiraled for several months. For as long as I could remember, I'd lived a strict existence. I rarely drank, I had a strict diet, rigorous workouts, and I kept women at a distance to not distract me from my goal. That goal being the Super Bowl." He finishes his coffee before speaking again. "When that finish line was no longer a part of my race, I gave in to the excess. I did all the things I never allowed myself. With great enthusiasm, I might add. I can't tell you what caused me to change. There was no sudden epiphany or spiritual awakening. One day, I knew I needed to pull back, find a balance, and set new goals. I can still get my Super Bowl win if I want, only it will be from a position of management or maybe coaching. I'm not sure yet, but it won't be from being on the field. And that's okay because I enjoy everything I have. I work hard, but I finally get to play hard, too. Maybe you need to adjust what your race looks like or your finish line."

"I'm sorry you lost that chance, Noah. Truly, I am. Thank you for being so open about it. I appreciate it."

"Of course. I told you I want us to be friends," he says. "Are you nervous about seeing Drew in Dallas?"

"God, yes." I laugh.

"If you need anything from me, you let me know." He reaches over and squeezes my hand.

Once again, I'm struck by how great of a man Noah is. He's honest, supportive, and seems one hundred percent genuine. Then again, my personality radar is on the fritz, so what do I know?

After we check into our hotel, we're only given a short time to settle before having to meet with the producers and crew. It lasts for hours. All the bases of our schedule get covered and a lot of other details that don't pertain to us on camera personalities.

It's late evening before I'm able to head back to my hotel room. In the elevator up to my floor, I realize I never texted Drew that I'd arrived. I pull my phone out and start typing as the door opens to my floor.

"Text me if you want to catch dinner together," Noah says as I step out.

"Thanks. I'm beat, though. I'll probably just order in some room service and binge some shitty reality television," I reply just before the doors shut to take him up to his floor, and I press send on the text to Drew.

ME:

At the Live, Room 408.

The sound of a phone notification down the hall brings my head up.

He's here, standing at the door to my hotel room. One arm above his head as he leans on the jamb.

My heart stumbles as I take him in. His large body that used to give me a sense of security whenever he was around. His chiseled jaw, always dusted with perpetual two-day-old growth. And those eyes, his piercing hazel-green stare.

They say the eyes are the window to the soul. They, whoever they are, say a lot of bullshit. I don't see the soul of a man who willingly broke my heart. If I had, maybe I would've never fallen so uncontrollably in love with him to begin with.

I wouldn't have pined through my adolescence, secretly watching every move he made. The way his thumb rubs his index finger when he's thinking hard wouldn't have been something I noticed when I was only nine years old. It wouldn't be a sign I looked for when I was concerned about his mental state, because I wouldn't have cared at all. He would've just been my brother's annoying best friend.

Maybe I would have met a sweet, adoring man. One who'd have worshiped me to at least the point of faithfulness. We'd live a happy life in the suburbs somewhere, just like all the millions of other women out there in the world.

But that's not what I got. Life delivered me a boy with dirty knees and messy hair, whose mere presence had my heart beating in time with his, and I never looked back.

"I know." His deep voice carries to me. He holds his phone up, showing he received my text.

"I thought you didn't get in until tomorrow?"

"Changed my plans," he says when I stop right in front of him, his bulk blocking my door. "I missed you."

I missed you, too.

I can't say it. I don't tell him I think I've been missing him for months. Or years, even. I don't ask where he's been, where he went. Why I've missed him. Because I know the answers.

He left me for her even when he kept coming home to me.

"Can I come in?"

Still, I say nothing. My throat feels constricted. I'm not sure I can speak without breaking down. Instead, I stare.

"Let me in, June."

With the heaviest of hearts, I do.

He follows me in, watching me closely as I drop my handbag on the dresser and kick my shoes off into the closet, then head to the mini bar for a bottle of water. Anything to avoid looking at him. Anything not to acknowledge his enormous presence, occupying too much space and sucking up all the air in the room.

"Stop," he clips out in a demanding voice.

He steps to me, so close I can feel his warmth, his breath rustling my hair. Reaching around, he removes the water from my grasp and sets it aside.

"Turn around, June." I do and his arms encircle me, the gentleness breaking me all over again. "Shh, just let me hold you," he says when my breath hitches.

Minutes feel like days as I struggle to shut my brain off and live in this moment. A moment where I'm the most important thing in Drew's life. Not football, not sex, not Lorelai. Drew holds me as he did on our wedding night as if I'm cherished. As if he's a bubble protecting me from all life's dangers.

Now I know the biggest danger comes from inside my home.

"You look beautiful," he tells me, and I step back from his embrace. The dress I'm wearing drapes off one shoulder. My hair is up. The silver scar on my neck is in full view. "You did in the pictures from the other night, too. But I hated that you dressed up for him."

Anger rushes through me with his accusation.

"I didn't dress for Noah any more than I ever dressed for you."

"Bullshit."

I narrow my eyes on him. "At least I get dressed as opposed to undressing for other people."

"You should watch that smart mouth of yours with me, June," he says, eyes flashing to my lips. "Or I'll find a way to shut it up for you."

"Do your worst."

Drew's eyes bounce between mine. Calculating or deciding, I can't guess.

"Are you threatening me with a good time?" he asks, his voice cautious but laced with excitement.

"How the fuck would I know? It wasn't me you were showing a good time to."

He stills, every muscle instantly rigid.

"Do you think you're ready to find out?"

"I've been ready for ages. You never gave me a chance. You never asked me what my fantasies are. Instead, you just went out and lived yours."

"You do not know what you're talking about," he bites back at me.

"Bullshit," I say, throwing his word back at him.

His mouth forms a thin line and he's back to staring at me. The subtle changes don't go unnoticed by me, though. Drew leans ever so slightly closer to me. His jaw ticks, nostrils flare. I know the signs of his arousal well as his darkening pupils enlarge.

"Do you want to fuck, Drew? You can pretend I'm her."

He flinches, and my heart is racing so fast, I'm not sure I'd even hear the words over the rushing of blood if he answered me. I don't know why I just asked him that. I shouldn't be instigating any kind of sex, let alone whatever kind of angry sex I'm pushing for right now.

I'm jealous, though. Jealous of Lorelai. Of Drew. Of everyone who gets what they dream of. I want my turn and I want answers. And I want them both from Drew right now.

"Do you picture her when you have sex with me?" I ask.

His hand quickly finds my messy bun and tugs, causing my face to upturn to him. His eyes are ablaze in a way I've never seen.

"Let's get one thing straight, June," he says slowly, precisely. "In my mind, I've only ever had sex with you. Every. Single. Fucking. Time. It's you I see, always you. Since the very first time."

The crack of my hand on his cheek echoes through the room. My reaction to his words surprises us both. I hope his face burns as much as my stinging palm does.

"It should have been me. Every single time, it should have been me."

Drew slowly loosens and undoes his tie. So silently, he moves. Barely letting out a breath while his hands work at the length in front of him, looping and pulling at it. I don't know what he's doing with it until he suddenly spins me around, pulling both arms behind me. With a quick tug, he binds my wrists with his neckpiece.

I gasp at the sensation it sends through my entire body. Every nerve ending has birthed new life. Turning me back to face him, Drew places one large palm on my chest.

"Do you feel how hard your heart is beating? That's excitement, and if I hiked that short-as-fuck dress up and shoved my fingers in your cunt, it would be soaking wet."

This dirty talking man in front of me isn't someone I know. It's a side of him he's never shown me. I hate that he's right. I hate that his words make me so hot. I hate that he's never said them to me before.

"Is this how you talk to all your other women?"

"How many do you think I have?"

I fucking hate him. He should give me this moment, where I'm the top dog. Where I get to ask all the questions and he answers obligingly. Where I get to be snide and rude, and he takes it all. I want all of that and I want him to fuck me like he does her as well.

Maybe I hate myself even more than I hate him.

"Again, how would I know? You should tell me."

"Do you want to know?" He whispers the words over my cheek.

"Not want, need."

"Four," he answers after a pause.

"Currently?" I ask angrily as my blood boils and my heart screams in despair.

"No. None currently. There were three before Lorelai."

"Elaborate, and if you have ever loved me, you'll not speak her god-damned name again," I say, using Dr. Fillmore's prompt.

Drew moves behind me and slowly unzips my dress. He takes as much time with the dress as he does with the words. Creating a mix of anxiety and thrilling excitement at the same time.

"The first time, I went to a private club. Confidential. Discreet. Picked some woman at random. Never even asked her name. Her hair was similar in color to yours. That made it easier. And also, harder."

My vision blurs, fists clenching with biting pain. I blink rapidly to keep the wetness at bay. Drew pulls my dress down below my breast, hikes the skirt up to my waist, then moves back in front of me, all while speaking in such a nonchalant manner. As if he's only reciting a scene he saw once in a movie. Not remembering something he lived, something he did. To us.

"Do you still need more? There may be no going back from this."

"There already is no going back, Drew. I can't live with all the questions. Tell me the rest," I say, choking out the words.

"I didn't have sex with that woman. She went down on me, and I hated myself. I didn't go back for months. Every time you looked at me, I thought you knew what I had done. Every time you told me you loved me, I wanted to vomit from the betrayal, the guilt." He kneels in front of me, eyes never leaving my face.

I stare down at the stranger in front of me. I would probably slap him again if he hadn't tied my hands behind me.

"You broke us for a blowjob?"

"Not just a simple blowjob, but yes." His hands drag down from my waist to my feet, taking my skimpy panties with them. "Do you want me to show you?"

More than almost anything.

"I don't think you have it in you to show me. I am your pretty trophy wife, not your dirty, secret whore, remember?"

The swat to my ass cheek startles me and I jump even though I don't hate the sting of it. It only edges up the sexual frustration I'm trying so hard to ignore.

"Don't slut-shame, June. It's beneath you."

Asshole.

He says it to shift the balance in power. He knows it, I know it. We both know it works.

"You're right. I should put all the blame on you, the husband who thinks his wife is too fragile to fuck properly. But I'll still reserve a healthy portion for Dollface."

He shoves my panties in my mouth when he stands up. I glare in return.

"Another change in plans. That mouth of yours is trying my patience."

I mumble a fuck you as best as I can. It comes out sounding like a garbled moan when his fingers encounter the juncture of my thighs. His other hand tangles back in my hair, holding my head in the position he wants it. Like the rest of my body, tangled and trussed up, completely at his mercy.

He kisses me roughly, pushing the lace further into my mouth. Stealing what little air I could get around my undergarment. Suddenly, his mouth disappears from mine. Just as quickly, it finds a new place to kiss. There isn't any other way to describe what he's doing to me. He's making out with my pussy like his life depends on it. His tongue drops to explore my entrance, fucking me with it. Making my knees weak and my legs shake. As if he notices, he easily lifts me, only to reposition me in a sitting position on the end of the bed.

He wastes no time taking up the position between my legs.

"I've missed you so fucking much, Junie."

I watch everything he does, the careful attention he pays me as he sucks on my clit while his fingers thrust in and out of me. After a short time, he stalls to pull my lower lips apart and blows soft air on me. It makes me shiver with need. I try to close my thighs, push him out, the sensation too much.

He swats my inner thigh. Not hard or sharp, a mild warning. It's the combination of that followed by the quick suck to my clit and the two fingers pumping in and out that makes me explode in an intense orgasm. Without warning, it burns through me, decimating everything but the toe-curling sensation that draws my whole body tight. A scream finds its way around the lace clogging my throat as I clumsily fall back on my tied hands.

Through blurred vision and rough breaths, I watch Drew pull the panties out, then he flips me over to untie my hands and pull my dress off me completely. He's everywhere all at once. Lying next to me on the bed, pulling me onto him. His arms surround me, hands rubbing down my arms and massaging my wrists.

Neither of us speaks. I'm unsure what to say at first. Thank you? Why couldn't you have done that five years ago? Do it again? It all makes me angry at him. And myself.

Without looking at him, I push for more answers.

"Tell me about the rest."

"June." He sighs. "Can we just be still?"

"No."

"Fine. The second time was also at the club. I didn't go with the intention of anything more than watching. Or getting myself off while watching others. I was still feeling the acute sting of guilt. I numbed it with whiskey. So much so that when a woman approached me, I agreed. She didn't quite do it for me and I convinced myself I'd never go back."

"But you did. You sought out another woman, again."

"Yes. Months later, after my convictions faded. I went back and there was a different woman. One who reminded me nothing of you, thinking that would be better, that I wouldn't be able to pretend and therefore wouldn't be able to perform," he whispers. He's pulling the pins from my hair, massaging my scalp as he does. "I wish I could tell you that was the truth."

"You came for her? Like the two before."

He doesn't answer with anything more than a choked sound of affirmation. I'm glad he's feeling some shame now. Glad that I'm not the only one gagging on it. Why this information hurts is beyond me because of course he came for them. Shared that part of him with strangers and with Lorelai. I knew this already, in the deep, dark places of my mind I prefer to never visit.

"Were those two just blowjobs or more?"

"One of each."

Crawling off him, I move to the other side of the bed, clawing to get the covers pulled down. I'm so cold, my whole body shudders with the chill that works down, down, down into every cell.

"I hate you," I whisper.

"I know."

"Go away."

"Junie," he begins.

"Stop calling me that! It's too much. It's intimate and familiar and we aren't those things. Not anymore," I cry out. "I don't think we ever were."

Drew moves to kneel next to the bed, face to face with me. He cups my cheek, and it's all I can do not to snuggle into the warmth of it that seeps through the tears trailing out of my eyes. I hate that my stupid body hasn't caught up with my heart and my head.

"You're killing me, you know that? You're the love of my life, June. I can't see you as anything but mine. My Junie. Please don't ask me to tell you things that will hurt you. I hate it," he pleads.

"This isn't love."

"Bullshit. It is love. It's fucked up, it's damaged, and that's my fault. But it is love. The undying kind. The type that makes you stupid and makes you hurt, but it lasts forever."

"I don't want your kind of love."

"Whether or not you want it, it will always be yours."

"Leave."

"I'll go after you're asleep. At least give me that."

"I don't owe you that, Drew. I don't owe you anything."

"No, you don't owe me anything. I'm the one in debt so deep that it will take me a lifetime and more to repay. But I can't leave until I know you're peacefully sleeping, okay?"

I don't answer. He doesn't leave. He stays, a sentry to the nightmares that plagued me for so long. I never considered the effect they had on him. That's my fault, and I'll own that part of our sad saga. But I'm not to blame for his chosen coping mechanism.

When it becomes clear he has no intention of leaving my side, I close my eyes, shutting him and his deranged view of love out.

CHAPTER 12

June

Crawling out of bed the following morning, I'm spent, stripped down, and pissed off that I keep getting woken up by others either calling me or showing up at my door. The room smells like Drew. That pisses me off, too.

I pray it's not Drew with the incessant knocking this morning. Last night was intense. I'll be struggling with reconciling the pleasure mixed in with all the horrific pain. All the images my mind wants to create of Drew and strange women. Of Drew visiting a sex club, of him even knowing about a sex club.

My life feels split in two. One world that I live in and another that I never even knew existed.

I know kink exists, of course. That a large group of people live it, openly, every day. I'm not naïve to it. I just didn't realize it was living with me, hidden away in the shadows.

Wrapped up in the hotel-supplied bathrobe, I go to open the door. It's not Drew knocking, thankfully. Noah stands there looking bright-eyed and fresh-faced.

I hate him, too.

"I was downstairs getting coffee and ran into Sally. She'd like to get breakfast with us, but you weren't answering your phone," he says, eyeing me suspiciously.

"Sorry, I'm moving slowly this morning."

"I see that," he says slowly, as if he's working something out in his head. "I think we need some rules, June. Rule number one, don't apologize to me unless you have caused me actual offense. Which, as of yet, you have not."

I balk. Noah isn't saying anything wrong, per se. But his tone feels like a reprimand, and I had enough of that last night to last me through the day.

"Yeah, okay. Whatever." I move to the closet, needing to decide what to wear today.

"Tell me what happened."

"Drew happened. He was waiting for me when you dropped me off on my floor yesterday."

"And?"

"Noah, I like you and I'm trying to trust you, but you're not my BFF who I spill all my tea to," I say, turning to him.

"I get that." He laughs lightly. "You don't need to give me any more details than you want to. However, you will undoubtedly see your husband today, and if you want help bringing him to his knees, I'm your best bet."

"Oh, you are, are you?"

His playfulness leaks through my waning armor, nearly forcing a smile out of me.

"Yes, June. Only another controlling man with a jealous asshole side can tell you exactly what will hurt a controlling man with a jealous asshole side."

I study him for a hot second. Noah is a conundrum. Nice, caring friend on one hand, something maybe a lot darker on the other. It's impossible not to wonder how much he and Drew have in common.

"I don't want to hurt him, Noah. Just make him crawl. Far."

"On it, my sweet June. Go shower. I'll pick your outfit."

While all of this is beyond weird, I decide to just go with it. Every decision I've made for my own life hasn't panned out the way I expected. Why not temporarily hand the reins to someone else? Self-deprecating is not an attractive attribute, and if I'm honest with myself, not every life move has ended up ashes in the fire. This job, for one. So far, it's been great. The team has been amazing. And maybe I found a new friend in the enigmatic Noah Anders.

"You have impeccable taste in underwear," Noah calls out when I shut the shower off.

Oh my God.

"That's such a violation of my privacy, Noah."

"Is it, though?" he asks.

"Yes!"

"I think not. It's not on you. It's just fabric."

"I assure you it is."

"Agree to disagree. Hurry up, buttercup, I'm starving."

In the ten minutes I was in the shower, Noah rearranged my entire closet, separating it all into outfits, complete with underthings, shoes, and sticky notes for when I'm to wear each outfit.

TODAY

TONIGHT

PRE-GAME SHOW

GAME

POST-GAME

AIRPLANE HOME

"Are you a fashion fairy?"

"I'd prefer revenge demon."

"You're enjoying this," I respond.

"Greatly." He grins. "I don't know what happened between you and Drew last night, but I imagine he'll have certain expectations for your reaction today. Be unexpected, June." He holds up today's outfit. He's picked out a men's suit jacket style dress, oversized, dark blue with lighter pinstripes. The front sports a double-breasted buttoning. However, those sit low, below a deep plunging neckline trimmed by wide lapels. I meant it to be paired with a bodysuit, making it far less revealing. Noah has not handed me that bodysuit, or any other item to wear underneath. Except for a bright orange eyelet lace bra, also plunging. A simple pair of flats is set out. The ensemble leaves all attention on my breasts.

The outfits he's arranged are nothing at all like anything I've ever worn before. They're my clothes but styled in ways I'd never do for myself. He's put together looks with an edge; with a feminine strength I've never let show.

"How are you so good at this?" I ask.

"I was a psychology major before I entered the NFL draft."

"Figures. I wondered why it's been so easy to open up to you."

"Right? Now go get dressed. I can practically smell bacon from here."

Twenty minutes and a haphazard braid-crown later, we meet Sally in the lobby restaurant. Sally's great. Capable, practical, but also witty. She has a shock of bright red curls that complement her personality, if hair can do such a thing.

Noah and Sally have known each other for years and worked together off and on for different football related projects. He shows her the same familiarity he shows me and I wonder if he makes simple friends with everyone he meets, or maybe just women.

The difference between me and Sally is that she has that same comfortability with him, whereas I still have moments of questioning his motives.

Sally must pick up on my mood because her attention turns from slapping Noah's hand away from her bacon to me.

"June, can I ask something personal? With the promise that I will not use it in production, of course."

"Sure," I tell her, with just a dash of skepticism.

"If it's too sensitive a subject, I completely understand," she says, and I expect her to ask about Drew and the tabloid press coverage of his very public infidelity. She surprises me, though. "Can I ask about the scars?"

"Sally," Noah says sternly.

"Noah, no. It's okay," I start. I had told myself I was over hiding it. Now it's time to prove it. "It's not something I talk about, but I am no longer hiding it either."

It's now or never.

"I had a stalker when I was in college," I begin, my hands going to my thighs under the table. "It started as something like harmless attraction. But the more I rebuked him, the more determined he became in getting my attention. One night, in my final year, he found me walking alone back to my dorm and, um, he attacked me."

"Oh my God, June. That's horrible. I'm so sorry," Sally exclaims while Noah's hand finds mine under the table, silently unclenching my fist and winding his fingers with mine.

"Thank you," I say. "It was a rough time in my life, but family and therapy and a lot of work later, I'm okay."

"Did they catch the guy? You knew who he was, right?"

"They didn't have the opportunity. He committed suicide after the attack, before the police found him. I was in the hospital unconscious while all that was happening."

"I can't imagine how hard that must have been for you," Sally says. "Did you have a long recovery?"

"I did. I was in the hospital for a long time, therapy for much longer."

Noah still has hold of my hand, his thumb rubbing back and forth in a soothing motion. I'm doing well speaking about it and not showing my normal anxiety ticks. All of which surprises me.

"Is this something you're willing to discuss, or would you like me to make sure the subject never gets broached? I doubt it will, but you never know, and I'd like to be prepared."

"You know, I think I'm okay either way. Let's not worry about it for now," I say with confidence. With a new sense of self.

"Well done, my sweet June," Noah says as he presses a kiss on my cheek.

Which, of course, is when Drew walks into the restaurant. His eyes lock with mine, then quickly flash to Noah.

"Be unexpected, June," Noah whispers to me. As Drew approaches, Noah brings our clasped hands above the table, still holding mine for a beat. Long enough to be noticed, then he releases it, only to move his arm around the back of my chair. It's a possessive move and Noah completes it all without ever sparing Drew a single glance.

"Mind if I join, or is this a confidential work thing?" Drew asks. The only chair available is across from Noah, next to Sally.

Noah's words echo in my skull. Be unexpected. Drew would expect the prim and proper June. The ladylike June who would never speak out in public about personal issues. Not this new snarky, speaks-her-mind June. Okay, so she's still emerging, but now is as good a time as any to let her out to play.

"Are you here alone?" I ask him.

"Of course," he answers, eyes narrowing on me. I only give a shrug in response, as if I couldn't possibly know if he had company in his hotel room when he woke up this morning.

He takes his seat and introduces himself to Sally, who looks equally uncomfortable and awed by my husband's presence. I understand. He has always had that effect on people.

"You remember Noah, I'm sure," I say. "I think you fucked the same woman in college."

Sally releases a little gasp, but there is a commiserating twinkle in her eye.

"Yes," Noah says, "though I don't keep in touch with her these days. Nice to see you, Drew."

"Right," Drew mumbles.

"I was just explaining to these two how I got my scars."

"You were?" Surprise shows all over his face. He knows I don't talk about this with strangers as much as he knows I don't easily make friends. Me telling two people I don't know well is a tremendous deal.

I hum around a sip of coffee.

"Were you two together during that time?" Sally asks.

"No," I say.

"We got engaged while she was in the hospital," Drew says at the same time.

"So, you were dating when the attack occurred?"

"Nope," I say, popping the word. "We went straight from something sort of like friends to married without all the usual in between."

"Huh," is all Sally says. "I guess you move fast, Drew."

Noah chokes on a laugh, or a piece of bacon, I don't know. But now it's Drew who looks uncomfortable. Something that happens often these days, but I'm still not used to his fractured confidence. He used to walk around with the same air that surrounds Noah. That big dick energy all

NFL quarterbacks have. Even the ugly ones have it, that extreme swagger. Drew's is fading fast.

I love to see it. I hate it, too. There is an awful lot of hate in my world right now. This desire to hurt him, to let others hurt him in my presence; it makes me small. He makes me feel small. My life is an emotional minefield.

I finish my coffee and push my plate aside, knowing all eyes at the table are on me.

"Thank you for breakfast, Sally," I say to her. "I'm going to excuse myself. I have some work to get done." I stand slowly, leaning over the table to give a bit of a show before I leave. Thankfully, I make it to an elevator just before the doors shut.

It's been only weeks since Los Angeles, not enough time to not be sad over it all. But long enough to learn that I don't have to keep ranking myself lower than others. I don't need to sit at that table for Drew's sake. He can weather whatever Noah and Sally throw at him without me.

The next several hours of my day are free time. I use them to catch up on blog posts and emails that I've been ignoring for the past several days. I also check in with my mom, who expresses her concern for me, for Drew, for our shit show of a marriage.

"Honey, have you talked to him since you moved?"

"Yes, he flew into Dallas early. I saw him last night," I tell her.

"How did it go?"

"Not well, Mom. It's hard to look at him the same, knowing he's been with them."

"Them? There were multiple?"

Well, shit, guess that cat is out of the bag now.

"Um, yeah. I... I think the others were like one-time things," I stammer out. There is rustling on her end, and she mumbles something that sounds an awful lot like she's going to kill that little shit, but I can't be sure. "Listen,

Mom, I'm glad you called, but I've got to get to a meeting. I'll call you tomorrow, okay?"

"Of course, June. I love you."

"Love you too, Mom."

I lied to my mom. I don't have a meeting until dinner, but it simply isn't a conversation I want to have right now. It's one more thing to feel shitty about myself for. The list of those is piling up quickly. It's not so easy to stay in anger. I wish it were. Anger is like a warm, fuzzy blanket protecting you from the freezing cold of depression and self-loathing.

I try writing a post about a new café I had visited in New Orleans Uptown, but it somehow turns into an open letter to cheating husbands. It's nonsense, cathartic ramblings fueled by heartbreak and rage and a bone-deep depression from knowing you somehow aren't enough.

That's at the core of every feeling. Which is utter bullshit. I'm the victim here and I can't quit blaming myself. I should think Drew wasn't enough. He wasn't strong enough to resist his urges. He wasn't brave enough to confront me when he was having problems. It's a "he" issue, not a "me" issue. Yet, I'm here, wallowing in my low self-confidence.

I'm at it for twenty minutes when there is another knock on my door.

"You told your mom?" Drew is incredulous when I open it to him.

"Ah, did you get scolded for being a manwhore who broke her daughter's heart?" I ask, turning my back to him and walking back into my room.

"It was a full hour and I think I was able to speak all of four words."

"You deserve it."

"I know," he says, contrite.

"Why are you here? I'm busy," I lie.

"Are you? I got a call from Fillmore. She had a cancellation and wanted to know if we could talk."

"Now?"

"Now."

"Fine." I sigh.

"Really?"

"Yes, Drew," I say flatly. "Video call?" He nods, and I pull it up on my laptop.

"Good afternoon, you two," Dr. Fillmore greets us. "It's been a while. June, how was your move?"

"Great, actually. I'm enjoying the city and all its history."

"That's wonderful. How about you, Drew? Are you ready for your game tomorrow?"

"As ready as ever." One thing that makes Drew such a great quarterback is how easy it is for him to compartmentalize. His home life, personal matters, everyday stressors—none of it affects his game. It's a skill he learned as a kid. His dad always pushed him to be the best on the field, even when his dad had a rotating door of unstable women at home. Drew's father sank into alcohol addiction after his wife died. It caused a lot of problems for my husband in his early years. Drew learned quickly how to shut it out.

I'm just now seeing that he uses those same skills in our marriage, and it makes me feel foolish for not noticing before now.

"Perfect. Let's get updated on you two. Have you been on another date?"

Neither of us answers.

"Elaborate, please," she says and because I'm still in whatever red space I was in while writing my post, I do as commanded.

"Not exactly. Drew didn't speak to me for over a week after our last session with you. Until he saw pictures of me out at a work dinner with another man. A man who turns out to be the ex-boyfriend of his mistress, by the way. That's probably an important detail for you to know," I ramble along. "When he saw the pictures, he accused me of having sex with him. Then he showed up to Dallas a day early, waited at my hotel room door, told me about all the one-night stands he had, gave me an orgasm the likes I've never known, and made me cry. I'm not sure we can call any of that dating."

"One, she is not my mistress. Two, I was trying to give you space. Three, I didn't accuse. I asked," he says, holding up his fingers as he lists how he sees the situation.

I open my mouth to retort, but Dr. Fillmore cuts me off.

"Both of you, please stop. You're heated, and that is understandable. However, I need you to calm yourselves. Let's sit here, in this moment, full of feelings, and count to twenty. When we're done, we'll use feeling statements, not accusatory or defensive ones. We'll also pretend we have gags in when the other one is speaking. Listen to each other, truly hear the words."

After the designated twenty count, she asks me to start.

"Okay. There's a hollowness inside me that I've never known before. Unless my imagination conjures up images of Drew with faceless women or with Lorelai. Then all that empty space overflows with such rancor, I think I'll suffocate on it. I feel less than, little, small. Like I might just disappear. Then I have moments of the opposite. When I feel full of new life and new experiences. I don't know how to balance it all. So many times, I've wanted to call him and share all these new feelings and accomplishments. But how do I do that when he isn't my closest confidant anymore? I don't know how to tell Drew that I don't think I can ever forgive him for choosing her over me, or that I want him back. Because how can both be true? I'm utterly confused, all the time."

I stop to take a breath, a moment to slow my racing heart. Drew's palm runs a circle on my back. I want to tell him to stop touching me, but the truth is I need the comfort.

"Both can be true, June. Do not devalue your own feelings by dismissing them as impossibilities. Did you conjure these images before your discussion with Drew last night, or did they start after?"

"I've had them since I walked in on him and Lorelai. Different ones. They were playing on a never-ending loop at first," I answer.

"And today? Still a loop?"

I ponder her question and realize, no.

"No, today has been better. Surprisingly."

"Is it?"

I don't answer, just give a small shrug.

"Perhaps this warrants more communication, and we can see if these conjurations continue to decrease. Sometimes you need to know the specifics to calm the imagination. I wouldn't suggest that for everyone, but it seems to have helped in your case."

"Okay," I agree, though I'm doubtful.

"Your turn, Drew."

"I feel like the biggest asshole on the planet for making June feel all the things she is. She's turned cruel and defensive, two things she never was before, and that's my fault. There's no love coming from her anymore. It's terrifying and the stress of that makes me want to find a release. But the only release I know is what caused all this to begin with. I caved to that when the pressure of moving and leading a new team was weighing on me. I won't cave to it again. But, despite how she sees herself right now, I see how much she's growing. I'm proud of her, but I'm afraid she's growing away from me. I feel"—he emphasizes the word, as if it's the word that is causing insult instead of the feelings themselves—"like we never should have gotten married."

I die a hundred deaths. My heart numbs as my veins go ice-cold. There are no words I can imagine him saying that would hurt me more than those. Even with it all falling apart around us, I'd never give up the good times we've had. The loving moments, the laughs, the millions of kisses.

I'd rather lose his love than to have never had it at all. It hurts that he doesn't feel the same.

"Do you think there is a way for the two of you to grow together?"

"I want there to be."

"Do you have any ideas on how to do that?"

"I think we need to connect at a more basic level. The dates would be perfect, but my cheating keeps getting in the way," he says. "We need to get through that somehow first. Fight it out, maybe. There can't be any make-up until then."

"I'd suggest discussing rather than fighting, but you may be on to something. Those feelings we hold in when we're feeling hurt or guilt need to be let out before they can ever be let go. Now, why do you think you shouldn't have married?"

I'm going to hyperventilate. I'm bleeding out in my hotel room, staining everything red, and I don't think they even notice. But the hand on my back is still there, moving up to knead at my nape. I focus on that.

"We weren't ready. Or I wasn't, I guess. I wasn't capable of being what she needed. A man who could help her heal. Instead, I broke her more. And now she hates me. If we'd stayed in the friend zone, at least she'd love me like she did before we married. It's not the love I want, but I'd take it over what we have now in a heartbeat."

"Can you be the man she needs now?"

"Not yet."

CHAPTER 13

June

NOAH:

How are you doing, my sweet June?

ME:

Hanging in there, just finished up
a couple's therapy session.

NOAH:

I'm here if you need anything. See you at dinner?

ME:

Yep, thanks Noah.

"June?"

Drew hasn't left my room yet. It's clear he wants to talk more. I've run out of excuses to keep him at bay. He knows I have nothing on my schedule for the next few hours.

"Are you sure you want to do this now? You have a game tomorrow."

He steps into me, hands resting on my cheeks, thumbs caressing them.

"Baby, you know I can play through anything. We need to do this."

"I'm scared," I admit. He swallows hard, as if he is, too. "There is so much I don't know about you. I hate that."

"I do, too," he says. He catches a rogue tear with his finger and sucks it into his mouth.

Everything stills, the room falls away, the world outside of the space between us vanishes. The only thing left here is a fractured woman and a man holding a hammer in one hand, glue in the other. This conversation can go either way.

And I'm terrified. My fingers shake as I angrily brush away another stray tear. The sadness that crosses his features tells me he notices.

"How did Lorelai find her way back into our lives?" I ask, plunging into the deep end and waiting to drown.

"The club. She was there the fourth time. She was in Seattle for some conference."

I hate this club with everything I am. It's quickly becoming the bane of my existence.

"We chatted, got caught up on each other's lives. When the subject changed to why we were both there, we realized we could help one another. No strings."

"You had strings, Drew," I say in a broken whisper.

"You and I are not past tense." His hands have tightened, tangled deeper into my hair. He's trying to keep me from running, but all I can think is that I'm going to have to redo my hair. These are the effects of depression on your brain. In the middle of the storm, it's the inconsequential that feels like the biggest of details. I shake my head to ward them off and focus on arguing with his statement.

"Don't deflect. How does she help?"

"You know this already. I discussed it in therapy. She's just a tool I used to ease that part of me. Don't make me give you the details, Junie."

"Stop calling me that," I hiss, wounded. It's there in his eyes, his reluctance to take this where I need it to go. So, I swim down deeper. "Do you tie her up?"

"Sometimes."

"Do you spank her?"

"Yes."

"Choke her?"

He nods.

"Come in her mouth?"

Another nod, this one accompanied by a grimace.

"Did you… Oh, God. I hate you for making me do this. Did you have unprotected sex with her? Is there any chance she could be pregnant?"

There is no nod. No sound. My knees shake for a split second before they give out.

Is this how it ends? This is when I grow smaller and smaller and smaller. This is when I fade away completely.

"Stop it. There is no chance. None, June," Drew says as he catches my weight when the last bit of strength I have leaves me. I'm lifted into his arms, but that only makes me cringe.

"I don't believe you. You paused, and you're a liar, anyway."

"I didn't answer because I couldn't believe you believed I would chance that. I know you hate me right now, but it's still shocking, okay?"

There were long discussions after the doctors told me it would be hard to carry a baby to term. Days when I didn't feel whole. Not because I'd ever had dreams of being a mother. I hadn't. I was still so young, it'd never crossed my mind. But the possibility was always there in the periphery. And having a piece of you, a tangible, physical piece, ripped away—it's jarring and painful.

Jonas had taken the decision away from us. We decided we were okay with the outcome. That if we ever wanted children, there were other options. Options that would allow us to help children with great need.

Him impregnating someone else was never an option. I don't know why the idea that his whoring around could lead to it hadn't crossed my mind before. Now that it's here, it won't leave.

"I can see it, you know? Lorelai, fat with your child. Pictures of the two of you together, splashed on TMZ, your hand on her swollen belly."

He's sitting on the bed now, holding me on his lap, though it feels more like I'm levitating. Weightless because I'm missing more and more parts by the minute. Soon I'll be nothing but dust in the air.

"Stop that," he snaps. "None of that is even a remote possibility. Now or ever."

"Did you use a condom every time?"

No answer. He doesn't fucking answer and bone-deep sorrow washes over me.

"I'm going to be sick," I say, scrambling to get up and rush to the bathroom.

I heave out every bit of my breakfast, plus more. Probably the remnants of my obliterated heart, too.

After a quick brush of my teeth, I exit to find Drew staring out the window.

"How do you know she can't be pregnant? How did you know you wouldn't bring an STD home?" I'm resigned truly to hate him now. I've been saying it with no heat behind it. Oh, how I feel it now.

"I know for several reasons," he responds hesitantly.

"Jesus, Drew. Explain! Quit making me do all the work."

"I know because I made her sign a contract with clear inclusions. Birth control was one. Monthly testing was another. I also made her sign an NDA. They all had to sign that. I took every precaution to protect you."

Who even is this man? I can't believe I married someone who makes women sign NDAs like he's Christian fucking Grey.

"What good is a monthly test? She could pick something up between tests. She could have lied about birth control. Truly protecting me would include not betraying me at all. Besides, you gave me your hotel room number, explicit instructions on how to find you with her! None of that is protection. It's all betrayal."

"It's not like I was fucking her on a weekly basis, June. And you were never supposed to show up!" He turns to face me, and I gasp at what I see. It's not guilt. Nor pain.

"You're mad? You don't have the right. I would have given you anything, Drew. Fuck, I would have given you it all! Whatever you wanted. I've been so over the moon for you my entire life that I would have put all my dreams and fantasies aside to give you yours. Hell, some of them I did. And you're mad at me for finding out that you like to fuck other women instead of me?"

"I'm not mad at you. Fuck, June. I'm mad at myself. For what I've done to you and our marriage. For what I know comes next. I'm angrier than I've ever been in my life, but none of that is directed at you."

His chest is heaving, eyes glassy, hands shoved in the pockets of his sweatpants.

"What comes next?"

"You tell me to leave you alone. I do it and I hate every fucking minute of it. You focus on your career, and you continue to grow. All while I watch from the outside, wondering why I'm such a fuck-up. You eventually catch some feelings for someone else. It won't be love because you'll only ever love me. I've always known that, and I took advantage. But it will be affection and trust. It will be enough for you to give them a part of you that was also only supposed to be mine. From there, I don't know. Maybe you give up on us completely. Maybe I spend the rest of my life alone. I'll be content, if you're happy, but I'll always be miserable without you. Because every day we're apart, every fucking minute you aren't there for me to see and touch, it kills me. It fucking guts me, and I will never hate anyone more than I hate myself for this."

I'm in tears by the time he finishes. One of his own now trails down his strong cheek. I'm a sobbing mess, however.

He wraps me up in his arms, pressing a few kisses atop my head.

"Just not Noah, okay?"

Oh my God.

"Why not Noah?" I ask, pushing away from him.

"He's dangerous and I don't like him."

"You don't even know him. I don't think you ever did. You just took her word."

"I didn't take her word. I saw what he did to her!" He's angry again, like a colossal bear huffing and puffing. His emotions are as crazy of a rollercoaster as mine are. We're quite the pair.

"Of course she showed you," I say with a roll of my eyes. "Did she tell you it was her idea? Or that she pressured him into it when he was unsure?"

"No, because that isn't the truth." He looks startled. Maybe even confused.

"Are you so sure? He told me his side of the story. How he was in love with her, and she asked him to experiment with her. How he feared the idea because neither of them knew what they were doing. He said he needed to think about it. Then she went out and partied with you and some of your teammates, rubbing it in Noah's face, prompting him to agree. She brought the crop. She begged him to hit her harder with it, and he felt horrible! Does any of that sound plausible?"

He blinks.

"Oh, let me guess the rest! I bet you'd fucked her a time or two before that. In typical Drew McKenna, star quarterback fashion, you didn't give her enough repeat sessions. Did you? Until after mean old Noah hurt her, that is. Then she came crying, and you acted like the big hero. Am I close?"

Blink, blink, blink.

"Wow, you really are a pussy-whipped cliché, aren't you? Her cunt must be like a gold-plated vice."

"Fuck you, June."

"Did you always like controlling, rough sex? Or was she your first? Was it her idea with you, too?"

The answer is all over his face. My stomach riots at the realization that Lorelai is the woman who introduced Drew to the type of sex that caused our marriage to erupt into so much chaos.

Without another word, he leaves.

I guess we're done fighting it out.

I'm stunned when the door closes. Not only because he left so abruptly, but also at my outburst. Drew's right. I've gotten mean. I'm not altogether sure it's a bad thing.

What is glaringly bad is how I look. I take a look at myself in the mirror above the room's dresser. Puffy, red eyes stare back at me. Makeup ruined, mascara streaking down my face. My hair is a disaster. Most of which a shower and redo will fix. Except for my swollen under-eyes. That's going to take extra effort.

Leaving the room like this is no go.

ME:

I need help. Bring ice.

NOAH:

On it.

Ten minutes later, he arrives, a bucket of ice in hand. He winces when I open the door.

"The fuck did he do to you?"

"Answered every question I asked," I say dryly.

"Was it better not knowing?"

"No. Don't get me wrong, this feels awful, but I needed to know." I watch as he grabs a hand towel and fills it with ice.

"You're one of those," he says. "Lie down and put this on your eyes."

"One of who?" I do as he says, grabbing the towel from his hands and moving to my bed.

"The type who needs all the gory details. It makes sense, it's the journalist in you, probably. No guessing games with your type, just facts."

"Fair point."

He's right, I see things without shades of gray. Black and white. Yes or no. Truth or lie.

Husband or enemy.

"Ugh," I groan.

"Would you like to talk about it?" Noah asks from somewhere on the other side of the room.

"Our therapy session was rough. I told him I didn't know if I could ever forgive him. He told me he didn't think we should have gotten married."

Noah makes a low oohing sound.

"She suggested we talk more about the whosits and whatyados of his infidelity. I asked him about Lorelai."

I hear him open the mini-fridge, the clink of ice cubes plopping in a glass. He mumbles something about my nonsensical words, but whatever, I'm sure he understood enough. A moment later, a cool glass is in my hand.

"Maybe I asked too direct of questions. I threw up, Noah, that's how awful it was," I cry.

"Sit up, take a sip," he tells me sternly. My eyes are blurry, but no more tears are spilling out when I remove the towel. I down my drink, enjoying the sting of the whiskey as it sears my throat.

"Mmm," I moan at the small satisfaction.

"Stop doing that," Noah says, his eyes dark. I swallow hard. I know Noah is attracted to me on some level. It's easy to read his flirting. The heat currently directed at me is a new level. And his timing is awful. I feel like a flea clinging to life on a soaking wet dog.

"Um, I confronted him about what happened between you two. And her."

"I can guess how that went," he says while making his own drink.

"She's beautiful. I guess I get it."

Noah goes rigid.

"Stand up, June." His tone compels me to comply. It's a demand laced with arrogance that he knows I'll follow. "Turn around."

I jump with surprise when the swat lands on my ass. Quick and sharp.

"Lorelai has nothing on you. Lower yourself to her like that again and you won't sit comfortably for days."

Damn.

"You just spanked me," I say, incredulous.

"You deserved it."

"I'm sorry, what?"

"You heard me," he says smugly and takes another sip.

"What gives you the right?" My voice edges with a slight fear that Noah picks up on immediately. I didn't mean for it to be there. I'm not afraid of Noah. Old habits and all that… I'm never easy in the presence of men. Noah has been an exception, never showing me anything that gave me unease. Until just now. I don't like hands on me when I'm unprepared.

"I'm so sorry, June. You're correct. I don't have the right. And given what you've been through, it was horrifically careless of me. You never have to be afraid of me. I promise you that," he says contritely while holding my gaze, and I believe him. "I hope you can forgive me for not gaining consent beforehand. Give it to me now so the next time you say stupid shit like that, I can correct it."

"No."

"What was that?"

"No?"

"Is that a question?"

"No?"

"Are you giving me permission to do it again when you misbehave?"

This is like the Twilight Zone. I don't even know what's happening. I want to say yes and because I want to say yes, I should say no. Right? While the unexpectedness of his swat was something I didn't like, I can't say I didn't like the actual spanking itself.

I have no idea what that says about me.

"I thought you weren't into this kind of thing?" I ask.

"I never said that."

"But, Lorelai—"

"Was a mistake I made when I was inexperienced. That's no longer the case. I sought the knowledge I lacked then, and like I do with everything worth doing, I perfected the craft."

Oh.

"Oh."

"Are you consenting, June?" A smirk grows on his stupid, pretty face.

"For you to punish me?"

"Not to punish. To correct a behavior."

"That sounds like the same thing." I narrow my eyes on him.

"You aren't saying no," he says with a smile.

My phone chimes with a notification. I use the opportunity to avoid confirming or denying.

LOVE:

How is it going? Have you seen Drew yet?

ME:

Saw him, it went terribly. I'll explain when I'm back in NOLA with copious amounts of booze.

Also, Noah just spanked me and wants permission to do it again.

LOVE:

WHAT!?!?!

ME:

Gotta go, dinner meeting. TTYL.

LOVE:

JUNE!!!!

I set my phone down and turn back to Noah, who is casually leaning against the wall, watching me, humor on his face. This man sees right through me. I'm certain of it.

"Thank you," I say with sincerity.

"For what?"

"The ice, the distraction, the apology, all of it. I appreciate it." I smile and give him a small shrug. "And for the record, I believe Drew is completely wrong about you."

"You're welcome and thank you for giving me a chance. For trusting me when I know that can't be easy for you. I know this is all an awkward position for you to be in. I'll let you get ready now, but I'll be back in a while to take you down to dinner."

I lie down and place the ice towel back over my eyes. That turns out to be a horrible idea when I wake up from my nap in a small puddle of water.

Gross.

There are several texts from Leighton when I check the time on my phone.

LOVE:

I cannot believe you are leaving me hanging like this.

You are the worst best friend in the history of best friends.

Please tell me he spanked you with his dick? And that it's huge.

There is a text from Noah, too. A message with a link labeled 'Boss Bitch'.

NOAH:

Play this when you get ready for dinner.

Clicking the link opens a girl power playlist to rival all girl power playlists that have come before. I push play, drop my phone on the bathroom counter, and start the shower as "Flawless" by Beyoncé fills the room.

An hour later, I'm applying the last layer of lipstick when Noah arrives to escort me to this dinner. It's kind of a big to-do, I guess. It won't just be network people there, but some higher-up execs and owners of the teams, local celebrities, retired players who may be in town for the game and their respective plus-ones. I'll know plenty of people and even more will know who I am.

Drew McKenna's wife. Or maybe even Drew McKenna's jilted wife. What I need to be is June, an independent woman.

Noah shows up exactly when he said he would and carries a small shopping bag with him.

"What do you have there, Mr. Anders?" I ask when I move to the side to let him pass. He doesn't immediately answer, opting for a silent trek to the far side of my room.

"Come here," he calls gruffly, with his back still to me.

I move to stand next to him, wondering what this is all about.

"Noah?" I call when he doesn't acknowledge my presence. He turns then, eyes traveling down my body. The slow seduction sends chills through my limbs and makes my nipples pucker under the slight fabric of my dress. It's blush, just a shade darker than my skin. Thin spaghetti straps hold up a simple triangle bodice above a flared skirt that falls to just below my knees. Strappy black heels complete the look.

Since Noah is the one who set the ensemble for the night, he knows I only have a scrap of white lace underneath. The way he is looking at me, he remembers what he's chosen. He doesn't miss that my body is reacting to his perusal.

I don't miss his notice. His lips part ever so slightly, and his breathing deepens. Following his lead, I let my sight fall down his form, taking in his perfectly tailored black suit that stresses his wide shoulders and fit form. He doesn't move a muscle until my eyes stop where there is clear evidence of a large, hardening penis behind the fly of his pants.

Noah takes one quick step forward, his chest brushing against my nipples.

Holy mother of fucking God, he smells amazing.

How does such a light touch set my entire body alight? As if I could explode in orgasm just by him breathing on my breasts right now.

"This is not how I expected tonight to go, June."

"What do you mean?" I ask, looking up at him. His gaze bores into mine.

"I was expecting another fun time with my new friend. Her name is Sweet June," he says with a wink. "The woman standing in front of me right now, the one who called me Mr. Anders, making my cock twitch? Sweet isn't the word I'd use to describe her."

"What word would you use?" I say only after I swallow down the feelings clogging my throat.

Instead of answering, he reaches into the bag he brought with him and pulls out something made of leather. One hand reaches out and lifts my left arm, then slips the leathery strap over it. He repeats the action on the other arm before he moves behind me and sets to work on the dainty gold buckles.

It's a body harness of some sort. The thin black straps crisscross over my chest to enhance my breasts, and another encircles my waist. After the task is completed, he comes back to stand in front of me and makes another path down my form with his blazing eyes.

"Fucking fire, June. You are the heat that will scorch every man in the room tonight and it's my honor to be the one by your side."

I blink several times. Noah is unexpected, always surprising me.

"Can I see it?" I ask him.

"Go look." He nods to the mirror. I do as he says and take in the simple way he's converted me from almost angelic to just shy of dirty, and I smile. The harness isn't heavy or blatantly sexual. There are no garish O-rings, just buttery leather and discreet buckles. He's made me look high fashion, not dungeon kink.

"Did you listen to your playlist?"

"I did. Thank you, Noah," I say, turning to him. "You're more than just a fashion demon. You're like my very own fairy godfather."

"Oh, fuck no, stop that train of thought right now before you get your second spanking of the day."

"Promise?" I ask teasingly.

He reaches out to pinch my chin, gently tilting my face up to his.

"Be very careful what you say to me tonight, June. You've got me feeling very dangerous," he says, rubbing his thumb across my bottom lip. "And I promised myself I was going to be good with you." He lets go and sticks his thumb in his mouth, sucking off the lipstick he took with it.

"We should get going, playboy," I say.

"Mmhmm." He walks toward the door, grabbing my clutch on his way. He holds his arm out for me and I take it, letting him lead me.

The dinner is exactly as stale and stuffy as you'd expect. We've been here for all of twenty minutes, and it already feels like a lifetime. I've got my phony face on, the one that says I'm always pleasant, I never speak out, I'm every public relations person's dream to work with.

There have been plenty of looks tonight. For both me and Noah. Stares and rumors spreading through the large, garishly designed dining room like a virus. I've done a good job ignoring them, and any time I stutter at it, Noah is there, whispering some affirmation in my ear. Which, yeah, probably adds to the rumors, but oh well.

He has yet to leave my side, opting to guide me through the room, introducing me to people I don't know, and allowing me to return the favor for him. We're approaching a small group near the bar when my fingers tingle with nerves.

One man is a past teammate of Drew's from college, Nathan Park. He and Drew were good buddies then and after they were both drafted to the same team. We spent a fair amount of time with him and his wife, Sarah. I like them. Nathan knows Lorelai, of course. He likely knows their history to an extent and the current situation. I don't know if he's spoken to Drew since our story broke, but it's likely.

"Hi, Nathan," I say, stepping up to the group. "It's good to see you."

"Hey, June," Nathan replies, stepping in to give me a quick hug. "You look beautiful tonight."

"Thank you. Do you know Noah?" I ask, stepping back to make room for Noah to enter the conversation.

"I don't think we ever met formally. Just on the field several times." Nathan holds his hand out to shake and Noah accepts.

"Nice to meet you, Nathan."

"Where's Sarah tonight?" I ask.

"Home. She's pregnant again and doesn't want to travel."

"Congratulations," I tell him genuinely. "Send her my love, will you?"

"Of course. How are you doing?"

"I'm great, staying busy, and happy to be starting something new." I keep it vague, since it's not his business, for one. Two, I don't want to get into anything in this room with these people. The few other people standing around have taken notice of who Nathan is talking to and turn to us.

One man is an executive from ESPN and asks how we're getting along with plans for our upcoming show. I see Nathan visibly ease when he realizes Noah and I are coworkers. Conversation flows and I try to enjoy myself more.

Eventually, I excuse myself, wanting to use the restroom before we sit down to dinner. I find the restroom down the hall from the ballroom and take care of all necessary business, plus put on a fresh coat of lip stain. As soon as I exit, I hear familiar voices. It's easy since one of them is raised.

"Because I don't trust you, Anders."

"Whether or not you trust me is irrelevant."

"Nothing about my wife is irrelevant," Drew says. I quietly move closer to where they are arguing. They didn't try very hard to find a private place, standing down a side hallway. Anyone visiting the restroom could overhear.

"Make your point, Drew. I have dinner to escort my lovely date to."

"My point is this. If you hurt her, if you leave a single fucking mark on her, I will end you. Do you understand me?"

"Finally, something we can agree on. I wouldn't dream of ever hurting June. Your wife is charming, kind, smart, funny as hell, and one of the most gorgeous creatures I've ever met. I would be lucky to have a chance with her. Any man would. She's something you should have cherished, Drew, not tossed aside for a conniving lesser woman."

My hand covers my beating heart. Hearing Noah speak of me like this does great things for my battered ego. It's comforting to know someone sees the parts of me that are having a hard time shining through these days.

"I know exactly how special June is, you piece of shit. And I won't let you manipulate her into believing that bullshit you fed her about Lorelai. I know what you did to her."

"I know what I did to her, too," Noah says, heat behind every word. "It's not anything I ever denied, if you remember. I disputed how it happened. And it's something I regret to this day. But make no mistake, Drew. I'm not that same stupid doe-eyed boy and I know exactly what I'm doing now. It's unfortunate you don't, nor do you truly know who you're doing it with."

"Lorelai has her issues, but she's not a manipulator."

"You're a fucking fool if you believe that."

I step around the corner then, sensing that their conversation is escalating to a level that soon will be out of control. They're both too strongheaded to back down. Besides, I want Drew to know I heard him defend her.

"That's enough," I say, drawing their attention, my voice full of bitterness.

Drew stares at me. His jaw drops as he takes me in.

"Noah, could you please get me a glass of white wine? I'll see you back at the table in just a moment."

"Of course." He places a hand on my shoulder, then lets it slide down my arm as he steps away. Noah takes his time retreating, perhaps not sure of the state of Drew's temper. Or maybe he just wants to do some eavesdropping of his own.

"You have a game tomorrow. What are you doing here?" I ask my husband.

"I came to talk to Noah," he answers almost dazedly. His hand reaches out, fingers curling around the leather straps that cross over my cleavage, pulling me toward him. "What the fuck do you think you're wearing?"

"A harness."

"Why?" His voice is a harsh whisper he has little control over.

"It was a gift, and it makes me feel sexy. It makes me feel confident and beautiful in a mysteriously edgy way."

Drew pulls me even closer, so close I strain my neck to look up at him. He brings his face down to mine, nose to nose.

"A gift from Noah, I presume."

I nod, though, he wasn't asking a question.

"One day, I'm going to fuck you raw while you're wearing this and nothing else. Fuck you so good you won't have a single memory of any man's touch but mine. That asshole won't be a thought or even an idea in that pretty head of yours."

I rise onto my toes, bringing my mouth nearly to the same height as his.

"Had you been fucking me like that for the last five years, I'd never be tempted to know what another man's touch feels like. What his body could do to mine, what pleasure he could bring me. How full he could make me." I dart my tongue out to give the slight cleft in his chin a small lick, followed by a quick bite. "And maybe it would be me you'd be so defensive of, instead of her."

"June," he starts.

"Have a good game tomorrow, Drew," I purr as I walk away.

I make it back to the table with my head held high. Noah stands as I approach and pulls my chair out for me. Drew follows me in, conveniently finding an empty seat next to Nathan. He stares at me as I sit.

"He liked the harness, didn't he?" he whispers in my ear before taking his seat once again.

I look at him, studying his wide smile. He winks.

"You knew he'd show up?"

"I made a calculated guess."

"Fucking wizard," I say, making him laugh.

CHAPTER 14

June

Thanksgiving in Dallas passes quickly with our busy schedule. I spend the entire game with broadcasters and announcers, promoting all things Super Bowl related. I try to focus on the game when the chances arise.

I still love watching Drew play. The butterflies, the adrenaline, the anxiety—it's always there when he's on the field and it never waned. I still root for my husband. Wanting the best for him is as ingrained in me as it always has been. Despite everything, I still want him to have good things in life.

He wants a Super Bowl ring. That won't happen this season. The team hasn't been a cohesive unit. The offensive line is crumbling, and he's having a harder time finding his wide receivers down the field.

But Drew is still young and healthy and it's never easy with a new team. There's time and I have faith he'll get there. I only wish I knew if I'd be by his side when he does.

I opt to skip dinner that night and order a room service turkey burger instead. Not only is it my first holiday without Drew since we've married, it's the first holiday I've ever spent completely alone. It doesn't make me sad when I stop to think about it. I'm oddly at peace with it here in a strange hotel room with my version of turkey dinner.

I speak to my mom and Reed, who are together at her house. And Leighton, who flew to her dad's house for the weekend. And Noah, who calls to check in on me.

Drew doesn't call. Ignoring the twinge of pain I have over that, I text him halfway through my dinner.

ME:

Congratulations on the win today.
Happy Thanksgiving.

I finish my meal without a word from him. There is no reply by the time I go to sleep and nothing when I wake up, either. I'm proud that I didn't end up drowning in nightmares of what he was doing and who he was doing it with.

I return to New Orleans and bury myself in work, determined to be the best at this job. To get noticed and be in demand after this contract is over. I research every idea and topic we've discussed in our meetings, immersing myself in the local history and culture. I check out several high school football programs, dragging Leighton and/or Noah with me to games.

That turns out to be an amazing experience, watching kids in love with the football, starstruck when they notice Noah in the crowd of spectators. As always, Noah is beyond charming to the athletes, their parents, and coaches.

Noah and I have gotten closer, our friendship stronger. He's still a vicious flirt, but it's mostly harmless. In fact, I find it empowers me, and I think that's his point. Noah is the same way with Leighton, but not as extreme.

She doesn't get little swats when he doesn't approve of her behavior, though. I do. Rarely, but there have been a couple of times. They're always delivered with a smile and a small lecture on how I shouldn't look down on myself. I've taken it to heart, and I'm better about not falling into that hole. I'm no longer comparing myself to Lorelai ten times a day, at least.

Noah would tick a lot of boxes for a single woman on the market. In another lifetime, his attention would be thrilling. It would be flattering, and he'd be a man I could fall in love with. Some days, when I look at him, I see those same beliefs reflected on me. Noah's got baggage of his own to unpack.

I know with certainty that we're not meant for each other, but there is something kindred between us. Perhaps that is all born of our awful connections with Drew and Lorelai. It's there all the same. I trust him, and at this point in my life, that speaks volumes.

So, it shouldn't surprise me in the moments I see him look at me with longing. Or when I catch myself looking at him and feeling… things I should only feel about my husband. Those moments shouldn't shock me. My hunger for him or my need to explore should feel like a natural progression to the course my life has taken.

People feel this after betrayal. Revenge, rebound, call it what you like, but I'd say it stems from an intense need to feel wanted. To be seen and desired, to just fucking feel anything real.

At times, I think I'm ready to give in, to let go. The urge to, grows every day. So far, I've resisted. Mostly by staying busy and distracted.

Leighton, the constant all-star sidekick, goes along with all my whims. She's tagged along with me to the strangest of places, popular tourist ones and some off the beaten path alike. We've been on nearly every ghost tour in the city in the month since returning from Dallas. She even indulged my whim to traipse around the deserted husk of the old amusement park on the east side of the city.

It was abandoned after Hurricane Katrina. A place that once, if only for a few years, brought joy to many, now lies in waste, haunted by the ghosts of better times. I relate all too well. Noah pulled some strings to get us legal access, though we could have snuck in like so many urban explorers before us. This was one of the adventures he refused to accompany us on, claiming he didn't have the proper shoes to muck around in such a place. Always the dandy, that one.

Turns out, I enjoyed it more because it was only Love and me. The silence, strangely, like a warm blanket wrapped around us while we explored what looked much like I'd imagine a post-apocalyptic world would look like. We took some amazing pictures, and both of us may have found a new appreciation for places long deserted.

I text Drew every few days to check in. He's still not talking to me or scheduling time for us with Dr. Fillmore. He only responds to a text of mine once or twice a week and it's never more than a few words. I'd be more worried if I didn't know he was still in regular contact with my brother.

Reed says Drew's focused on 'things.' A vague response, but if it was something bad, Reed would tell me. I assume it's the team, the last few games of the season. They're not playoff contenders, but they don't have to finish at the bottom of the division, either. I understand that. I know his ethics and how hard he works, not just for his goals but for all his teammates, as well. What I don't understand is how he asked me to put in the work while he all but ignores me.

I miss him every day. And every day, at least once, I question who he's spending time with. Is he missing me, too? If he were, he'd call. But days go by, and nothing changes. I'm finding some peace, some happiness in my everyday life. Confidence grows in me by the hour. I am proud of what I'm doing, what I'm accomplishing.

It would be a lie if I said I didn't wish Drew were with me while I'm doing it.

My attention the past few days has shifted from all things New Orleans to Christmas preparation. Mom, Reed, and Larry are all flying in to spend it here with Leighton and me. The holiday falls on a Sunday and Drew's game that week is the Thursday before. His schedule absolutely allows him to travel here and spend it with us.

I just need to extend the invite, which I've been dragging my feet on, because I don't think it should come as an impersonal text message. It's only a week away. If I'm going to do it, I need to do it now.

Christmas won't feel right if he's not here, regardless of how furious I still am with him. Making the phone call scares me. What if he answers? What if he doesn't? What if he accepts? What if he declines?

You won't know if you don't try.

I press his contact on my phone and pace my balcony while I listen to it ring. I'm about to end the call, convinced voicemail is about to pick up and I won't know what to say, when the ringing stops.

"Hi, June." Even though I'm the one who told him not to call me Junie, it still hurts when he doesn't. It's an endearment only he has ever used, and he's been using it for as long as I can recall.

"Hi."

"Everything okay?" he asks after a pause, and I want to scream that of course nothing is okay. That's not true, though. A large part of my life is more than okay, amazing even. If I break it all up into little pieces and make two piles—one good, one bad—the good would far outweigh the rest. It would be just a speck of bad. Yet when pushed all together, the bad bleeds into the rest, tainting it all.

"Yeah, everything is fine."

"Why are you calling?" He sounds, I don't know, put off maybe. As if I'm a disruption taking up precious time he doesn't have to spare. Or maybe that's just my head reaffirming all my own fears.

"Um," I stammer, trying to keep the hurt at bay. "I was calling to invite you to Christmas. But I'm sure you already have plans, so it's okay if you can't make it."

There's another long pause and I wish a hole would open and suck me down in it so that I wouldn't have to hear his reply. This was a stupid idea. I should have asked Reed to call with the invite so I wouldn't be in the position of waiting for my husband to break my heart all over again.

"It's fine, Drew. Don't worry about it. I get it. I hope you have a good Christmas, whatever your plans are," I blurt out. Realization hits me like a truck; I no longer know how to talk to my husband.

"June," he says, and he sounds exhausted.

"Drew, honestly, it's fine. I'm sorry I called." I end the call before he can say anything. He tries calling back almost immediately and I send it straight to voicemail, but he doesn't leave a message.

He doesn't try again.

The little urge that I've been tamping down for days, weeks even, grows bigger and bigger while I fret over Christmas, Drew, and the current state of my life. Until it's as big as the sun blotting out all the darkness that is my ruined marriage.

There's nothing here to distract me from it. I analyze it, examine it from every angle, run every imaginary calculation.

All the equations come to the same basic answers.

Yes.

Do it.

Why not? There isn't much left to lose. The trust between me and Drew is so fractured I don't know if it can ever be repaired. Certainly not when I still don't fully understand his drive for sexual release with other women. I'm more and more convinced that I won't, can't, be sympathetic to the plight until I have a similar experience.

Often, rebound relationships are a subconscious thing. I'm making a conscious decision to betray my splintered marriage vows in the hopes of better learning how I might mend them. Maybe that's the dumbest idea on the planet, or maybe it's the only hope I have left.

Being so lonely for physical connection may be driving my decision, but I'm not sure that's such an awful thing. We're all just animals at our base level. We chose to be more; we chose to live by the human rules of love and fidelity. I'm choosing to ignore those rules, for a time, anyway.

I press call on a different contact number. It rings twice before a deep voice answers, one I'm becoming increasingly familiar with.

"Is there a sex club in New Orleans? Or nearby?" I ask. The line is quiet on the other end. I can't imagine I've shocked Noah; he seems like the type who is impossible to surprise.

"When was the last time you spoke with Rebecca?"

Noah, with his brief background in psychology, encourages talks with my therapist. It's not unusual for him to ask if I've had appointments. This time, however, he's asking less because he wants me to keep working on my mental health, and more because he thinks I've lost it altogether.

"Two days ago," I answer.

"Have you discussed this idea with her?"

"Of course."

"And her opinion is?"

"Her opinion is that it's perfectly healthy to explore, sexually and otherwise, as long as I do so thoughtfully and safely."

"So, your first idea was a sex club?"

"I'm not asking you to drop me off on a street corner to be picked up by a john, Noah. Drew went to a sex club and since there were non-disclosure agreements involved, I assume it's a controlled environment. That's what I'm looking for. Besides, you'll be there with me."

Dead silence responds. I must have surprised him, again. It takes him a minute, but he does finally find a few small words.

"I will be?"

"Please, Noah? I know this is a huge ask. I do. I need to do this with someone I trust. Also, someone who knows these kinds of things."

"Damn it, June," he says with exasperation. It deflates me completely, just as my earlier conversation with Drew did. The sun sets on all my newfound ambition to try something new.

"It's fine. I understand. I just thought that because you had experience with that sort of thing, you'd be able to help," I babble. "I'd like to see—well, I'd like to learn more about what I like, what I want. And maybe get a better understanding of what Drew was looking for. It's probably a horrible idea."

"Stop," he barks.

Like every time he shoots me a sharp command, the impact of his words compels me to obey. It's the intended effect. He's very good at telling me what to do.

I'm very good at liking it. It's a dangerous combination.

"I'm glad you trust me. It's flattering the way you put so much faith in me."

"But?"

"It's not the idea I'm hesitant about, it's the venue," he says calmly, and I remember this is Noah. Easy to speak to, non-dramatic Noah. We can discuss this without me melting into a puddle of self-deprecation. "This isn't something you dive into head-first. I know you're curious and I understand that. But before you make any decisions, you should be sure. You need to be clear about what you want, what you don't want, and understand the ramifications that may come from it. If you decide on something, we'll discuss the best ways to go about it."

"I am sure."

At least, I think I am. Convincing myself is easier than convincing Noah, however.

"Are you?"

"Yes."

"I'm not taking you to a place where you could get caught up in something you'll regret. If you want to play, my sweet June, you come to me." His voice, usually so smooth, comes out heated and raw, sending blood rushing to every erogenous zone my body has.

The call ends before I have a chance to form a response. Not a minute later, while I'm still staring dazedly at my phone, a text comes through from Noah. His address and a door code for his building. No time, no date, no further instructions.

It takes me hours to work myself up. Also, to make myself up. Deciding what to wear to possibly have sex with a man who is not your husband is no easy task. In the end, I decide to be blunt.

I arrive at Noah's doorstep in a bundle of nerves that doesn't settle much when he opens the door to me. In the short time I've known him, I have never seen him dressed down in anything less than business casual. Even that is rare. Noah is a suit man, typically three-piece and tailored to perfection. Today he's dressed in those stupid gray sweatpants that are every woman's kryptonite. Nothing more.

Blond men have never been my type. Granted, my type was always Drew. Regardless, Noah's dirty-blond hair, slightly mussed, framing his striking features, does things to my body. It's been years since Noah played in the NFL. You can't tell by his body with all its rippled muscles and zero body fat in sight. I always feel small next to him, but tonight, without the barrier of his impeccable clothing, he's a giant in front of me.

"You took your time."

I nod in agreement while I unbutton the lightweight trench, turning my back to him so he can take it from me like the gentleman he is.

An image he promptly ruins by swatting my ass.

"I expect better communication, June." He's crowding behind me, his words delivered as mere fact, not a sharp reprimand. But his stance, so tall and close, makes me want to apologize, anyway.

"I'll do better," I placate. Then I take the leap and untie the belt of the silk kimono wrap I have on. It slides slowly off my shoulders, down my arms, and ends in a pool between my feet and Noah's.

I'm left standing in a white bodysuit that covers me in a completely sheer delicate lace. It's sexy and naughty while also giving a sense of innocence and virginity. It's everything I am and want to be in a piece of lingerie. I mean, I'm not virginal, in any real sense. To certain things, I suppose I have a serious virginal point of view, though.

The soft intake of air behind me ratchets up my pulse. I concentrate on the thrum at my wrists and temples, rather than trying to guess what Noah is thinking. Or what he might do next. The steadily increasing thump calms me, somehow.

Harder to block out are the things I want him to do. With all the nonstop analyzing I've done since finding out about Lorelai and the women before her, I've concluded that I like a certain amount of dominance in a man. I wouldn't say I'm masochistic or a submissive, even; I'm too stubborn for that. I do enjoy being bossed around and manhandled a bit in flirty or sexual ways, with consent and trust.

I want to be told what to do, forcefully and directly. At the same time, I want to disobey and push him to the edge.

I'm hoping Noah will appease some of that desire tonight.

"Drew is an idiot," Noah whispers. Then louder, he says, "I can't understand how he doesn't fuck you against every surface and in every position every day. You're goddamn intoxicating, June."

My head drops slightly. I can't understand it either and there is just no getting used to the fact that he hasn't. Or that he has with someone else. All that pain swirls with the pride I feel when Noah says I'm perfect. When he uses my name, ensuring that I know he sees me. Not someone he wishes were here, not some woman from his past. Whatever woman who caused him to be the way he is. He sees June McKenna, not Lorelai Simmons.

He doesn't touch me as he moves away from me and heads straight to a large sofa. I've never been here before, so I allow myself a minute to get my pulse under control and take in the space.

It's small, like so many living spaces in the French Quarter, made to feel larger by being an open space. To the left is a small kitchen. Ahead are several narrow, yet tall, glass gridded doors that open on to a wrought iron balcony. The walls are a deep aubergine, a royal color that exudes warmth. A feel enhanced by all the dark, carved moldings throughout the space.

It's a masculine space but comfortable and homey, too. It suits him.

Noah sits on the sofa facing the doors, his back to me. The lights are dim, but a glow from the night outside shines perfectly on him.

"Come here."

I take a long moment to move to him, because of course I do. I'm excitedly terrified and eagerly apprehensive. The heels of my shoes tapping on the well-worn hardwood floorboards let Noah know when I'm close. He relaxes further back into the sofa and spreads his thighs wider. I stop only when I'm standing in between them, staring down at him while he stares up at me.

Never breaking eye contact, he reaches to his side and grabs a throw pillow and drops it at my feet. Holding out his hand to steady me, he commands, "Kneel."

I take his offering and drop down.

It's insanely intimate to be in this position, so close to him, so bare, sharing so much air. As if I can see into his mind. His desire to ravage me exactly how I want to be ravished. His need for touch and to be touched. A hesitancy that mirrors my own. It's all there, and so much more, right there in his steely gaze.

I'm not alone in any of the feelings pumping through my veins.

One hand moves to cup my chin. His thumb gently strokes my lower lip until I open wide enough for him to slip it in. It pushes in as far as it can, pressing down and allowing me to curl my tongue around it.

Sweetness invades my taste buds, sugar and something more biting. Cinnamon, maybe. Closing my lips, I suck in a slow, steady rhythm.

"We're only taking this so far," he says. "Only as far as either of us can handle, but far enough to get what we need. Understand?"

I nod just enough and let my teeth descend so that he can't pull his thumb out yet.

"I want you, June. So much. Too much, in fact." His grip tightens, and I ease up. Moving his thumb in and out in a slow and steady pace, he continues, "I want those long legs draped over my shoulders or wrapped tight around my waist. I want these plump lips and warm tongue touching every part of my body. But I know what will happen once I have you."

He pulls his hand back, giving me a chance to respond.

"And if I want all those same things?" I ask.

"We'd both end up in the same position at the end. Both indulging each other in the efforts of trying to fuck some other lover out of our system. Both chasing the past while tangling our futures tighter together. You'll want me to fuck you every day because I'm that good. I'll want to fuck you every day because I can already see you'll follow every instruction with just enough attitude to keep me guessing. We'll be exciting together, explosive."

Noah pitches forward, clashing his lips to mine with force. He reaches to steady me, grabbing my arms, dragging his hands down to mine and placing my palms on his thighs. His muscles move under my fingers, and I clutch at his sweatpants, wanting them to disappear. Wanting more skin, more heat.

He tangles his tongue with mine, and the same spicy sweetness from his touch coats his mouth. I lap at it, meeting his efforts equally.

When he finally breaks away, my chest is heaving. He's affected as well. I can feel it in the tightening of his pants. I move my hands up and in, almost there. Almost.

His eyes have grown darker, just like my cheeks.

"The problem is, you'll never be her and I'll never be him."

"They aren't here. We are," I counter.

"Yes, so we can play but only so far."

"How far?" Frustration bleeds into my voice. It can't be helped.

"Far enough to get us both by, not far enough that Drew will never forgive you."

"He deserves to feel what I feel."

"Absolutely. But I know you well enough now to know your heart will always be his. Even if you haven't admitted it yet, you want reconciliation. And I want that for you, even though he'll never deserve you. You're one of a kind, June. The type of woman men fall in love with. I can't chance that. I can't fall in love with you when you're already in love with him," he says and strokes my hair away from my face. "I'll give you some relief, some comfort. I'll take the same in return. But I won't obliterate either of us in the process."

I should be glad he knows me so well. Thankful, even, that he's invested in my happiness.

So why I am angry at his words? Oh right, I'm horny as hell.

And lonely down to my bones. Which should only make me more grateful to Noah. Lonely people make horrible decisions. I'm only lonely in the romantic sense. My life is full otherwise. I'm busy with work and the exploration of a new city. I have friends and family both readily available for adventure and conversation alike.

Only one part of my life is lacking.

"Please don't make me beg," I say quietly.

"Oh, I'll make you beg. But you'll like it," he replies with smugness. "The first lesson you've learned quite well already. Showing up in this little getup. The second is eye contact. Your eyes don't leave mine unless they're on my cock. Understood?"

Holy shit.

"Am I going to see your cock, Noah?" I ask, keeping my eyes on his the entire time.

His only response is a playfully wicked laugh.

CHAPTER 15
June

Christmas arrives quickly. My family flew in a couple of days early and checked into a quaint boutique hotel around the corner from my condo. Mom came over early today to cook Christmas dinner for us all here. Reed and Larry are out for a walk, something Larry enjoys doing so much that he never misses a day. Leighton is expected later as she had to cover Midnight Mass until the wee hours of this morning.

My entire day passes in a daze. I'm thrilled to have everyone here and they are all having a wonderful time catching up. Including Reed and Leighton, who play this ridiculous game of trying to keep their distance but continually gravitate to one another all the same.

I wish they'd just sleep together already.

We all know how great they would be together, and none of us understands why they both fight it so hard. I've asked them both in the past. Reed's answers are always evasive, and Leighton's are always some form of disgust.

But I watch them when their focus isn't on me. I see how they hold each other's attention. I see every time Reed tenses up when he sees a man hit on her in public, and how she side-eyes any woman who gets within a two-foot radius of him.

It's even more obvious today since we're in the tighter quarters of my condo. Each time one of them realizes how close they've gotten to the other, they shift away. It's comical and impossible not to giggle at their teenage antics.

My brain is scattered today, so I'm sure I'm only seeing half of their strange behavior. Even so, it's a lot.

It's the first Christmas since Drew entered our lives that he isn't present. As a kid, he'd spend the morning at home with his dad, who was usually too hungover to remember what day it was. But he'd always find his way to us before dinner. There were always gifts under the tree for him and a place at our table. Just like there is today, in the hope that maybe… just maybe.

We haven't spoken since the awkward conversation where I invited him and promptly hung up. Which means we haven't spoken since I spent the night with Noah.

We slept together, in the truest meaning. We slept. We didn't have sex. There was a copious amount of touching and there was more kissing. Mostly, we talked, and he tutored. Noah told me of some of his personal experiences, discussed at length certain things he likes and behaviors he expects from his partners.

Admittedly, it was the strangest fucking experience in my entire life. I expected to feel shy or uncomfortable around him after that, but that didn't happen. The man has an uncanny ability to always make me feel at ease.

Even after he made me cum on my own fingers while he restricted my airflow with his big hand while giving explicit instructions with a gravelly voice.

That was as far as it went. I never did get to see his dick. Though it was pressed against various parts of my body, I never saw it, and he wouldn't let me touch it. And after hours of my endless questions and his patient answers, he held me. He tucked me next to him in his bed, rubbed my back, and made me tell him all the reasons I love Drew. All the reasons I don't want it to end.

I've evaluated a lot about that night. I talked to Rebecca about it, too, asked her if it could possibly be a bigger betrayal than Drew's. Because mine wasn't just about sex. It was a different kind of intimacy, more meaningful than fucking, for sure.

In the end, I decided not to beat myself up for it. I took what I needed because it was offered in friendship and trust. If the lightness in Noah's attitude since then means anything, he got what he needed out of it, too. And I refuse to feel bad about that.

Nothing more has happened since that night. We've gone right back to the relationship we had before, as if the night never happened at all.

Noah took my family and me out to lunch the day after they arrived, before he took off to Lafayette for the holiday. He was flirty with my mom, who loved it. Larry talked to him about football and Reed kept a pleasant distance. He wasn't rude, only resistant to accept Noah as easily as the rest of us have.

I get it. I even expected it. But he also sees that Noah brings a support system to my life that I need right now, so he's been quiet about his biased opinions.

We sit down to dinner when Mom has it all prepared. The entire place smells like every childhood holiday I can remember. Roast turkey has always been something she enjoys cooking but always reserved for special occasions. The food is passed around with easy conversation that I feel detached from. I'm taking part but not present. Here in body but not mind.

My gaze constantly travels to the empty chair at the table. I'd hoped he'd show up, regardless of my fumbled invite.

My melancholy, much like my anxiety, is a downward spiral. It starts off with a bit of control, but it quickly picks up pace the further down I get until it's unhinged and takes a life of its own. I'm atop the mountain right now. I've only taken a few steps, but I feel the urge to keep going.

It gets harder to swallow. My throat feels thick as my eyes stay glued to that empty chair. To the void in the room as large as the hole in my heart.

He didn't even call.

"Reed?" I ask, my voice watery with tears I fight to swallow down.

He looks at me from across the table and his smile vanishes.

"Hey, Baby Girl, what's going on?" His entire face shows his concern.

"Is it over?" I ask in a small voice.

"No, Ju. No." There is a strong confidence in his quick response. I don't understand how he can be so sure.

He hasn't even fucking called.

I blink to let a single tear escape and race down my cheek. I wipe at it, hoping it takes the sadness with it. Reed reaches across the table for my hand, pouring some of his strength into me.

"Are you sure? He didn't call." I know it's ridiculous. I know I haven't called him either. There is no logic in how I feel about Drew. There never has been. I gave him all the love I had in my little six-year-old body that first day he showed up with ruddy cheeks and dirty shoes.

It only grew and grew over the years. With every visit, with every birthday celebrated, every milestone shared. Every time I found him hiding in Reed's room by himself, looking for a quiet place to nap or to hide from his dad for a while. Every time I saw him watching me when no one was watching him. My love for him grew because he fed it and I nurtured it until it blossomed into a beautiful fucking lie.

"I'm sure. Trust me," Reed says, snapping me out of my fog.

I wipe away another tear at the same time the call box buzzes. Reed's lips quirk into a sympathetic smile.

And that's all I need to know who's at the building's entrance. I'm out of my seat and out my door before anyone can question it, taking the stairs as quickly as I can in the four-inch heels I had no real reason to wear today other than I wanted to feel pretty. Then I'm pushing the front door to my building open to let my husband into the lobby.

Because he's here.

He's here and so am I and so is all this tainted love shared between us.

He drops the bags he's carrying. One is his overnight bag, the other laden with perfectly wrapped gifts. He drops them because he can see I'm shaky and needy, so needy for him. For reassurance that not everything between us is lost forever.

He holds his arms to his sides just enough for me to leap into them. I wrap my arms around his neck and bury my face in as a sob escapes me.

Because it's not a family Christmas if he's not here. But he is now and I'm feeling grounded for the first time all day.

I don't know what it means for us, but I won't question it just now.

"Hey, June. Shhh, baby," Drew says as he tightens his hold, one hand cradling my head.

"You're late," I cry.

"I know. I'm sorry."

"I didn't think you'd come."

"Look at me," he says. I do. I look. I see. Devouring him because it's been too long. Because he's beautiful and I still love him, even if that love is mixed up with a lot of other emotions now, too. "I'll always be where you need me to be, okay?"

My eyes flit between his. "Where did you need to be?"

"I wish you didn't feel like you had to ask me that."

"I do, too," I say sadly.

"I missed you. So much. I know I've been missing in action, but I've been trying to figure my shit out. For us," Drew says into my lips before delivering a gentle, sweet kiss. "Climb on."

"I can walk."

"No." He shakes his head. "I'm not ready to let you go yet. Jump up, I'll carry you."

I rise onto my toes and tighten my arms. "I'm on the third floor."

"Good, that much longer you'll be clinging to me." Drew's hands cup my ass, and he lifts so I can wrap my legs around him. "Hold tight."

He bends slightly to pick up the bags he had dropped and begins making his way up the stairs.

"You smell good," I say absently. I don't mean to complicate our situation. I'm just overwhelmed by how much I've missed him. How comforted I still feel with his arms around me. His smell, which is always oddly woodsy and fresh, makes me feel like I'm home.

"You do, too. Like turkey, and I'm starving."

I smile into his shoulder. "I tried to help Mom with the cooking."

"Is any of it still edible?" he asks with a laugh.

"Doubtful."

I say nothing more until we reach my door, but he doesn't set me down right away. Instead, he snuggles in closer. His face buries in my hair, and he sighs softly.

"I know nothing has changed between us, and I'm not here to push."

"Okay." I nod. "It's Christmas. We shouldn't fight on Christmas. I still kind of hate you."

"I know," he says with a sad smile. "Thank you for wanting me here, anyway."

"You're family. It didn't feel right without you." I open the door and let him walk through.

My mom jumps up from her chair and takes a step away from the table. Drew freezes where he's at. His hand clenches a little, a sign that he's not sure how this is going to play out.

"Hi, Janet," he says with more apprehension than I've ever heard from him.

"Come here, son," she calls. He's moving before she even has all the words out. She wraps her arms around his colossal frame, and he lifts her up, her feet dangling off the ground. I avert my eyes. I'm weepy enough as it is.

My mother is the only mother Drew has ever known. I know she's mad at him, but she could never stop loving him. I'd never want her to, no matter how much hurt he deals me. I'm thankful they're getting this moment, for both their sakes.

I sit back down next to Leighton, who grabs my hand under the table, giving me a comforting squeeze, which is both needed and appreciated.

Drew and Mom are still embracing, whispered words flowing between them. I hear Mom tell him they'll talk about it later and she pushes him toward the empty seat.

Conversation picks up rapidly, very little directed toward me, and I add that to my list of things I'm grateful for tonight. Everyone is giving me a moment to take it all in. So, I do. I take in the love between us all, how unconditional it is in its giving. The smiles shared, the jokes, the laughter—I absorb it all. I listen to the accomplishments they've made over the past year, the new goals made and met.

They all ask me more about how work is going, what we've filmed so far and when they'll start airing the pieces. Noah comes up a couple of times, but Drew is on his best behavior and other than some tension around his eyes, he shows no sign of discomfort about the topic. If he cues into any bashfulness on my end, he doesn't give it away.

Mom shares a memory of Dad from a Christmas I was too young to remember very well, but Reed and Drew have some recollection of. They chime in here and there and everyone laughs and starts up on other stories from our childhoods.

For me, it's equally heartwarming and heartbreaking.

We move from the table to the deep sofa and armchairs that look out onto my balcony, which I've decorated with twinkling lights. I set up a small tree in the corner, and gifts spill out from under it. Drew adds to them with ones he brought with him.

They're exchanged, and I take that in, too. We purchased everything with care and consideration because we know each other so well after all these years.

Leighton being Leighton, gave me a box full of highly inappropriate sex toys and lingerie that I know is ridiculously overpriced for how little fabric there is. I laughed when I opened it. My mom blushed. Both Drew and Reed looked wholly uncomfortable. Larry, like the trooper he is, took it all in stride.

Drew has outdone himself, as always. My mom turns sixty in the spring. My dad had promised he'd take her to Ireland for it. It's where her grand-parents came from, and she's always wanted to go visit the place where they fell in love. My dad had been saving up for it when he passed away. Drew remembered and has gifted her, Reed, and me with the trip.

She cries because she's so happy that he's honoring my dad in such a way. I cry because I notice he doesn't include himself in the plans.

Then I cry a little more because I'm afraid I want that too much. I'm afraid I'll forgive him too quickly and he'll hurt me again. I'm afraid I won't forgive him at all.

I can't win, but maybe I have nothing left to lose anymore.

Drew steps in front of the chair I'm curled up in, leaning down to my level. He thumbs away a few tears that are still escaping from my eyes.

"I have something else for you. Something I want to give to you in private, okay?" he asks me gently.

I only nod, not trusting my voice.

Shortly after gifts and desserts, Mom announces she's ready to go back to her hotel. Leighton offers to drop them on her way home, and everyone gathers up their belongings.

"Where are you staying?" I ask Drew, who is standing by my side. He's hardly left it tonight.

"I don't know. I figured I'd go with Reed, see if they have a room available. Or just bunk with him," he answers with a shrug.

"You could stay here," the words vomit out between us, and I wish I had some magic to make them unheard. "In the guest room, I mean."

"I… Are you sure?"

No, I'm not at all sure. In fact, I'm rather unsure of the idea altogether.

"It's fine. It doesn't have to mean anything."

"Doesn't it?"

"No. It's just a place to sleep. You in your bed. Me in mine."

"Except you'll have all those fun new toys in bed with you," he says quietly against the shell of my ear, then walks away to give my mother a hug goodbye.

I pretend I didn't hear him and busy myself with cleaning up the last of the remnants from dessert. Pick up a bow left on the floor near the tree, carry a wineglass to the kitchen sink. Diversions have become my favorite thing around Drew.

Soon, we're alone, and I've run out of distractions. I show Drew to his room, smiling at how large he looks in the small space.

"You look like a giant in a dollhouse." I laugh.

"It's like a bedroom for a sprite." He smiles at me. "Mind if I shower?"

"Go right ahead. Towels are in the linen closet in the hall."

"Thanks. You going to bed?"

"Yeah." I nod. "It's been a long day."

"Sure. We need to talk in the morning. I still have that last gift to give you." He cups one of my cheeks. "Thank you for today."

I smile before retreating to my room. Putting away all the gifts I received, I hear the shower start and once again look for a way to keep my mind from focusing on Drew. Leighton's box of goodies is as good as anything.

She went on an Agent Provocateur spree, it seems, as I now have an array of panties, bras, suspenders, and a corset. All black, all dangerously sexy. All barely there. Arranging it on the bed, I play with different combinations. Some of them are nothing but straps. I'm not sure how I'm even supposed to wear them.

Listening to be sure the shower is still running, I strip off today's outfit until I'm completely bare. Standing in front of the mirror that leans against one wall of my room, I study myself. New Orleans has been good to me. Instead of losing weight from the constant burden of sadness keeping my appetite down, I've gained a few pounds. In all the right places. My hips are a little rounder, breasts a little heavier—probably from all the creamy sauces, the buttery side dishes, and the flaky pastries.

I'm not mad about any of it.

I grab one bra that looks the most complicated. After a moment, I have it on and clasped. Then I slide my legs into a pair of panties that, besides a small piece of fabric to cover my vagina, are just bits of ribbons.

My brain registers that the shower has shut off, but I'm focused on what I see in front of me. I look strong. A confidence there that I've never had before warms me up. I've spent so much time feeling weak. Feeling anything but beautiful.

Tonight, scars and all, I'm comfortably pleased in my own skin.

I think about walking all this newfound swagger next door to Drew's room. But after a minute or two of rumination, I decide that's not what's best. My day included a mini-breakdown followed by profound relief. Both of which I don't fully understand. Adding more content to my already over-flowing emotional baggage would be stupid.

Besides, this moment is for me. I don't need his validation. I'm giving it to myself, maybe for the first time ever. And, damn, it feels good.

After stripping back out of my new sexy underwear and slipping into a much more practical set of pajamas, I sleep like a baby.

CHAPTER 16

Drew

I slept like shit. Not only because the bed was made for a child-sized human, but June sleeping so close kept me awake. So many times last night I almost got up and went to her. Even if it was only to hold her, to have her close.

I miss that, having her nearby.

There was even a moment I considered sneaking in and watching her sleep. That's how desperate I've become. Thankfully, I let that creepy urge pass.

Every time I thought about her sleeping so close, I stopped myself from rushing to her. If she wants me, she knows where I am. The hardest habit to break for me is my selfishness because I never saw it as that where June was concerned. She always wanted to give me what I wanted to take, and I failed to see how one-sided our relationship has been.

So, last night, I didn't take. And today, I plan to give. A lot.

The only time I've been more terrified is when I got the call that June was in the hospital. This will be a big shift in power. A huge step in balancing the scales weighing our marriage.

Not a single one of my instincts agrees with it. I'm a controlling fuckwit. My sessions with Dr. Fillmore have shown me all the ways acting on my twisted instincts damaged my marriage. She told me I should look at this time, my separation from June, as a reboot. A pause in our lives to install upgrades and rid myself of the bugs diseasing my system.

Which means an abundance of self-reflection. Little did I know I was never being honest with myself about who I am. Or was. I'm not the same person I was growing up. I'm not even the same man June found in that hotel room.

Stupid when I think about it… I've been so eager to control situations and other people. Yet I couldn't control myself. The truth of it is, I didn't even see what I was doing with June as control. But it was, just much more subtle in its execution. I've never told her what to do, not directly, but I've carefully guided situations to get what benefited me from them.

With Lorelai, it was direct. I gave implicit directions for her to follow. And she would, start to finish.

At least Lorelai signed up for it. June was blind to it all.

I'm taking Fillmore's advice—and dammit, she has a lot of it—to heart because June is my world, and I want her whole. Even if that means she can't be with me. Even if it means I put my ego and my needs aside. I can do it. I will do it.

Despite my crappy night, I'm up before her. Not surprising, she was dead on her feet by the time our family left. I played a huge part in that. Emotionally, I ran her ragged. I should have called her to tell her I planned on coming for Christmas. I should have told her a lot of things.

The strong aroma of coffee fills the air from the pot I set to brew, when there is a light knock on the door. I expect it to be Reed and Janet. That's not who darkens the entryway, though.

Noah Fucking Anders.

The man I've hated for years. So sure have I been in my spite for him that I find it impossible to see him the way June does. He can't be both people. The cuntfuck who traumatized Lorelai all those years ago and the man who June trusts wholly in such a short period of time. Unless he's playing June. Or Lorelai played me.

If the latter is true, I'll have a hell of a lot more self-reflection to work on.

"Fuck, man, why are you here?"

"Good morning to you, too, Drew. I have a gift for my sweet June," the fucker says in his fake polite tone. It's annoying, like he's placating a child. Or sweet-talking a naïve woman into his murderous lair.

"She's still asleep. You can leave it with me, then go," I say through clenched teeth. The blond asshole just laughs.

"I'd rather wait. Perhaps you could offer me a cup of coffee."

"Turn around and leave, Anders."

"Calm down, Drew. I already said I'm only here to drop off a gift. I'm not here to fuck your wife."

Baiting the bear may not be his wisest choice. If I thought June would forgive me, I'd take this smug bastard down a notch. That's just not an option. She likes him. I think she even needs him, no matter how much that fucks me off.

"You'll never get that chance."

"Awfully confident for a man who broke her heart and let her run off to the other side of the country," Noah taunts.

"Fuck you."

"No, fuck you, Drew," Noah says, visibly annoyed now. "I've only known her a short time and I know how special she is. You've had her your whole life. You should know that better than me. Yet you still screwed it up in epic fucking fashion. You deserve to lose her, to feel every bit of the pain that trails her like a shadow every day."

He's known June for mere weeks and he's already so tuned in to her. He's already willing to go to bat for her. Before I can come up with a way to defend myself, he continues.

"You know what she did the first night I took her to dinner? When I was walking her home, we passed a homeless man. She made me walk her all the way back to Brennan's to have them pack up a meal, complete with appetizer and dessert no less, to take to him," he says, smiling. "Most people do nothing more than step around, maybe toss a coin. That's not June's style, though I suppose you know that. Every day I'm with her, she does something similar, something small to her but monumental to whoever is on the other end. The kids at the schools we visit, folks in the parts of the city that society ignores, strangers on the street; she treats them all as equals and shares whatever she has. No questions asked and no recognition needed. She's fucking amazing."

"I know," I say, resigned to some brow beating. I hate that it's coming from Noah, but I deserve it regardless. "I know."

"Then tell her, show her. Fight for her, like she's fighting for you every day. Because she is. She hasn't lost any love for your stupid ass. Fucking earn her, McKenna. The way you're going, there will be a day very soon when someone like me picks up every beautiful piece of her. Unlike you, I'd never let her go."

Noah gives a wink over my shoulder, cuing me in to June eavesdropping behind me. I don't know how long she was there, but I know I don't come out of this smelling like roses. That fucker does.

"Noah, hi. I didn't know you were coming by today," she says, sounding groggy, and it pisses me off that he showed up so early and woke her up. Pisses me off more that they're both so comfortable with him popping by in the early morning, unannounced.

But what right do I have to be angry about that?

"He was just leaving," I say, failing to sound casual.

"No, I wasn't," Noah says, moving around my bulk to enter the room. "I have a small gift. I came to drop it off and see how your Christmas was."

"It was wonderful. Thank you for this," June says as she takes the small package from him. "How was yours? Your brother made it home?"

"He did, and ours was wonderful, too. They'll be heading this way for New Year's and are excited to meet you."

I pace behind him, worried. I can't be here for New Year's. Not with the team's schedule. Although I'm giving June the reins in our relationship, I can't say I'm pleased with the idea of her using them to start spending less holidays with me and more with him.

"I'm excited to meet them as well." She peels back the paper on his gift to unveil a book. One all about the haunted houses of New Orleans. "Thank you, Noah," she says, stretching up to kiss him on the cheek.

His hands go to her waist, and he presses a kiss on her forehead. It's a small, innocent action, but one that inflames. That forehead is mine. That's where I kiss her. It's where I rest mine when I tell her something I want her to truly hear, to feel. And he's wiping his fucking lips all over it, while his dirty hands softly grip her through her dainty, short, silk wrap.

I realize I'm being an idiot, but she's barely covered, dammit.

"Okay, out now, Anders. My wife," I say with emphasis, "needs to get dressed so we can talk before I have to leave."

"I'll see you later, my sweet June." He gives a small wave as he heads back out the door.

"That was rude, Drew."

"I'm not particularly worried about being polite to him," I reply as I go to pour a cup of coffee. When I offer her the mug, she wraps her hands around it and breathes in the strong aroma as if the smell alone will wake her up. Some days I think it does.

"You should be."

"I should be kind to a man who would try to steal you from me for nothing more than an act of revenge?" I ask with a raised brow. She wouldn't be... hasn't been, nice to Lorelai. I don't blame her, not at all. And yeah, okay, not the same situation.

Fuck, I'm stupid.

Her ire rises, taking a strong hold on her by the looks of her rosy cheeks. I'm being dismissive of her opinion, something else I've learned I need to change. Noah around my wife keeps me from being able to think clearly.

"This isn't a conversation you want to have with me, Drew," she says curtly.

"I think it is. I know you need to work with him for another couple of months, but I don't like you getting so close to him outside of that. I've already told you I don't trust him."

"And I already told you that I do trust him. More than I trust you right now. Certainly, more than I could ever trust your bitch girlfriend."

"Dammit, June, I get why you hate her, but she's not the person you think she is. She's not evil."

I know I've fucked up, again, as soon as the words are out of my mouth. Defending Lorelai is about the dumbest fucking thing I could have done just now. Evident by the way June's fingers tighten on the mug I just handed her. As if she's struggling not to knock me upside the head with it.

There are about a million things I could have said to piss her off. But I think I picked the one at the top of the list.

"You're going to stand here and defend a woman who fucked you knowing you have a wife? Seriously? All while you degrade a man who wouldn't do the same thing to you. Who even are you right now?" She stares at me as if she doesn't know who I am.

It kills me. Just not as much as the idea of Noah leaving his mark on her does.

"Bullshit, June. He'd absolutely do the same thing, if you'd only give him the chance."

"I did give him the chance. I practically threw my naked self at him, and still, he didn't fuck me!"

What the hell?

I stumble back away from her. Shocked by what she's just admitted.

The knowledge that she was getting so comfortable with him concerned me, but I didn't think she was already teetering on the edge of having sex with him, or anyone for that matter.

I convinced myself I had more time. This is June. She doesn't rush into situations, especially not intimate ones. I'm beginning to understand the depths in which I've broken her. The changes I pushed her to by being so callous with our marriage.

While I've been keeping a safe distance to work on myself, to fix the problems that got us here, she's been growing into the woman she always should have been. The one I was supposed to support, to nurture. Instead, Noah's been the one doing it while I stayed away so as not to cause her more harm.

Panic knots my stomach at the idea that I've lost her. I've taken too long, severed us to the point we are no longer mendable.

"I was so ready to take control of my life, to explore the things I want. I was done waiting for the scraps of you she leaves behind," she continues. Her fingers shake around the mug so much that the hot liquid spills over. She doesn't seem to notice the burn of it. "I went to him for help. For relief. For a little fucking release. To feel wanted! I kissed him. I touched him. I let him touch me, and I liked it. Enough to go further, if only he had agreed. But he didn't. He wouldn't. Instead, he held me while I cried over you. So, spare me your bullshit opinion about her being a better person than Noah because that is a damn lie."

I've backed farther away from her as she's yelled, as far as I can get in the small kitchen. My knuckles grow white from where my hands grip the countertop behind me, bracing myself. I think I might pass out from it all. The hurt, the bone-crushing pain, and that guilt that I'm sure I'll be living with until my last breath. Eyes closed, I try to shut it out, shut it down and slow my racing pulse.

"Don't you dare do that. Don't compartmentalize this. You feel it, Drew. You feel it like I've had to. Picture it, see his hands on my naked body. See him giving me all the things you ran from," she says in an angry sob.

Fucking hell, I see it. My mind will never unsee the pictures it's conjuring of the two of them together.

Opening my eyes, I take in every detail of her face. I finally understand. I fucking get it now, how I've made her feel. What I've caused her to live with.

I get it, and I want to fucking stab myself in the dick for it.

I would too, if she only asked. She won't, though, because the look that keeps flashing in her eyes, the one she is so desperately trying to keep out… it's one I know. It's the same one she had when she opened the door to me last night.

Need. Not need for Noah. Need for me. That look sets my tipsy world back to straight. It brings life back to focus. June needs me to be the man she deserves, and I'll walk through whatever hell she throws at me to deliver that man to her.

Right now, Hell's landscape looks a lot like the fight we keep starting but never quite finishing.

"I didn't come here to argue with you. I wanted to spend Christmas with my family. With the woman I love more than anything in the world," I say, grabbing the envelope I'd set out earlier and moving toward her again. Erasing the distance I built between us. "Now, all I want to do is fight. With you and him."

Lies. I don't want to fight with her. Noah, sure. Not June, though. She can't move forward until we get through this part, though.

"Fight with me, then. I'm not stopping you."

"Fine. Tit for tat, June. I answered your questions. It's your turn now."

"Ask."

"Has he hurt you?"

"No, he'd never."

I scoff at her immediate answer.

"How many times have you kissed him?"

"I wasn't counting, but several times. Only the one night."

My head tilts to the side sharply, neck cracking. I don't like that answer, at all.

"How has he touched you? Specifically, June."

"Mostly he's hugged me, held me. That night, he caressed me in all the places you'd hate, except there. His mouth was on most of them, too. I came on my hand while he told me what to do. Afterward, we slept in the same bed, him holding me all night. And... and he's spanked me a few times. Usually when I'm putting myself down. He doesn't like when I do that." Brutal honesty—asked for and given.

I drop into a crouch, every part of me rigid with anger. One hand gripping my hair, the other crumples the envelope I still hold. I audibly strain for breath, like a raging bull about to explode out of its pen.

"Fuck." I'm shaking now too, with the image of them in bed together. Naked and tangled. We're quite the pair, my wife and I.

"I touched and kissed him, but only above the waist. He didn't allow more than that."

How do I make her stop?

"Is that supposed to make me feel better?"

"It's supposed to make you feel," she says. It comes out hoarse from choking back emotions.

"I feel it all, Junie. Every fucking bit of what I've done. How could you think I don't?" I stand and move closer now. She tilts her head up to keep eye contact.

"Because you're gone. I moved away, but you're the one who disappeared."

"I'm trying to give you space. I thought that's what you wanted." My stare bores into hers.

"You're giving me whiplash, Drew. One minute you say we need to fight it out, the next you're giving me so much space I feel like I don't exist to you at all."

My free hand comes up to cup the side of her face as I bend down to her forehead to forehead, taking back my spot.

"I have never been blind to you. Not since the moment I first saw you, your hair in braids that were coming undone while you rode your bicycle up and down the driveway because your dad wouldn't let you follow Reed down the block. You're burned into every part of me. Every day you're not with me, I die a little faster." A tear falls from my eye and lands on her cheek. She closes her eyes, shutting out her suffering... or mine.

"Except the days you spend with her?"

Fucking Lorelai. It all comes back to that.

"Did you miss me any less the night you were with him?"

"No. I missed you more."

"Then why do you think it would be any different for me?" I ask.

"Because you were with her for a year. Because I know for a fact you didn't spend those nights with her thinking about what you want to do with me. Or crying in her arms while she asked you to explain all the things you love about me. That's how I spent my time with Noah. He wasn't fucking me in the ass," she says incredulously.

I'm never living that down.

"Look at me, please." I wait until those gorgeous dark earthy eyes that I lose myself in open up to me. "You seem to be under the impression that I was with her all the time. That's not the case. It was less than a handful of times, over the year."

"Is that supposed to make me feel better?" she asks, using my own words against me.

"No, I don't think I can say anything to make you feel better. But I know I've done an awful job at helping you to understand the situation. Both how we got here and what I'm doing to try to fix it," I say, then press a kiss on her forehead, marking my territory. "While I've been trying to give you space, I've also been talking to Fillmore nearly every day. I'm working out a lot of issues, not just regarding you or sex, but old shit with my dad. The death of my mom, too. That's why I've been quiet. I didn't want to be an unhealthy presence in your life. Not like before. I want to be what you deserve."

"You should have told me that before. All of that," she cries. All I can do is nod in agreement. She's right, of course.

"Come sit with me," I say, leading her to the living room area. Taking a seat on one of the oversized armchairs, I pull her down on my lap.

She must see something on my face that frightens her because she clamps her bathrobe in one hand and my shirtsleeve in the other.

"Drew?"

"I have that last gift to give you, remember?" She nods, and I continue, "I don't want you to freak out about it. It's something I put a lot of thought into, something we need to discuss."

That panicky feeling starts again when I gently rest the envelope on June's lap, and she looks at it like it's a package of C4.

She slides an unstable finger under the seal, prying it open, feeling the large stack of papers inside. Beginning to pull them out, she stops abruptly when she's able to see the heading of the top page.

Then she drops them like they're laced with poison.

"Why?" she asks through the tears stinging her eyes. Her airflow stutters with the beginnings of hyperventilation.

I toss the envelope off her lap so that I can adjust her to face me, her legs straddling me. Clasping her face, I force her to look at me, while I try to caress the stress away.

"Keep breathing, baby. Just listen for a minute, okay? Our whole lives, I've taken control. Even when we make decisions together, I know you let me take the lead. I have all the power," I say, wiping tears off her face with my thumbs. "It's another thing I've taken advantage of. This is me giving it to you. It's the most important decision of our lives, and it's all yours."

"No," she says in a wobbly, watery voice.

"That's up to you, Junie."

"Then take them back!"

"Baby, calm down," I say, peppering kisses over the areas my thumbs just traveled. "I'm not telling you to sign them. I'm not even asking you to. I just want you to hold all the cards."

"I don't want that hand. I can't believe you'd do this to me. As a Christmas gift, Drew, what the fuck?" Her words come out in gasping sobs that are like needle pricks to my heart.

"Junie," I say, laughing a little. It's not funny, but her reaction is like a balm to my own anxiety over the situation.

"It's not fucking funny!"

"No, it's not. But you're fucking adorable. Here I was terrified you would sign them upon sight and instead you're ready to murder me for handing them to you."

"I'm not signing them. You're taking them back."

"No, I'm not. You're going to keep them until we work through everything. But we need to talk about how you're reacting to them."

Her immediate descent into hysterics over the words 'petition for divorce' tells me more than any words she's said regarding where we stand.

She's still mine.

"Just because I'm not ready to sign divorce papers, doesn't mean I'm ready to forgive you." She struggles to calm her breathing as her panic ramps up. I hate overwhelming her this way, so I distract her in the only way I know how.

Sealing my mouth to hers. Replacing her breath with mine as I move my hands, one to her neck and one to her lower back, holding her to me as I taste her for the first time in what feels like years.

I keep it short, just long enough to give her nerves something else to think about.

"I know it doesn't mean forgiveness. I'm fully aware of the strong possibility that you will never give me that. But it does mean something that you're so adamant about giving them back to me unsigned," I say, pressing another kiss on her wet cheek. "Really hear me, June. You get to choose. If you decide I haven't earned you and you sign those papers, I won't stop trying. I'll spend every day of my life trying to make you love me again. Whether we're married or not. If you need to start over, need me to do everything right a second time around, I will. Sign them and I'll court you, and someday when you're ready, I'll give you the wedding you always deserved."

"Drew," she whispers.

"I'm not done. You need to keep these for another reason, too. I know you and how your heart works. So, I know that if we're tied together, even by just a piece of paper, you won't allow yourself to truly feel anything for another man. Fuck, it kills me to say that to you."

June's fingers find my mouth, pressing my lips together as if she can push the words back in, but they keep flowing. Seeping through her fingers, bringing things she thinks she's not ready to hear with them.

"If you think you can love someone, even him, sign them and love without guilt. Even then I won't stop trying to be the man you should love, the man you deserve, but that decision is yours."

Her eyes flick between mine, trying to find signs I don't mean what I say. She won't find insincerity. I hate that this is a possible outcome for us, but I meant what I said.

Love doesn't mean keeping her chained to me if it isn't what makes her happy. Above anything else, I want that for her.

My love for June is unconditional. Fully and completely. No matter what she's done with Noah, I forgive her for it all. I can't tell her that I wish she could do the same for me. There's a difference there, after all. The betrayal of our marital vows is not equal in its execution. I'm the one who put conditions on her love for me.

There isn't time to dwell on that just now. I have a plane to catch. A season to get back to, a team that depends on me. Though, I'd rather stay right here. I've considered retiring after this contract is up. I haven't discussed that, like many things, with June. We have the money, more than we could ever spend. We don't need any more. It's just an excuse I use to keep myself in the game until I win that elusive championship ring.

But I'd give it all up for her. If it would help, I'd leave it all behind and never look back.

"I need to leave," I say, kissing her lips softly, reverently.

"Already?"

"Already. I'll be back soon. Only three more games." Standing up with her held tight in my arms, I settle her onto her feet but don't let go. "There's another choice in that envelope. Don't lose it. It's precious."

She looks at me in question.

"I'll miss you," I tell her. "I'm sorry for everything I've done. I'm sorry I pushed you away. I hate every bit of this, but I understand, okay? You do whatever you need to do. I'll love you through it all."

When she opens her mouth to respond, maybe to repeat the words back to me, I steal them by sealing my mouth to hers again.

It's not a hungry kiss. Nothing like the ones we've shared since that day in Los Angeles; those have been heated and angry. This is gentle, kind, apologetic.

It's wrapped in an unknown future, but it's a promise all the same. A promise that we'll always be some version of us. I cling tighter to her, trying to convey all the words I don't know how to say.

Only time can convince her. My word is shit to her now.

What a complicated web my life is.

CHAPTER 17
June

Drew's gone and Reed stands in his place. I don't know how that happened. Time must have been lost in my state of dazed and confused.

"Baby Girl, say something?"

I blink a few times and his form comes into focus, my mother standing beside him, looking equally concerned.

"Sorry. Why are you guys here? I thought we were meeting later."

"Drew called early this morning. He said you would need the company. Honey, what's happened?" my mother asks as she leads me to sit next to her on the sofa.

I stare at the envelope on the coffee table in front of me and recount all his words.

"He gave me divorce papers."

A shocked gasp escapes my mom, her hand going to her heart.

"He wants a divorce?" Reed asks, his confusion clear as day.

"No. I don't think so," I say. "He said he wanted me to have the power. To end the marriage or to be free to love someone else."

"He didn't," my mother gasps out in some weird, elated revelation.

"Mom, it's not romantic. It's twisted."

"Oh, I suppose that's all in the way you look at it."

Reed grabs the envelope and pulls the papers out. When the envelope drops back to the table, a soft thud escapes. Picking it up, I stick my hand inside and pull out the object.

My wedding ring lies in my hand.

The other choice is putting this delicate heirloom back on my finger.

"Oh, honey," Mom says, full-on crying now.

I close my fingers around the circle tightly enough to feel the edges of the stones, letting them ground me.

"Ju, what is this?" Reed asks, confused, still flipping through the divorce papers.

"What?" I ask back, holding my hand out for him to pass me whatever he's looking at.

"These properties, there's a whole list of them."

"What?" I ask again. When I look down at the pages, I see he's right. But I don't know what any of it means.

There in the listings of all shared properties are a number of addresses listed as shared residences, eight of them. All would go to me if I were to sign the papers. I frantically begin reading through the documents from the beginning and become more and more shocked as I go.

"What has he done?" I ask in disbelief.

"What is it?" my mom asks, worried now rather than elated at Drew's warped sense of romance.

"This can't be right. It says I'd get sixty percent of his earnings. Forever."

"Oh," my mom says. She's back to sighing romantically.

"Mom, stop. This is messed up. He cheated on me, he didn't steal all my money. Why would he do this?"

"That's how you see it, June. That's not how he sees it," she replies. "He probably thinks this is his penance."

"You should have expected it, honestly," Reed chimes. "Of course he'd want to take care of you, however he could, until the end of days. I swear sometimes it's like you two don't know each other at all."

"Reed, this is not okay. It's so unfair to him. I'd never agree to it." I roll my eyes.

"Don't then," he says with a shrug and a grin. "But can we get back to the list of property assets? That's the part I don't understand."

"What assets? The house?" Mom asks.

"Houses. Apparently, he owns seven that I know nothing about."

"That he'd give all to June, outright, in the event of a divorce," Reed says.

"Seven? Where?"

I flip back to that page.

"Salem. Chicago. Bangor. Savannah. San Antonio, and two here in New Orleans."

I'm dumbfounded. Gobsmacked, actually. I need more big words for how utterly confused I am by all of this. Sure, I can see Reed's point on the money situation. It's very much in keeping with Drew's personality to ensure that I'm well taken care of. He doesn't care about money at all for himself. The man would live a happy existence if you stuck him in a studio apartment with just sweatpants to wear and salads to eat. He's never been particularly materialistic, even though he dotes on the people he loves.

Giving me that much of his money forever is ridiculous. Despite what he says, chances are he'd eventually fall in love with someone else. Or even Lorelai, as much as that idea induces me to vomiting all over the floor. No future woman would be happy about this sort of arrangement. No future family. He makes an amazing amount of money right now, but that won't last forever.

We've always lived frugally compared to how we could. Drew isn't the only one who doesn't splurge. I shop, don't get me wrong, but I stick to the lower ends of the designer scales. I don't have a closet full of Louboutin or Hermes.

These papers give me an even higher percentage of all our savings.

If I excuse the ridiculous financial aspect of these divorce papers, I'm still at a loss for words on these properties. Why does he own so many, and why don't I know about them?

"Are these his fuck pads?" I ask Reed.

"June!" my mother scolds.

Reed scoffs but doesn't say no.

"Oh my God. Is he giving me houses he takes his girlfriend to?"

"That can't be right," my mom says.

"We're going. Right now." I grab my handbag from the side table and head for the door.

"Ju, maybe you could get dressed first, yeah?" Reed says.

I look down to see I'm still in my pajamas.

"Fine!" I stomp off to my room, slamming the door behind me.

Twenty minutes later, I'm fully clothed and ensconced in a hired car with my mom and Reed. The properties listed in New Orleans have addresses next to each other in the Garden District. It's not a long drive, but long enough for my mind to wander as we pass by one beautiful old house after another.

This area isn't one I've spent too much time in. I've come to visit the cemetery, eaten at Commander's Palace, and walked around the neighborhoods some, but never for very long. It's beautiful. Alive with the same Crescent City charm you find in the French Quarter. Yet, nothing at all like it. It's quieter, only a few pedestrians out strolling at this time of day. The houses are grander, the gardens larger and more mature.

I can see why Drew, and Noah, would choose to buy here. It would be a great spot to live, to raise a family, to grow old with the ones you love.

This isn't a neighborhood you come to for one hot night with your mistress. Maybe I jumped to a ridiculous assumption. Of course I did.

Maybe I need a lobotomy. This brain of mine is fried.

The car stops in front of a Greek Revival Creole cottage. It's painted robin's egg blue, with clean white shutters framing each large window. The landscape has been freshly tended with mowed grass and trimmed shrubs.

There are two sunny yellow doors, one marked with the letter A, one with the letter B.

I exit the car and don't wait for Reed as he tends to the driver, or for my mom to catch up. There's an aged and patinaed fence surrounding the property with a narrow gate along the walkway, allowing entrance to the front porch.

Lifting the latch, I walk up to the front door with the A, less and less confident in my initial idea the closer I get.

Another envelope awaits me. This one is small and white, taped to the front door. My name written in Drew's telltale messy script.

I pull the tab open as Reed and my mother catch up with me.

"What's that?" Mom asks.

I hand her the envelope, then unfold the small note.

> Junie,
> If you haven't yet, go to the other address first. You'll find more information there.
> I love you,
> Drew

I hand the note to my mom and start walking again. They follow, hypothesizing all the way along the short walk out of this yard and into the next. The homes both sit on St. Charles and the streetcar approaching is the soundtrack currently playing along with the rapid beat of my heart.

A magnificent center hall home greets me. It's desperately in need of love and attention, but that doesn't detract from how fabulous it is. She's a gorgeous, white, majestic queen that's stood the test of time. A wide porch covers the entire front of the house on both the lower and upper levels. With tall columns stretching to the roof that make her look even taller than she truly is.

The walkway is lined with jasmine bushes on either side, and I imagine what it would smell like in the warmth of late spring as I walk along the path.

"Nicely played, Drew," Reed mutters behind me amusedly.

There's yet another envelope taped to the peeling red door, my name decorating this one as well.

Junie,

I knew you'd come here as soon as you looked through the papers. I'm sorry I didn't tell you in person. They were always meant to be a surprise. A gift I'd give to you when I retired and had the time to indulge all your dreams with the attention they deserve.

I started buying the properties a few years ago. They're ready for you to do what you will with them. They're all reportedly haunted, except the one next door. All need a lot of work, but I know that's what you wanted.

This is the newest purchase and was the hardest to get. But when I saw the listing, I knew it was meant to be yours.

I snagged the duplex next door when I was closing on this property. I've had a contractor in there to make all necessary repairs, so it's ready for our family to move in. I bought it for them. One half for Love and Larry, the other for Reed and Mom.

I knew you'd want them to have their own space close by. I also knew Leighton would never do this on her own. So, I made the decision for her because I'm a controlling asshole like that. I'm sure she'll agree.

Whatever you decide, I know you'll make this a home.

All doors open with your dad's birth date.

I love you, Junie. Always.

Drew

Holy. Hell.

My hand falls to my side, the note dangling from fingers I can't seem to get control of today. Mom gently removes it. By the time she's done reading it, her face is covered in silent tears.

"Oh, my boy," she cries.

I can't bring myself to press in the code. One side of my heart is full of love for this ridiculously grand gesture. The other half—okay much less than half because holy hell this is amazing—wonders about the timing of it all. Handing me divorce papers in the morning and gifting me a dream right after is heavy-handed, any day of the week.

Except, holy hell, he bought my family homes, too.

"Do you want to go in?" Mom asks.

I do. Also, I don't want to at all. This is a house you make a home.

I don't want to make plans for a home until I know if I'm making it for myself or for us. If this is to be our home, I don't want to enter it for the first time without him. I want him there while I imagine what color to paint the walls, which furniture goes where, what can be restored and what needs replacing.

If this ends up mine and mine alone, I won't be keeping Drew's taste in mind while I make those plans.

"No," I answer her.

"Are you fucking kidding me?"

"Reed! Language."

"I'm serious. Maybe I'll explain later, but right now let's go see your place."

"I'm not moving, no matter what Drew's note says," he grumbles.

Reed has taken so well to his hipster lifestyle in Seattle, his comment doesn't surprise me. It's bullshit, though. If Drew and I weren't in Seattle, he wouldn't be either. He'll always follow us. If we're in the same place, that is.

One of these days, I'll have to admit I still see my future with Drew. That day isn't today. Today I still feel the bitter sting of Lorelai. It's dulled some, but not enough. I want to trust my husband; I want to forgive him. Two things that take a lot more time than what I've had.

"Let's call Leighton. She and Larry should be here," my mom says.

I hit Love's contact and when she answers, I ask how quickly she can get here, but I leave out the reason why. She needs twenty minutes, so we sit on the porch step and wait, not wanting to go in without them.

This gift should be given by Drew. Even if I understand that he's giving me control, he should be here to see their faces when they walk in. With that in mind, I decide to record it with my phone, and I have it ready when they pull up.

"What's going on?" Love asks, concern and confusion taking over her features when she sets her sights on me.

"Oh my God, so much I don't even know where to start," I say.

"How about by telling me where we are?"

"That's not such a simple answer. This morning Drew handed me divorce papers," I begin but am stopped by her reaction to that news.

"That dumb fucker!"

Mom lets out a scandalized gasp, but let's be honest, she's heard worse from all of us before. It's just a game she plays, and we all allow it. It's kind of adorable.

Larry only nods in agreement with his daughter. What can I say? The man loves me.

"He doesn't want me to sign them, I don't think. His words were something along the lines of letting me hold all the cards. Whether we're done for good, we try again, or divorce and he has to woo me all over—it's all up to me."

"Wow, that's some diabolical crazy shit."

"Thank you! Mom thinks it's romantic."

"Who said diabolical crazy shit isn't romantic? Not me." Love laughs. I sigh, and she ignores it. "That doesn't explain why we're here."

"He bought me that house," I say, pointing next door, "and a handful of others."

"What?"

I pull my phone out of my pocket and unlock it. Hitting record, I point it at her.

"He bought this duplex for our family. You and Larry get a side, Reed and Mom the other."

Squeals loud enough to wake the dead at Lafayette Cemetery down the street fill the air. Regardless of all my strange feelings or misgivings, I can't help but love her excitement. Larry looks shell-shocked. I go to stand next to him, wrapping my free arm around him, and rest my head on his shoulder.

"He said he knew I'd want you all close," I say just loud enough for him to hear over the tall blond bombshell currently celebrating on the small front lawn.

196

"In different circumstances, I'd tell you he's a good man. In this situation, I'm going to tell you that he's got a good heart, but you need to smack that brain of his around a little. You hear me?"

"I hear you, Larry," I say with a genuine smile.

"What are we waiting for? Let's go in! What side is mine?" Leighton asks Reed.

"I have no idea, but I'm going to say mine is the better side," Reed says.

"No way, you don't even live in this city. I should get the better side," she protests.

"Bullshit, I'm his best friend and his brother-in-law. That gives me all the power here, blondie."

While they continue their argument, I step up to door A and punch in the code. I don't enter, just open the door wide, then go do the same to door B.

Leighton rushes into the first door and like I knew he would, Reed follows. Still smiling, I choose the second door.

It opens to a small living room. I walk through it to find an eat-in kitchen complete with new appliances, at the back of the house. There is a small bathroom off to the side that also houses a washer and dryer. Another door leads to a shared backyard and detached garage. It's all very clean and has been updated in the last couple of years. Fresh white paint covers the walls. The floors, which all look original, have been refinished and are a beautiful dark mahogany. A fireplace grounds everything with floor-to-ceiling exposed brick.

I take the stairs up as Larry and Mom enter through the front door, finally deciding to take a gander of their own.

Above stairs holds two bedrooms. One sits in the front of the house, the other in the back, a large bathroom connecting the two. The rooms are good sized and the one in the front has a fair-sized closet and a second fireplace, giving the room more character. The walls here are all white as well, leaving a blank canvas for Leighton. Or Reed.

I can picture her here. Her eclectic taste spilling into each corner of every room. With the second room set up as a home office and guest room combination. It would sure be nice for Larry to be able to stay with her on his visits, instead of a hotel.

I head back downstairs and toward the other unit, noting that Mom and Larry are in the backyard.

It's surprisingly quiet when I walk into unit A. The layout is identical to the other side, and so are the finishes. Doesn't seem like they'll have much to argue over. They'll create something if they can't find it. Of that, I'm sure.

I walk up the stairs, listening for my brother and best friend. I'm about to turn to the left, to the front bedroom, when I hear them.

"Kiss me, Reed."

"Hard pass. Thanks."

"You've done it before. I don't know why you're so scared now."

"I'm not scared, blondie, I'm repulsed."

Leighton gives a loud huff and I promptly retrace my steps back down the stairs and out the back door. Reed kissing her in the past is news to me. While I'm nosey as hell about it, I won't pry. They'll tell me about it when they want to.

For now, I'll play the fool. After all, I'm quite good at that.

CHAPTER 18
June

Everything shifts after Christmas. Drew keeps in constant contact, checking in regularly throughout the day, as his schedule allows. Each night, he calls. It's how we've ended every night since he flew back home.

Drew focuses the conversations on me, mostly. Taking a newfound interest in my career. Not that he wasn't invested in it before. Examining it with fresh eyes, I know that it was always me who pushed it off for his benefit. He'd grumble about me making sacrifices for him, but he'd always relent because it's what made me happy.

I discussed that with Rebecca this week. My need to take personal responsibilities. The brunt of our marital problems lies with Drew. I won't transfer those onto myself, but I won't blame him for the decisions I made freely, either.

In any case, it's nice to have so much of his attention. It reminds me of the early days of our marriage, when I was still recovering, and he doted on me. I think we both took advantage of each other then. I leaned on him more than I should have. He used my mental health issues to avoid the larger problems.

Despite our current situation, our relationship over the past week feels healthier than it ever has before.

He does ask me about Noah, and I don't omit anything. I don't give the finer details of my time spent with him, but I give enough for Drew to understand the nature. I've not spent another night with Noah, not like that first, where I was utterly spent and passed out in his arms. We do, however, talk often about sex, desires, needs. Noah's willing to help me understand the things Drew is still hesitant to share with me. Or the things I feel too vulnerable to bring up with Drew.

Those things comprise a lengthy list. Noah is delicate with me, thoughtfully giving me information I desire to have, but never pushing past the limits he's set. He encourages me more and more to talk to Drew. Every day, that gets the tiniest bit easier. Every day, I get the tiniest bit closer to acceptance, if not forgiveness. I'm not there yet.

Years could be spent with me worrying about why there continues to be a divide between us. That's a hole I try very hard not to fall into. Knowing Drew is trying to sort it all out before he shares it with me, is all I can hope for.

Noah helps fill that gap for me. Patiently describing to me the things he likes and why, tutoring me on the acts I can do that would bring Noah pleasure, and therefore, possibly Drew, too.

It's all so surreal. Like I'm living in an alternate dimension. Yet, it's working. I grow stronger and less depressed by the day. So, I ignore the strangeness of being a sexual apprentice of sorts to a friend I hold dear.

And I do hold him dear. Noah is an invaluable presence in my life. There have not been any more naked petting times between us. He knows that the conversations I had, the reactions I had, with Drew over the holiday changed my trajectory. That doesn't mean he's stopped his affection outright. He's still keen on holding me, comforting me, after we've had a long talk. That's for him as much as it is for me, and I'm happy to be able to give it to him.

New Year's Eve with his family was a great time. Leighton went with and hit it off with Noah's brother, Connor, who's only a slightly smaller and darker version of Noah. Leighton didn't say, but I suspect they spent the night together. Since she was quiet about it, it means she likes him more than she wants to admit. She's always been an open book about men she sees as nothing more than a good time.

Drew is careful not to comment negatively when I tell him of my talks with Noah. They make him uncomfortable and boorish, but he understands I'm doing it for the purpose of better understanding him. Until he's here, until we're both willing to have these talks with each other, he bites his tongue.

Sort of, anyway. He doesn't have to say words. I understand his silence, his sighs, his quiet, frustrated groans all the same.

What can he say? He, too, found someone else to fulfill a part of life he wasn't willing to fulfill with me.

He's asked me to fly home for his last game of the season. I've agreed, albeit somewhat reluctantly. Of course I want to see him play. I miss that more than I can say. It's the other wives and girlfriends that I don't particularly want to encounter. Suffering through it won't be pleasant, but I'll do it for him.

It will be a quick trip, as our first live segment airs in only three days. This week, we filmed a couple of the stories, and I must say, I'm enjoying it even more than I anticipated. Which is telling, since I expected to like it very much. I've never been so satisfied by work before, so proud of what I'm doing.

Maybe to some, that would sound superficial. I'm just a cohost of a show to promote a sporting event, if you break it down to simple terms. Yet, the stories they're encouraging us to share speak to the heart of the city. Stories that don't get such national coverage most days.

My trip to the abandoned Six Flags, for instance, prompted Noah and me to dig further into the story. We brought in the people who had made a documentary of it not long ago and helped develop the story further. We're hoping the coverage prompts some pushback to help the property owners who are suffering from depleted home values due to the giant eyesore.

It feels amazing to be helping, even in such small ways, a city that I hope to spend much more time in.

Being back in the Pacific Northwest feels amazing as well. Even if just for the night. I didn't fly in early enough to go to either a hotel or the house first. I'm not sure where I'll stay, honestly. Going home is the choice I'm leaning toward. Despite how great Drew and I've been getting along, I'm not sure it's the wisest choice. Either way, I didn't commit to anything and likely won't until I need to.

After landing, I head straight to the stadium. It's early yet, but pre-gaming is in full swing, regardless of the team's standings. Fans here are always supportive and the proof can be seen by how many are at the stadium already.

Casey, the team's family liaison, meets me at the designated entrance and walks with me to the suites. He started this position the same year Drew started for the team, so we bonded over being newbies. We chat about his wife and newborn daughter on the walk, and I realize just how much I've missed being away these past weeks.

It makes me sadder than I'd expected. Totally my fault. I fight this part of Drew's career, the family aspect of the team. Always blaming my inability to trust easily, something a stalker ingrained in me. But I didn't have that problem with Noah, or with anyone on the ESPN production team.

That's one more thing to talk to Rebecca about, why my default is an easy distrust of the other players' wives and girlfriends.

One exception is the first face I see when I enter the suite. Candace is married to the team's tight end, Bryce. She doesn't often come to the games; their four young daughters are a lot for one person to handle. She's here today, though, redheaded girls all in tow.

"June! I was hoping I'd see you today. It's been forever," she greets me with a one-armed hug, balancing a newborn in the other.

"It's good to see you, Candace. You look amazing," I tell her. She hasn't lost all the weight from her last pregnancy, but the added pounds that linger look good on her, and she glows with a bright smile. The players are always surrounded by Barbie doll types, so it's refreshing when you find one who doesn't conform to the standard and is comfortable with that.

I've never conformed to it either. Not with my scars and especially not with my size. I wear a size six, but most of the women I've encountered through Drew's career would consider that plus-size. It's fucking ridiculous and I've always hated it.

But then, Lorelai is much closer to the standard than me, so maybe they all know something I don't. Fuck that, though. I will not compare myself to that woman ever again.

"Thank you, you do too," she says, a little conspiratorial. I'm once again wearing an outfit that's more revealing than I'd worn to previous games. It's cold as hell outside, though, so no dress. Instead, I opted for snug jeans, an off-shoulder chunky knit sweater cropped just enough to highlight my scar, and my new favorite badass heeled combat boots.

"Yeah, well, we do what we have to, right?"

"Lady, yes. And you do whatever it takes to have that man begging at your feet. Looking like this"—she waves a hand at me—"you'll have every single man on this team pushing him out of the way to get to you."

"From your lips," I say, mustering a smile. I'm glad she's not pussyfooting around the subject. Everyone here knows what's happened. How could they not?

"For real, honey. You need anyone to sit with, you sit with me. You need to chat, you come chat with me. You need to escape it all, you run away to Aruba with me. I got you."

"Thanks, Candace. That means the world. You have no idea," I say, this time with a genuine smile.

"I have some idea, but that's a conversation for another time and with a lot of wine."

Before I have the chance to ask what that's all about, Candace and Bryce's three-year-old, Jolie, comes rushing up to her mom.

"Mama, can I has some food? Millie says it's not for me." Millie being her sister who is only two years older.

"The food is for everyone, baby. Just let me change the baby's diaper first, okay?"

Jolie's bottom lip juts out in the most adorable pout and tears pool in her wide eyes.

"I can take her," I offer. "Any food allergies I need to know of?"

"Thanks, June. These kids are four whole handfuls," she says. "No allergies. They're all garbage cans. Just like their daddy."

Jolie nods vigorously in agreement.

"Come on, sweetheart," I say, holding out my hand. She doesn't take it, and her eyes narrow on me.

"Mama, is she a stranger?"

"No, this is June. She's QB Drew's wife, remember?" Candace answers, grinning like a Cheshire.

Jolie's eyes quickly change to big old saucers. For the entire game, she shadows me and asks me every question she can think of about Drew. Some, several times. The cute-as-a-button child has a huge crush on my husband.

"What's QB's favorite food?"

"Salad."

"Nobodies like salad," she says in disgust.

"QB Drew loves salad." The look of disgust doesn't diminish with my reply, but neither does the look of adoration she's been wearing all day.

"Maybe you should eat salad so you can be like QB," Candace prods.

"No, thanks, Mama," she says, and I giggle. Jolie doesn't notice, though, because our team has just gotten the ball back and her eyes are glued to the field. They follow only two players, her dad and Drew. She's got a wonderful attention span for those two men.

We're sitting in the seats that are open to the rest of the stadium, the suite doors shut behind us. I hear them open for a moment when someone either comes to join us or decides to head back inside. The chatter flows out every time. Once I caught some comments that probably were not meant for me to hear. But then again, with some of the cattier women here, maybe they were. It's exactly what I'd expect from them, so it's easy enough to ignore.

A few of the other players' family members have come out to say hello to Candace and me. None stay long. I get it, it's awkward, and it's not as if I have ever been overly friendly with any of them. I've overheard two conversations about me and my marriage. Both held the same sentiment; how can I stay with him after he cheated.

I do my best to ignore them.

Besides, Candace and I are quite busy keeping up with a newborn and three toddlers. Millie is entertaining herself by playing a game on a tablet. Samantha, the oldest—she's six and three-quarters, if you ask her—is happy as a clam with a plate of nachos in front of her. Elizabeth is asleep in her mom's arms. And Jolie is currently prattling on about how she hopes QB Drew passes the ball to her daddy on the next play, while she sits on my lap, twirling a strand of my hair in her small fingers.

The girl is a bit of a savant when it comes to football. Or at least this team. She knows things no three-year-old should know. She fires off stats like it's her job. Even if the game weren't exciting, I'd be fully entertained by her.

But it is exciting, and Drew is playing the best game of his career. He looks magnificent, completing nearly every pass. Although it hasn't been exclusively a passing game. They've run the ball plenty. Drew even ran it in once for a touchdown.

We're still down by three with less than a minute left in the game and forty-two yards from the end zone. Despite how well Drew and the team have played, which has been exceptional, their competition has been equally as good.

Everything about the next play lines up with perfection for our team; each player is exactly where they need to be. The line blocks are executed with certainty, giving Drew and Bryce the time they need to get in position. Drew's arm arches through the air, the ball sailing and landing precisely into Bryce's waiting hands, feet from the end zone. Bryce easily pushes away a player from the other team and strolls into a touchdown.

Jolie bounces in my arms excitedly as I stand to scan the field for possible flags. I see none. With two seconds left on the clock, we've just won the last game of the season.

"I knew it, I knew it!" Jolie can't contain her excitement. It's infectious. My smile grows as wide as hers as she throws her tiny arms high in the air.

Candace, the girls, and I celebrate in the suite for a while longer before heading down to meet the men. Both will have to linger and speak to the press before they'll be able to end their day. We go straight to the broadcast room, Jolie still clinging to me, rattling off random facts and various questions.

"What's QB Drew's favorite food?"

"Scrambled eggs," I answer as seriously as I can.

"No, it's salad!"

"How did you know?" I exclaim with false shock, and she giggles. "Do you want to sneak in with me and watch QB talk to the reporters?"

Her little golden eyes go wide again. "Yes," she answers in a conspiratorial whisper.

I glance at Candace for approval, who nods and waves us on. "You mind Miss June, Jolie."

"We have to be super quiet so that he can hear all the questions, okay?"

"Yes," she whispers again as I open the door and move to stand in a back corner of the room. Coach is still being hammered with questions. I lean against a wall and adjust Jolie on my hip while we wait it out.

She's not at all bored. In fact, she's riveted on the answers. I focus on her intensity. Jolie is the most entertaining creature I've ever met.

After Coach finishes up, Bryce comes out. As soon as he's at the microphone, Jolie begins waving wildly.

"Hey, baby," Bryce greets her with a big grin. When she sees the attention it garners from the press, the oohs, she buries her face in my hair. And now I'm giggling.

Bryce only takes a handful of questions; he's got a reputation for hating this sort of thing. He does what he must, nothing more. I respect him more for it.

"Okay, okay. That's it for me. I obviously need to go help my wife out, since she's recruiting June to babysit my girls," he teases, giving the crowd a wave as he leaves the stage and heads to us.

"She's fine," I reassure him. "She wanted to watch QB Drew."

"Ahh, QB Drew is her favorite," he replies.

"Will these vultures try to eat him too, Daddy?" Her voice is loud enough for half the room to hear, and laughs erupt all around as Bryce's cheeks pinken slightly. Obviously, some of his disdain for the dog and pony show has rubbed off on his daughter.

"We're about to find out," I tell her, pointing to where Drew is walking to the podium.

There have only been two occasions when I remember Drew dressing up for pressers after a game. Both times it was because the games fell on my birthday. Otherwise, he's dressed in some sort of athleisure.

Tonight, he's dressed to the nines. He's perfectly draped in a dark silver three-piece suit. Under it is a crisp white shirt, unbuttoned low enough to show the strong column of his neck. The vest is also unfastened in a completely casual manner that has all my sexual pistons firing in time.

There's a devil-may-care attitude wafting off him that makes me gooey and too hot. Drew with that big dick energy, a little reckless, a lot cocky… it's a whole vibe. Like earthquakes shattering my whole willpower type of vibe.

Luckily, a tiny palm with sticky fingertips lands on my cheek, distracting me from my lust spike.

"There he is," Jolie quietly announces.

There he is, is right.

As soon as he gets to the microphone, the queries fly. Drew takes the first handful of questions in easy stride. They're softballs, the type of questions I always wonder why reporters ask. The answers are always some generic versions of each other. The same soundbite every game isn't worth the effort, in my opinion.

Then he points to someone on the other side of the room.

"It's already being floated that this was a career highlight game not only for you but the entire team. What do you attribute that to?"

"You know, there are days when a few of us show up a little high on life for whatever reason. It's infections and can take over the entire team. We had that today. This was the first time Bryce had all his girls at a game. Tyson got engaged this week. Jimmy found out he's going to be a dad. We had a lot to celebrate this week coming into the game and we played like a team happy for each other. A team that wants to work for each other," Drew answers.

A smile takes over my face. Though, a sadness takes a little hold of my heart because I didn't know about Tyson or Jimmy's news. I've been so wrapped up in my own world, I'm utterly failing at being a supportive member of this team's family. Not that I was ever all that good at it to begin with.

"Are you saying that earlier in the season, collectively, you all were having bad days?" The same reporter follows up.

"I mean, no, not collectively. A lot of what happened this season falls on my shoulders. We're still a new team, learning each other's habits. And I used to think most of us could compartmentalize, keep our personal lives separate from the job. This season I learned that isn't true. Everything in our lives bleeds into it. Personally, I failed the team this season by not being the man I needed to be all-around. I failed myself. Mostly, I failed my wife," he says, finding me in the room. "She's here today, though, maybe giving me one last chance to earn back some of her trust."

Jolie's little hand shoots up in the air as Drew looks for the next journalist to call on.

"I see our newest reporter has a question," he says, grinning. "Ask away, Miss Jolie."

"What do you fink it will take to lead this team to the Super Bowl next year? Besides throwing the ball to my daddy more."

The room erupts in soft laughter and Bryce beams with pride at his little tater-tot.

"Great question," he says and Jolie's whole face shines like the face of the sun at his praise. "It'll have to be a team effort, of course. But for my part, I'm committed to being the best quarterback, the best man that I can be. One who deserves to have faith and trust placed in him. A man who follows through on his promises. I'll do everything I can to get us where we all want to be." His eyes never leave mine. He's not talking about football as much as he's talking about us. "And yes, I definitely need to throw the ball more to your daddy. He made the play of the game today."

Bryce, from either instincts or a keen eye, clues in on my emotions. He takes a step closer, wrapping his solid arm around me and his daughter.

"Do you believe him?" Bryce asks.

"I do," answers Jolie. But her daddy is looking at me.

"I want to," I say, my voice betraying how unsure I am.

"I do, for what it's worth," he says confidently, keeping eye contact with me. "I think he's actively trying to be worthy of you, honey. He's a different man these past couple of months. I know what it looks like. I recognize it in him."

"Maybe I haven't been very worthy of all of you," I say to him.

Bryce gives me a sympathetic smile; his arm tightening just slightly. "That takes time. We're a horrible bunch of reprobates. You'll get there."

"What's prepobaties mean, Daddy?" Jolie asks in a not so hushed voice, and we both grin over her head.

"Boys, baby. It means boys. You should stay away from them. Forever."

"Okay," she agrees.

Bryce and Candace's past may be a mystery to me, although it's evident there was betrayal. The strength they have as a couple, as a family, gives me hope. If they came out of it as such a strong, loving couple, maybe Drew and I can, too.

I've been looking at this as the end of our marriage. Of course I have been. Any woman would. If I look at it from a different angle, one of optimism, maybe this is what we've needed all along. Not his infidelity, by any means, but something that forced us to begin again. To start the way we should have started all along. Instinct tells me we need that. I only wish I could trust my instincts these days.

The presser ends not long after Drew ends his questions, and by the time I file out of the room, he's waiting for me.

"Need a ride?" he asks.

CHAPTER 19

June

Drew loads me and both our bags into his SUV before folding his big frame into the driver's seat. After starting the engine, he pauses. He doesn't look at me, just stares at his hands on the steering wheel in the ten and two positions.

Silence fills the air between us, thick with feelings I can't quite get a read on. Maybe the same thoughts going through my head are going through his.

Where do we go from here?

I need a partner who wants to be with me, in every way, as much as I want to be with them. I don't have enough faith in Drew to be that man, but when we married, I believed you fight through your problems. You stick it out in the hard times as long as you're both making efforts to change. What if I haven't put in the right effort, haven't given Drew the right chances?

Maybe I'm just an idiot. Or maybe I just need to make the decision to either be done or truly put the effort in to see if we can get past this. Only one of those tightens my chest and knots my stomach.

"Where to, June?"

My mouth opens to tell him the Edgewater. Instead, I say what I want most, "Home."

A slow breath releases out of him, and he shifts to reverse out of the spot. We don't speak on the drive, but halfway there he reaches over to take my hand in his. I still wonder how we fit together, but I'm not apprehensive at this touch. I'm not letting my head wander into a territory that makes me hurt or hate.

When my dad died, a social worker stopped by his hospital room to speak to our family. She told us to be where our feet are. Don't look back on the what-ifs, don't worry about what the future holds. Be in the now. It stuck with me then and I'm embracing it now. Whatever happens tomorrow, I want to just enjoy this night.

It's strange entering this house after so many weeks. Everything looks the same, but nothing feels the same. I catch myself scanning for items out of place, things that don't belong. Things that aren't mine. With some effort, I'm able to push the suspicion and insecurity away.

Drew drops his game bag by the laundry room door and reaches for my hand again.

"Are you hungry?"

"No," I say, shaking my head. "I ate at the stadium."

He nods, his eyes flicking between mine.

"Will you try something with me? It's something Fillmore suggested," he asks uncertainly.

"What?" My voice is just as uneasy.

"It's called soul gazing. It's supposed to allow us to connect without words. She said it aligns our heart chakras, whatever that means."

A huge grin grows on my face and his begins to mirror it.

"What?" he asks with a smirk.

"Who even are you, Drew McKenna?" My Drew would never know what a chakra was, let alone suggest aligning ours.

"I'm just a man in love with a woman who, rightfully, hates him."

My chest hitches, skips rhythm.

"I don't hate you."

"You hate parts of me, June. Things I've done. It's okay. You should." His head bows so he doesn't have to look me in the eyes.

"How do we do this soul gazing?" I ask, and he brings his face back to mine.

"Basically, we get comfortable and stare into each other's eyes for five minutes. No talking."

"Sounds easy enough," I say, but not even I believe the words.

"She said it can be very emotional. Are you sure you want to try it?"

I nod. I am sure I want to reconnect with my husband in some way. I don't have any hesitations about that.

"I'll take your bag up to the guest room. You have something comfortable to wear?"

I nod again.

"I'll go change, too. Meet me in our room when you're ready?"

"Okay," I answer. He starts to head away, but I stop him. "Drew?"

He turns back to me, question on his face.

"You looked good today. The game"—I let my gaze travel over him—"and the suit."

Drew flashes a cheeky grin, then darts upstairs with a little more enthusiasm, picking my overnight bag up on the way.

I don't immediately follow. Instead, I move to the kitchen and take my time downing a large glass of water. Let it wash away the dryness in my throat and the apprehension in my head. Only then do I go to the guest room to put my big girl panties on.

Or, in this case, my sexy, little lacey ones on.

I push the door to Drew's room open slowly, my heart racing. He's in small, skintight black boxer-briefs, slung low on his hips. And not a stitch more.

Drew has always been incredibly fit. His body is his career, and he tends to it with that respect. But, damn, whatever he's been doing these past two months has taken it to a whole other level. His muscles are more defined, his shoulders broader, that vee just above his happy place more pronounced.

"June," he says, and it sounds like a warning.

My gaze darts to meet his hungry one. Desire ignites in his eyes, sending shivers through my whole body. I covered my ridiculously sexy underthings with a short kimono wrap. Drew looks at me like he's got magical vision that allows him to see through it all.

"Come sit," he calls after he clears his throat.

He's arranged pillows on the ground for us. The lighting is dimmed somewhat, and my oil diffuser is puffing a soft blend of lavender and bergamot into the room. I take my place on a pillow, sitting cross-legged as I watch him sit opposite me.

"I'm going to set the timer, but if you can't go the full five minutes, I'll understand."

"Same for you, I guess," I say.

"I could stare at you forever," he whispers, sending another shudder through me.

He pushes a button on his phone and sets it aside. I follow the movement. Then I take a large gulp of air and look into Drew's eyes.

If anyone says this is easy, they're a liar. Eye contact is intimate. It's intimidating, terrifying. It's other-fucking-worldly what you see when you look with the intent to see past the surface and into the depths of someone's soul.

My heartbeat slows, my chest syncing in time with his so easily. Only seconds have passed, I'm sure, but it already feels like minutes. Drew's mossy eyes storm with so many questions and even more answers. I can hear it all.

Never again.

I fucking love you, Junie.

I miss you.

Never again.

I've never deserved you. I never will.

Come home.

Never again.

Need to touch you.

Never again.

Please, love me.

Never again.

I don't know what he sees in my eyes, but the despair in his slowly calms into something more wistful. Memories from our lives together play out in my mind. I remember all the times I waited, heart in hand, for the door of our childhood home to open to Reed and Drew barreling in. How Drew's reaction morphed over the years from cautiously friendly, to feigned indifference, to unconditional love. All the times I knew I was seen by him, even if it was from secret glances or sly nearness.

The first time he held my hand. He was still in high school, and the team had just won the state championship game. My whole family rushed the field to congratulate him. But it was me he hugged first, my hand he held while he received hugs from everyone else. He didn't let go until his dad took notice of it.

That memory is seared into my heart, forever.

The first time he kissed me is, too. I had just woken up in the hospital and it was as if Drew couldn't hold himself back from it. Like he couldn't live another minute without his lips on mine. It was tender, it was relief. It was life.

Drew's image blurs as my tears well up. I blink and one falls, racing down my cheek to wet my lips.

I want it all back. The happy memories, the years that I believed we were so blissfully in love and invincibly together.

I want it back.

I want it all back.

More tears fall, but I don't look away. I don't hide it. If I can see everything in him, he must see it all in me. I want him to fucking feel how much I've always loved him. How much I would do for him. How much I would forgive… and know what I can't.

Never again.

I love you.

I love you.

I'm so sorry.

The alarm on his phone goes off. We both flinch at the intrusion. Drew's leaves mine to shut it off.

I break. Silently, my body quakes with sobs.

"Hey, hey, come here," Drew coos as he wraps me up in his arms. Lifting me, he carries me into the bathroom. He sets me on the side of the large tub so he can reach over and start the water. I stare in a blurry daze as he adds some of my favorite bubble bath.

He pulls me to standing, unties my wrap, and drags it down my arms.

"Fuck."

I lift my face to his.

"What?"

"That is some insanely sexy underwear."

"Oh."

He gives me a soft smile. "I'll buy you more if this ruins it."

I'm about to ask what he means, but he's suddenly lifting me again and placing me into the tub. I pull my knees up to rest my chin on them as I watch him set two big towels out and shut the water off when the tub is nearly overflowing. Then he steps in to sit opposite me, boxer briefs still on.

"So, that was pretty intense, yeah?"

"I'm sorry I lost it there," I answer.

"Don't apologize," he says. "Can I touch you? Would that be okay?"

I give him a nod, confused by how gentle and hesitant he's being with me. Our tub is large enough that he easily spins me around, pulling me into his chest. I let my head fall back onto his shoulder, the rise and fall of his chest lulling my nerves.

Drew starts to massage my shoulders, slowly working down my arms. Between that and the warmth of the bathwater, my body is turning to jelly.

"It's hard to know how much of what was going through my head was something I saw in you or was just my imagination. You know?"

"Do you want to know what I was thinking?" he asks.

"Is that how it works? Are you supposed to tell me?"

"I don't know if there are rules to it, but I think we both know communication is exactly what we need."

"Truth."

Drew gently sits me forward so he can work the muscles of my neck and back. His thick fingers find every knot of tension in me.

"I was thinking how much I love you, how sorry I am for everything I've done. How I'll never do it again. I miss you. I don't even know how to tell you how much," he says before pressing soft kisses on all the places his fingers have been working. "I know those are just words and I need to back them up with actions. I will, though. I mean everything I say. More than I've ever meant anything before."

"Mmm," I moan when his lips find an especially sensitive spot. "Is this a form of aftercare?"

"I suppose it is. I should have been better at it with you," he whispers into my nape.

It makes me greedy for more. Needy to touch him, to tease... to please.

"I have something to say," I say, proud that my nervousness doesn't present itself in my voice. "We are not back together. Me deciding to stay tonight and whatever happens here changes nothing. We have so much to work through and I still don't know what we look like on the other side of that."

"I hear you," he says, his palm moving to my stomach and pulling me back tightly to his body.

"I need to know you're clean. I'm deciding to trust you to tell me the truth, despite having every reason not to. If you tell me there is no way you have anything, I'll believe you."

It's an enormous leap of faith, a first step in letting him know I'm willing to consider giving him a second chance. Which might be the wrong call, but I'm not willing to throw us away without a fight and I haven't fought for us yet. I've only fought for myself.

"I took your words to heart after our conversation in Dallas, June. You were right. I wasn't as careful as I believed I was. I can't tell you how much that pains me, baby. It's at the top of the list of reasons I'm hating myself for. I got tested as soon as I got back home. I'm clean." He hasn't released any hold on me. Instead, he's folded himself around me. Cocooning me in his strength.

"You haven't been with anyone since the test?" The question needs to be asked. I'd be stupid not to. If the answer is anything but no, I'm going to lose my shit, though.

His hand comes up to cup my face, turning my chin so I'm forced to look at him.

"I'm sorry I've made you doubt me. I want more than anything to repair that and I don't want you to think I'm not putting in the work, okay?" he asks. I nod for him to continue. "I haven't been with another woman since Los Angeles. You're it for me, and I wish I hadn't lost sight of that."

"Okay." I swallow down the array of emotions working their way up.

"Do you have anything else you want to ask me?"

"Yes, but I'm scared to."

"You don't have to be afraid of me, baby."

"I'm not afraid of you, Drew. I'm afraid you won't do what I ask."

He turns my face farther up to his, turning my body to rest sideways in his arms, and rests his brow against mine.

"Ask me, June."

I close my eyes and let the words fall out.

"Will you fuck me the way you like to fuck? No holding back. I can take it."

"Look at me," Drew demands.

I take a moment, afraid of what I'll see. When I meet his stare, I see all my feelings reflected at me. Drew wants this as much as me, but there is a speck of fear there, too.

"If anything makes you uncomfortable, you say stop. Do you understand me?"

"Yes."

"I mean it, Junie. I know you and how you suffer in silence. You cannot do that with me. If it does not feel good, you tell me to stop." His hand pulls my hair, winding it before he gives it a tug, as if to emphasize his words.

"Okay."

"Promise me. Say the fucking words."

"I promise to tell you to stop if it doesn't feel good. I'll trust you if you'll trust me, too."

His mouth clashes with mine so suddenly I slip down into the water. Drew steadies me by placing a hand low on my back, the other still tangled in my hair. His tongue forces its way into my mouth, and I moan at the taste of him.

I've missed this. The rush of lust, the bone-deep need. I can only hope it doesn't end with a sizzle like so many times before. I need an inferno. Passion burning away everything outside of the two of us, singing all my frayed edges and hurt feelings. Incinerate it all to the ground, giving us a fresh start at this life.

As quickly as our kiss started, it stops. Drew stands and steps out of the tub. I watch the taut muscles of his ass when they flex as he removes his soaking boxers. He wraps a towel around his waist, then turns back to me, reaching to pull me out of the water. He carries my wet body to the bedroom and stands me at the end of the bed, in the middle of all the pillows that mark the spot of our soul gazing.

"Remove my towel," he says, his voice rough.

I palm his chest, resting my hands on his hard pecs. Slowly, I drag them down, letting my nails tweak his nipples as they do. I feel every ridge of my descent.

"The towel, June. Now."

I look up at him through my lashes, trying for innocence that I'm sure my panting betrays. Disregarding his command, I don't rush. I'm terrified in so many ways, but I'm here to play, to push. To get what I want, to show him I can take but also give. If he wants to 'correct my behavior,' all the better.

When my fingertips meet the towel, I dip them in, running them along the edges around to his ass before I push it off completely.

I'm not sure if it's weird to be infatuated with a dick, but I love Drew's. Of course, it's the only one I've seen live in the flesh. Regardless, I cannot imagine a more perfect cock. Long and wider than most I've seen in porn, just slightly ruddier than the rest of his body, nestled between thick, strong thighs. I realize I'm biased, but damn, it's a good dick.

Right now, it's hard as hell. Ready.

"On your knees."

I still don't obey right away. Part of me wants to be a brat just to see what he'll do. Another part of me wants to do exactly what he says. The bigger part is the one that does not want to give anything to him easily because... honestly, fuck that.

So, I stay standing and watch as his eyes narrow on me.

"Do you want me to spank that ass, June?"

"I like spankings," I answer with a shrug.

Before I know what's happening, Drew has me pressed up against the bedroom door with my hands behind my back as he leans into me with his bulky frame. Heavy gusts of air puff out of him and onto my damp skin, pebbling it.

"Tonight, you don't speak to me about him or what you've done with him. In this room, you are my wife. You're mine to play with, not fucking his."

I laugh. It bursts out without my control or consent, totally ignoring how excited my body is to be this close to Drew. This close to fucking him.

"I don't think I'm the one who needs reminding that we're married."

"Fair enough," he grinds out, "but don't think I won't fucking punish you for that smart mouth, anyway."

"Feel free," I taunt.

"Get on your damn knees, June." He's no longer speaking pleasantly. He's worked up. On edge.

It's exciting, so I do what he says, and he steps in front of me again.

"Open."

I open my mouth, not wide enough for him to do anything with, but I open it all the same.

"That's cute. Open your mouth now. Show me that tongue."

I give a little snarky wink before I follow his instructions. Drew's lips twitch and his stance widens as one powerful hand reaches for his cock.

It's his right hand, his throwing hand, his dominant hand, and I want it to dominate me.

There isn't an ounce of fear there. I'm ready for this. I want this more than I can express. Watching him work his hand on his cock makes me hot all over.

Drew makes another small move forward, not close enough for me to put my mouth on him, just enough to leave me wanting more.

While I have no hesitation, I see it in Drew. The same something that always holds him back. The fear that he'll trigger an anxiety attack in me, or a nightmare, that I'll see another man in his place. That fright is bleeding through his desire, like it always has before. The longer he stands there, hand on his cock, eyes on my gaping mouth, the more of it I see.

I blink away the image as I snap my mouth shut and quickly fumble to my feet.

"June?"

Stomping out of the room on my bare feet, I slam his door shut behind me and walk into the guest room, straight over to the window where I rest my forehead on the cool glass. I don't care that the curtains are open and someone outside may see my nearly naked body. I don't care if they see my shattered ego or my heart bleeding out.

I hear Drew enter my room.

"It shouldn't be so hard to fuck your wife."

"You know that's not it, June. I told you why."

"And I told you I wanted it. I told you to trust me. I know what I like," I say to the naked reflection of him in the window.

"I'm scared that will change."

"I'm scared you never will."

"I already have. So much," he urges, and I turn to look at him.

"As have I, Drew. Do you want to know how? I've changed because I'm finally recognizing that I have fantasies, too. I'm beginning to see that they won't be met by you. That I'll have to find another man to satisfy them. Maybe I can ask Noah. He certainly does a great job in my dreams."

I know what I'm doing, provoking the beast. We're at a precipice here. We either get past this now, or we never will. I'm done playing the game by Drew's rules, the ones that give him all the power and me all the pain. I will not spare his feelings and I'm not above poking his jealousy to get what I want.

Three steps and he's taking up all my personal space. His hands on my hips, fingers tangling in the thin straps of my panties.

"Do you think it's a good idea to piss me off?"

"You had a chance to shut me up. You didn't take it." I shrug and give him an unimpressed look.

He yanks his hands and my brand-new pretty underwear flutters to the floor in scraps.

"Stay," he grits out as he walks around me to shut the drapes. He does it ridiculously slowly and I know it's a test to see if I'll do as he says.

"New Orleans has done you good, June," he tells me as he palms my ass from behind. "You've been eating better. Your curves have filled back out." One hand travels upward along my side until it cups my heavy breast. "I want to relearn them all. With my tongue. But first, you're going to pay for that smart fucking mouth of yours. Bend over and grab your ankles."

His hands guide my body down until I'm doing exactly as he says, my wet locks dangling down to brush the hardwood floors.

"Wider," he barks, grabbing my hips to steady me, and he uses his foot to widen the area between my feet.

Without warning, he delivers one quick slap just to the underside of my ass cheek. My body jerks with the force, but Drew's hands are there to stabilize me. His palm rubs the spot that stings, a few slow circles, then it comes down again. And again.

"Anders doesn't get this ass, June. It's mine. It's always been mine," he mumbles as he rubs the spot again with one hand. The other hand, the one that's been resting on the small of my back, drags downward through the crease of my ass and further. He dips it into the heat there. "This is mine, too. It's wet for me, not him. Say it."

I moan, but no distinguishable words come out.

"Say it." Smack.

"It's for you," I say between gasps.

Drew presses a kiss on the spot he's swatted, then another before dragging his tongue to where his fingers are. The sensation makes my legs shake. When his tongue dips in to taste me and he groans, I move my hands to the floor in front of me to brace myself.

His hands spread my cheeks farther apart, and he pushes in deeper, faster and faster until he's making love to me with his tongue. Occasionally, he delivers another light swat until I can hardly catch my breath from panting need.

That's when he moves to my clit and sucks it in a pulsing staccato that pushes my pleasure to the brink, then crashing over the edge. My arms give as the climax takes over and Drew's arms wrap around my thighs to hold me tightly as I fall apart in his mouth.

When the waves subside, so does Drew's touch, only briefly. Then he's pulling me up into his powerful arms. He studies my face.

"Are you okay? Dizzy?"

"A little, but I'm okay," I answer.

He kisses me, letting me taste myself on him. I want to climb up his body, get closer. Be closer. I want to be all over him and have him all over me. His hard cock presses against my stomach. My hand, a life of its own, reaches for it. Encircles it, thumbing the slight pre-cum at the tip.

"Stop that," he says into my mouth.

I don't stop running my fingers over his length or kissing him. I find I enjoy being disobedient.

Drew nips at my lip and stills my hand with his own. "Stop."

He moves to the bed, grabs a pillow, and drops it at my feet.

"Down."

"I'm not a dog, Drew," I say with a raised brow.

"No, you're not. You're a woman who let another man put his hands on you intimately. A woman who purposely provoked your husband's ire. You're a woman who needs to be put in her place. Which, right now, is on your knees."

"If I'm all those things, what the fuck are you?"

"The man who will spend the rest of his life regretting not fucking you into submission the first chance I got. Down, now, and open that god-damn mouth."

I drop to my knees and open wide, sticking my tongue out slightly.

"Good. A little lower. Drop that pretty ass between your feet so that pouty chin of yours is the perfect height to rest my balls on when I shove my cock in your mouth."

Damn.

I blush, but his words make me wetter, needier. I want him to do what he is talking about, but I'm not done being impish.

"You should have told me sooner. I would've been juggling your balls with my tongue for the last decade." I drop my ass down, lean forward, and open wide.

"Fucking minx," he mutters when he thrusts ahead into my mouth. "I know what you're doing. I'm going to fuck that sass right out of you."

Drew's fingers tangle into my hair, one above each of my ears, positioning me just so. He works himself in a little further with each forward motion. All the while rambling about my attitude, about how fucking good my mouth feels. Interspersed with his ranting are instructions for me to flatten my tongue, relax my throat, to look at him if I take too long of a blink.

I've already learned that lesson, so I do it, peering up at his muscular body. His chest ripples with every thrust. Nothing about him is relaxed right now. He's intensely focused on his mission.

Shutting me up with his dick as he fucks my mouth relentlessly.

And though I know I shouldn't let my mind go to a darker place, I can't help but wonder if Lorelai talks back to him. Or does she just easily comply? Did, past tense, my heart screams at me. I'd take bets she always does as told. That she's easy. Probably hoping if she gives him whatever he wants, without question, he'll keep coming back to her. She might have been right.

But fuck that.

Moving my hands from my thighs to his and pressing them around, I leverage my mouth off his cock. He's looking at me in question and I use the time to catch my breath, swallow hard. Keeping eye contact with Drew, I lick one palm, then suck my fingers into my mouth, getting them nice and wet before using them to hold his shaft.

Then I do what I teased, sucking his scrotum into my mouth while I keep working him with my hand. Drew rises onto his toes, giving me better access. Another groan escapes him. I'm not even sure he's aware of it.

"How are you so damn good?"

I smile as I trail my tongue around and then up, up, up to the head of his cock. I press a small kiss atop it, then a small suckle, then a small, playful nip. He draws back and shoves two fingers into my mouth, holding them there as his eyes flare.

"As much as I want you choking on my cum, I need in that cunt, Junie. Up." He holds his other hand out to help me, still holding fingers in my mouth. Presumably, so I can't talk back.

I circle my tongue around them as I stand. When I'm at full height, he removes them only to thrust them into the wetness between my thighs. He pushes them in a few times, then sticks them back in my mouth.

"Mmm," I sound around them before he pulls them out. All while I reach back to undo my bra and pull it off my body. "I've told you not to call me that."

Swiftly, I'm in his arms as he carries me to the bed and drops me unceremoniously onto it.

"Flip over."

I scramble onto my hands and knees. Before I'm even settled there, he's swatting me again. Light, but it still stings and makes me squirm.

A hand settles on my head and he pets me a few times, then winds the length in his fist.

"Brace yourself, baby."

Suddenly, he's everywhere. Pushing inside me, leaning over me, a hand on one breast as it tugs at my nipple, not so gently. Drew's so much bigger than me that he's nearly engulfing me, skin on skin everywhere. It's intoxicating.

He's moving inside me fast and hard. This isn't lovemaking. It's not even fucking. It's animalistic, raw, instinctive breeding. There is no thought, only feeling. Pure physical need to mate, to rut. He thrusts. I arch, pushing back at him with all the strength I have. Admittedly, it's draining fast.

My rhythm stutters, and he releases my hair to slap his palm on the burning flesh of my ass.

"Fuck, yes," I gasp.

"You like it? Tell me."

"I fucking love it," I say. "Your fat cock filling me up. I've missed it. I need it, Drew!"

"On your back," he snaps as he pulls all the way out of me.

I roll over and Drew drags me to the edge of the bed, pulling my legs straight up, my ankles resting on his shoulders as he stands.

"Those eyes never leave mine, you understand? I watch you shatter, and you watch me."

I nod in agreement, but as soon as he thrusts in, I blink long at the unfamiliar sensation the position brings.

"Eyes!"

I give them to him.

"It's me inside you, June. Me. Not him. This isn't one of your dreams, your fantasies. It's me," he chants as he pounds into me. Long, powerful strokes. It feels amazing. My body is ecstatic, but his mouth inflames my bitterness.

"Who is it you see? Who are you fucking, Drew?" I sneer. "Me? Her? Or some other nameless bitch?"

His fingers shove back into my mouth, thrusting in time with his cock. Faster and faster.

"You. I told you. It's always you. It's your perfect face I see, those beautiful eyes staring back at me. That love you've always rained down on me, even though I never deserved any of it. It's your heavy tits bouncing in my face, your tight pussy choking my cock. Your heart beating in my ears," he says breathlessly. Sweat rolls down from his brow. "Yours is the only voice that calls my name, that screams in pleasure as you explode around me. It's always fucking you."

Now it's him missing a beat as his body reaches its limit. I'm following closely behind with the swirl of his words in the air, the sight of his abdomen rippling uncontrollably, and the swelling of his already enormous shaft deep inside me.

And with the anger everything he says still brings out in me.

I clamp my teeth down on his fingers and break apart into a million shards of glass. My hands curl into the bedding and my legs tighten around his neck as my body convulses around him and brings him along for the ride.

He shouts my name, mine—not hers—as he fills me.

We're in the shower a short time later and I'm not even sure how we got here through the daze of sexual bliss. Drew lathers shampoo into my hair while he presses soft kisses all over my face. Everything has blurred edges as the water runs over my eyes. I keep them open. I don't want to miss the emotion playing over his facial features.

He gently tips my head back into the stream, rinsing out all the suds. Still, I don't look away. I trust him to keep it from my eyes.

He's good at that, after all.

"Say something," he whispers as he starts to massage conditioner onto my scalp.

"You still held back. Why?"

Pain bursts in his eyes, but he doesn't look away, either.

"It was your first time. Besides, if you saw your ass right now, you might not be saying that."

I push my fingers into my buttocks, feeling the soreness. Tomorrow won't be comfortable.

"I like that," I say with a small smile. "I liked it all."

"Nothing scared you?"

"No. It was tame compared to what I've imagined, to what I've fantasized." I pump some body wash into my hands and begin cleaning him as he's doing to me.

"Do you want to tell me about these fantasies?"

"Do you want to hear about them?" I counter.

"Fillmore told me I should focus more on what you want sexually. To find out where our desires meet and where they diverge. I think she's right." His thumbs massage the underside of my breasts, not cleaning me anymore, just touching. Like he always used to do. I've missed that the most.

"You've been talking to her about a lot of things, haven't you?"

"I told you I'd put the work in. I am." He nods. "Tell me what you dream about."

"Okay, but you can't get mad."

"Can't I?" he asks, standing taller. A move to intimidate. He forgets I'm feeling mischievous tonight.

"I dream of being tied up, tied down. Held down. Dominated. While you fuck me," I say, standing up on my tippy toes so I can get right in his face. "And another man shoves his dick in my mouth."

Drew's nostrils flare with rage, but I feel the effect my words have on him, evident in his thickening cock pushing against my thigh. He's hard again, ready for another round of whatever we just finished.

Again, it wasn't making love. I'd call it something close to a hate fuck, if I were obliged to examine it. I'll save that for therapy.

"Turn around," Drew says, deceptively sweet.

I give his chin a small bite before I do as I'm told.

"Hands against the wall," he directs as he lifts one of my legs to place my foot on the rim of the tub.

When he thrusts inside of me, it's without warning and so hard I lose my breath.

"Oh, fuck." I sigh.

He hammers with impressive speed, especially considering his stamina must be drained after round one. He reaches his left hand up to tangle his fingers into mine against the slippery tile of the shower. His other arm snakes through my breasts, his hand clasping my throat.

"That will never happen," Drew draws out the words, timing them with his thrusting. "Anything you want, Junie. I'll give you anything and everything. Except another man."

I hum, arching into him. "That hardly seems fair."

"Fuck fair," he growls in my ear and tightens the hand on my neck, making it harder to speak.

I don't relent in my efforts. Drew deserves to be pissed off. He deserves to hear these things. He deserves the regret and guilt he's bound to feel.

"So, if I want two men, or three, in me at once, I should go to a sex club?"

Drew's whole body tightens around mine, stealing more breath by both the grip on my throat and the force of his body thrashing into mine. Drew's thumb rubs back and forth on my scar. I recognize it, but it doesn't cause distress. His breathing stutters after a handful more thrusts and the touch at my neck moves to my clit. His fingers squeeze mine and his teeth gently pull at the lobe of my ear, pushing me to orgasm.

I cry out hoarsely.

"Fuck, baby, fuck," he grunts in my ear as he, too, finds release. So easily we've been together in that tonight, unlike ever before, in sync. One.

If only we'd always been.

The water cools, and I shiver. Drew reaches to shut it off, then grabs a towel from the hook just outside the shower door and wraps me in it. He doesn't bother drying himself, just lifts me into his arms and takes me to my bed.

He doesn't say a word as he pulls back the covers and tucks me in, nor when he walks around to the other side and crawls in himself. Ignoring the fact that I never agreed to sleeping in the same bed, he pulls me onto his damp chest.

"There will be no two other men," he says as he nuzzles into my hair. That's going to be a tangled mess in the morning.

"Maybe you should decide that after you talk to Fillmore again and figure out why the idea of it turned you on so much."

"Go to fucking sleep," he growls.

And sleep I do, with a wicked smile on my face.

CHAPTER 20
Drew

I wake up alone the following morning. That's not unusual after the season ends. I have a few more hours to spare now. The first few days are always slightly lazier mornings. The suit I wore yesterday is thrown haphazardly upon a chair, but the shirt is missing, and June's silky robe is still there.

Such a small detail, but the idea that she'd rather be wrapped up in my shirt than her own clothing feels like a monumental step.

June is plating food when I find her in the kitchen. That's... new. I'm about to ask her about it when my phone dings from where it's charging on the counter.

LORE:

This isn't fair.

I sigh, as another one pops up.

LORE:

You know what I've been through. Please.

I ignore them, as I've been doing for weeks now, and turn my focus back on June.

"What are you doing?"

"I made breakfast." She shrugs, handing me a plate.

"This looks edible."

"I learned a few things living alone."

"How many eggs did you char before you figured it out?"

"Quite a few, asshole."

I laugh but thank her and kiss the tip of her nose before sitting down at the breakfast bar to eat. She pushes salt, pepper, and my favorite creole seasoning over to me.

"I still haven't perfected that part... so they're bland."

"You did good," I say after I take a bite, and she visibly preens at my validation.

It makes my cock thicken, but that's not in my plans for today, so I tamp that shit down.

"Have you looked at the house yet?" I ask.

I mean the house in the Garden District. She told me she hadn't gone in, but never told me why. I never asked. Until now. Figured she'd tell me when she was ready, but my patience only stretches so far. I want to know that she loves it as much as I imagined she would.

What I want to know is if it's the house she can see us grow old in. Because I can see it. I do see it.

"No."

"Do you want to talk about why?"

Another text alert dings. I reach over and open the messages but quickly swipe them away.

"No. I'd like to talk about that," she answers, nodding toward my phone. There's a tension around her eyes that I know is my fault. I'll do anything to make it go away.

"What about that, specifically?"

"What has she been through, and what's so unfair?"

"You saw, huh?"

She gives a small tip of her chin in affirmation but won't meet my eyes.

"She's upset that I've placed distance between us. She wants to remain friends. I think that's a bad idea. For several reasons." I take a final bite and move to place my empty plate in the dishwasher.

"Because you can't trust yourself around her." She states it, not questions it. Fuck, that hurts. My back is still to her when my shoulders sag under the weight of her comment.

"No, June. I trust myself completely with her or any other woman. You can trust that too, when you're ready. When I've proven it. It sucks ass that you think so little of me these days." I turn to her. "I've come to understand that Lorelai and I used each other as crutches. Or excuses. Scapegoats, I guess. It's as unhealthy for her as it was for me. I'm better now, but she won't be if I continue to play that role in her life, even in a non-sexual way."

"Makes sense," she says before finishing off her coffee and heading for a refill. "What's she been through that makes her think you'd be sympathetic to her?"

"I don't think that's my story to tell."

June's expression shifts from thoughtful to pained. I rush to continue before this turns into another misunderstanding between us.

"It doesn't have anything to do with me. It's something that happened a long time ago, when she was a kid. I'd tell you if it had any bearing on either you or me. I swear," I say, taking the mug from her and refilling it myself. "She's got deep-seated issues from her youth and she's still entangled in it somewhat. I've helped her in the past, financially, to untangle some of it. I'll continue giving to an organization that helps, but I've cut ties to Lorelai. Fully."

"It's that bad?" June asks. Not defensively, but in concern. Worried about the woman who came between us.

Fuck, she's amazing.

"It is. I'll continue to help those who need it, through the charity. I don't need to have contact with Lorelai for that. Look, I'll block her right now. I don't want you to worry about this." My involvement in Giving Hope was substantial when Lorelai first told me of her past and the problems she was still facing. They once asked me to be a board member. I declined, but we still have a close working relationship, and they keep me apprised of the work they're doing.

June knows about my charity work. She even works alongside me. She doesn't know that this one become a pet project due to Lorelai, though. Again, it doesn't feel like my story to tell. Even though I trust June with it, I know she'd never tell anyone. It's not about that, I just don't like telling other people's trauma.

"Okay?" I ask, because I don't want her to feel like I'm withholding for my benefit or that I'm protecting Lorelai above and beyond how I would protect anyone's life story.

"Okay." June nods, content with my explanation.

"What time is your flight?" I ask, sitting next to her.

"Ten-thirty, taking the red-eye."

"Then I have you for the entire day." I let a wide smile take over my face.

"What have you got in mind?" she asks, eyes narrowing in suspicion.

"Groceries."

"I'm sorry, what?" she asks, laughing, obviously taken by surprise at my mundane suggestion.

"Let's go get some groceries. Your mom sent me her cookie recipes. I want to bake some today. With you."

Shock replaces the surprise. Janet guards her cookie recipes like they're the Holy Grail.

"How in the hell did you finagle those out of her?"

"It only came after hours and hours of scolding and lecturing. She even cussed at me. Pretty sure that was the key to her giving in," I answer sheepishly. Truth is, I talk to Janet every few days, at a minimum. We've always been close. She's the only mother I've ever known. Lately, she checks in on me as often as she does June. She worries about us. Honestly, it feels good. Feels like I have a parent for the first time in my life. It took some work to repair her broken faith in me, though. She trusted me to take care of the most precious thing in her life and I fucked that up. Janet made sure to let me know her feelings on that.

I hadn't realized how much my mother's death and my father's lack of concern for me had molded who I became. Funny how easily we lie to ourselves so we don't have to face our own pains. Dr. Fillmore has pushed me not only to evaluate those pains, but to face them, heal them, and move on from them.

I no longer hate my father for ignoring me until he figured out a way he could use me to his benefit. That doesn't mean I'll ever let him be part of my life again, but I understand now that he had his own issues he never dealt with.

My mother's death didn't just leave him lonely and heartbroken. Her cancer treatment nearly bankrupted us. My father worked tireless hours to keep our house, and any spare time he had was spent entertaining a revolving door of cheap women. I hated coming home to that, night after night. He treated them like they were worthless, and they never stuck around for more than a few weeks before he'd switch them out with a newer version.

It's hard to admit that I did that same thing to women, to a lesser extent. I wasn't cruel to the women I fucked in college. I treated them well during the short time I had them. I never made promises. I didn't give gifts. I fucked them, sometimes I fed them, then I moved the fuck on. Making it clear they didn't mean anything more to me than a place to get off.

It's a shitty way to treat another human. I assumed Lorelai knew that and was treating me the same. Now, I'm not so sure.

"All deserved." June laughs. I nod in agreement. "You must be feeling awfully brave today, offering to bake with me."

"A night spent inside you will do that to a man." I lean into her as I say it. She narrows her eyes in warning, a reminder to us both that we're still not an 'us,' despite our actions last night. "Come on, Junie, bake with me?"

That's exactly how we spend the day. By the time I have to take her to the airport, there are roughly eight dozen of various cookies scattered around the kitchen. That's not including the ones she completely fucked up, but that's another story altogether. I pack some up for her to take home and some for Leighton, then box some up to deliver to Reed.

I reflect on our day as I drive her to the airport. I think she does the same, since she sits so quietly next to me. It was a nice day without all our issues muddying everything up. We had playful fun the likes of which we haven't had since before I left for college. And while I flirted all day, I never took it very far. There were kisses pressed on the top of her head, her forehead, and what seems to be my new favorite spot—the tip of her nose. Each one light and sweet.

It was motherfucking torture. But I think she appreciated it.

"I should be able to get out of here in the next week or two. I have a few meetings and pressers, then I'll get the house closed up and head to New Orleans. I'll keep you posted on my timeline."

"Okay," she says.

"I can stay at Reed's, if you don't want me at your place. I'll understand."

"Reed's place doesn't have any furniture yet."

"No, but I can take care of that," I say easily. "I don't mind getting a room set up for your mom. I owe her that."

June scoffs. "How do you figure that?"

"She's taken care of me since I was eight. I owe her more than some bedroom furniture."

"Drew, you should talk to Fillmore about this. You don't owe her anything. You never have. Even if you did, buying her that duplex would have paid all your debts. And then some." She's always been concerned about the amount I spend on those I care about. June doesn't believe it's necessary. It's not. I know that. Also, I don't think she truly understands how fucking loaded we are. It's not a hardship for me to financially take care of those I love.

"I can bring it up, but I doubt I'll change my mind." There's no doubt. I won't change my mind.

"Speaking of… what in the world were you thinking giving me so much in those divorce papers?" This is a subject neither of us has broached since the day I gave them to her. Too unsure of the ultimate outcome to dive into those waters, we've pushed it aside.

"I made promises to you. I never meant to break any of them. I did, though, the biggest one. The rest… I'm keeping. No matter what."

"Drew," she starts, but I cut her off.

"We're not discussing it. The money is yours, whatever you decide." I've never needed much in life. Materialistically speaking. Wealth and status mean jack shit to me. Security does. I have more than enough invested to live off of the rest of my life. June's the same way. She spends such a small percentage of the money we have. I'd still give her the majority, though. She can use it as she pleases, and I'd keep only what I need.

"Hypothetically speaking," she starts, and I already know I'm not going to like the direction her brain is going. "If we were to split up, and you met someone else—"

"Never happening," I interrupt.

"But if it did," she persists. "And maybe you wanted to start a family. That would be much more difficult if you're giving me most of your earnings. You see that, don't you?"

"No, I don't see it. Because it's never happening." My fingers grip tight on the steering wheel. Thankfully, we're nearly to the airport because I'm quickly losing my shit here. "If you decide you want a divorce, you get what I laid out in those papers. I'm never remarrying anyone but you. Listen, I know my word means little to you, but fucking hear me, June. You are it for me. End of. There will never be another woman. There will never be another family. You are my family."

I know she's leaning toward trusting me again. Last night proved that, if nothing else. I won't push her on it. Society gives women enough as it is, calling women doormats for taking back their cheating husbands or boy-friends. Besides that old adage of once a cheater always a cheater. I get it. That happens a lot. Some of us can learn and evolve, however. I'm one of them. I'd never betray her again if she decided to give me a second chance. Fuck, I won't betray her again if she doesn't give me a second chance. I mean what I say. I'll never take another wife. There was never any girlfriend before her. There won't ever be one after her.

Regardless of what the paperwork says, in my heart, June will always be my wife.

Arriving at the airport, I exit the vehicle and grab her bag for her. Depositing it onto the curbside next to her, I move in close, invading her fragile personal bubble as I study her face. I stand on the street while she's on the curb, bringing her closer to eye level.

"My schedule is about to get crazy busy, but when you get down there, maybe we could continue with the dates," she suggests. "I… I think I want to start over."

I grasp her by the waist, easily picking her up and holding her to me. Burying my face in the crook of her neck. I still, holding on tightly, breath-ing her in, as she is me. I'm trembling, overwhelmed by her words, but my mouth grows into a smile on her skin. When I finally look at her, she's wearing one, too.

We're in this together.

"Thank you," I say. "For letting me try. For not shutting me out completely."

"I made promises, too. I'm trying my best not to lose sight of that," she says quietly. "For better or worse and all that." I set her back on her feet, then frame her face as I stare into her eyes. "We're fragile, Drew. We won't survive any more aftershocks. You understand? No more secrets, no more lies, no more surprises. You have got to talk to me."

"Fuck, I love you," I say on a sigh. "I'll never let you down again. I'm not saying this because I got caught. I'm saying it because I mean it. I'm not whole without you. I don't live without you. I'm never fucking that up again."

"I don't want to regret this, Drew. Please don't make me." Her voice shakes a little, the hurt still there. I can't imagine it ever going away. Not completely.

"You won't. I swear it." I hope she hears the confidence I feel.

She stretches up on her tiptoes to give me a quick kiss, then she turns and walks away. Taking my heart, my future with her. For the first time in too long, it doesn't feel like I'm dying as I watch her go.

I've had this growing idea since my conversation with June in Dallas. At first, it was just a niggling annoyance in the back of my head. Not niggling anymore. Now it's like a sledgehammer to my brain. There's only one way to get rid of it.

Taking a huge, calming breath that does nothing of the sort, I dial a number I wouldn't have thought I'd call in a million fucking years.

"Hello?"

"Anders. It's Drew McKenna."

"Is June all right?" he asks after a short pause. As much as it pisses me off that he's asking about June, admittedly, I like that someone's been looking out for her.

"She's good, on a plane back to New Orleans."

"Why the call, McKenna?"

"I need the truth, man. June told me what you said about Lorelai and that night in college. I think I'm finally ready to hear you."

Fillmore and I have discussed my need for this conversation a lot over the past few sessions. June doesn't have a warped sense of character. In fact, she's overly cautious with new people because of her past. That's enough to tell me that the person I've been thinking Noah is all this time is not who he is. It's become clear to me that I've suppressed seeing him clearly because of what that makes me in his life. A possible villain, a duped pawn at the least. Sure, he fucked up, but I was the asshole Lorelai used to take him down.

I don't understand why, and I doubt Noah can shed much light on that. I do know that Noah and I need to find some common ground and I need to be the one to offer that olive branch. June won't accept anything less; she doesn't deserve anything less.

"Drew. You know what happened. I told you the truth when you confronted me about it. I'm not a liar. Ever."

"Fuck. I'm inclined to believe you," I say, and it isn't a lie. The more I've analyzed it, the more Lorelai has become a volatile thorn in my side, the more I know it's true.

"You should. It doesn't absolve me of the role I played in hurting her, but I didn't do it with intent. I was in love with her. Causing her pain wasn't in my DNA."

I'm not thrilled about the role I played in our sordid history either.

"Why'd she do it?"

"You'd have to ask her, though I don't know if she'd give a straight answer. I assume she saw something in you she wanted, and she found a way to get it. Seems like she succeeded, at least somewhat," he answers, no lack of snark in his tone.

"Did she ever tell you about her childhood?"

There's another long pause. I don't know if he's trying to remember the things Lorelai told him back then, or if he knows the atrocities and is envisioning them. I can't say.

"She was always very vague about her past. She'd shut down if I pressed her on it. She told you, I take it."

"Yeah. It's partly why… anyway, it wasn't a good situation. I've cut her out of my life now. And I'm sorry for any role I played, unwittingly or otherwise, back then. It's one of the reasons I'm calling you."

"Apology accepted. You have the truth. What else do you need from me, McKenna?" Noah's always been a smug shit, so I expect this from him. There's more fuel to it now, though. Like he knows I know about his intimacy with June and is happy to flash it in my face.

"I'd like to talk about my wife," I say, trying not to grind my teeth to nubs. There isn't a bone in my body that wants to have this conversation, but my heart says I need it. Fillmore agrees. So, here we fucking are.

"Ask."

I swear this bastard is psychic.

"Are you in love with her?"

"Is it your business if I am?"

"I've said it before, and it hasn't changed. Everything about June is my business," I say. "I wouldn't blame you if you are. She's perfect. I don't know how every man who meets her doesn't fall at her feet. We're trying again. Officially. What I'm asking is if you and I are going to have a problem when I get down there."

"June wants this?"

"I'm not pushing her. June has control of where we go from here and this was her decision."

"Then no, we won't have issues. But you need to know that I won't stop being her friend," Noah says.

I'm feeling something like respect. After hating him for so long, it's a tough adjustment.

"I wouldn't expect you to stop. I owe you a thank you, Noah. Not just for this, but for keeping an eye out for her since you've been working together. I hate to admit it, but I think your friendship has done her a world of good. I really do appreciate that."

"She's special, Drew. Don't take it for granted again. For the record, I'm not in love with your wife."

"You like her enough to have naked play dates with her, though." June would call this our big dick energy taking over.

It is what it is.

Noah laughs. "A time or two, yeah. Not sure you get to judge, though."

"I'm not. From here on out, that shit stops. Clothes stay on when you're alone with my wife."

"Fair enough. From now on, we'll only take our clothes off when you are there, too."

Damn these two for continually putting that image in my head.

CHAPTER 21

June

Every day I wake up to a call from Drew and fall asleep just after another one. We're still on tentative footing, of course, but we're so much better at communicating since he dropped me off at the airport.

Our morning talks typically involve going over our daily schedules. It gives us both peace of mind knowing where the other will be, what we'll be doing, and with whom. In our first conversation after I returned to New Orleans, Drew requested that I not have intimacy with Noah again.

"You have an emotional and physical connection with him. I'm not asking you not to be his friend. I won't stand in the way of that. I even encourage it. Only that you come to me for what you've been going to him for," he'd said. Admittedly, it burned when he said it. Of course I wouldn't be having any more sexy time conversations with Noah now that Drew and I were making a concerted effort to work through our marital problems.

I let that go when I quickly realized this was Drew being vulnerable. Something I had asked him to be with me, so it wasn't very fair for me to get upset when he did just that.

This morning I'm up earlier than normal, giving me plenty of time to brew a pot of coffee and sit with it out on the balcony while I wait for his call. He sets an alarm to wake up much before he needs to just so he can be the first to greet me each day.

"Good morning, baby," he says when I answer his call.

"Hi. Did you sleep well?"

"Well enough, I guess. How about you?"

"Fine. Got a little cold, though. I woke up in the middle of the night and had to grab another blanket," I answer.

"Not too much longer and I'll be there to keep you warm." There's a pause then, because we haven't spoken about whether Drew will be staying with me when he gets to town or not. The subject hasn't come up, though we've talked about how much more he needs to accomplish at home before he can leave.

"I'm looking forward to it." There. That's done. A huge olive branch, tree more like, extended from me to him. He accepts with an audible sound of pure relief.

"There's something I thought about last night, and I wanted to run it by you."

"Okay."

"I was thinking I could put the house on the market before I fly out."

This is another subject we haven't discussed. Honestly, I haven't considered selling our Seattle suburbs house.

"I wasn't expecting that."

"I'm sure. I know you hate the house. I get it. I don't love it either. Maybe now is the time to find you something you can love."

"I… I don't think I want that." The answer is a shock for us both, I'm sure.

"No?"

"No. You have three years left on your contract. With that and everything we're going through, it doesn't feel right to add that move onto our plates," I say. "Besides, we have plenty of other houses that I love."

I adore that he's making me the offer, but it's just a house. I can make a better effort to make it our home during the season.

"You sure, June? We can make it happen. And you haven't seen the other houses yet."

"I'll see them when the time is right. Knowing you bought them because you knew I loved them tells me enough. I'm sure. If you're there, it's home and that's enough for me."

"If you change your mind, you tell me."

"I will," I confirm. "You have that interview tomorrow, yeah?"

"Yeah, last one on the schedule. Thank fuck. Almost have my calendar cleared. I'm still trying to drag Reed down with me. He's digging his feet in, though. Acting pretty strangely about it all."

I've noticed that, too. He's never been one to stay when Drew and I go.

"I overheard him and Love that day at their duplex. Something about them kissing before. I think his refusal has something to do with her."

"They've kissed?"

"Apparently. Neither has ever said anything to me about it."

"Weird."

"Yeah."

"Hmm, maybe I can squeeze it out of him. I'll let you go get ready for your day. Be ready soon, though, I'm coming for you."

"You fucking better be," I say with a grin.

Our morning talks are always lighthearted and easy. Evening ones, not so much. We tend to hold the heavier topics for those calls. There have been several conversations about what Drew is working through with therapy. A lot of it has to do with his father. They don't speak anymore, haven't since shortly after Drew was drafted into the NFL.

Growing up, Drew's father only ever saw him as a reminder of his dead wife. She was diagnosed with stage three, non-operable colon cancer when Drew was still a baby. Drew wasn't even four years old when she died. His father held on to a mountain of anger over it and generally treated his son with little love or affection. Drew was a nuisance until he figured out that his only child may be a cash cow.

When Drew got his first contract, he paid his dad to get out of his life. Like so many other aspects of his life, he shut away the hurt his father caused him. He's dealing with it now and I couldn't be prouder of him for it. It's long overdue.

He's also coming to grips with the idea that the way his father treated women, as disposable tools to get him off, impacted the way he saw women, too. With the exception of me. I was never disposable to Drew. That doesn't mean he knew how to treat me properly, however.

The effort is being made now. Drew may be a late bloomer in those regards, but I can't fault him for how hard he's trying to grow as a man and to make amends to me.

I made the mistake of cruising social media yesterday and reading through a multitude of strangers' commentary on my marriage. Not surprisingly, most of the male keyboard warriors didn't have any problem with me taking Drew back. A large portion didn't care at all about his cheating. The women were an entirely different story. No apology could ever be enough in their eyes. He'll never change. Once a cheater always a cheater, and the like.

Refusal to believe all that might be my downfall in the future. Except, isn't that what we expect of human beings? To learn, to change, to evolve. I don't believe that people must accept an apology, once given. Every situation is different. However, if it's sincere, from the heart, and comes with the best intentions… I want to try. And so, I have.

Getting ready for the day is done with care. Noah, the production crew, and I will be spending the day at the stadium. A full tour is on the schedule, as well as a few interviews with key event planners and the chef in charge of all things food. That will be my favorite part, of course.

It will be a long day followed by a fun night. The crew has deemed we go out once a week for karaoke. Evidently, Sally is a showstopper. What they don't know is that karaoke was Leighton and my go-to pastime in college. I've invited her to tag along. We're both abnormally excited about it.

Noah said there won't be time to stop home between shooting, dinner with the Saints' executives, and extracurricular events. I dress in black leatherette leggings and pair it with layers. Silky, lace camisole first, followed by a crisp white button-up and dark green blazer. I'll wear sensible flats for the tour and throw some fuck-me heels in my handbag for tonight.

As anticipated, the day is long. Noah deceived me when he said we'd be having dinner with team higher-ups. It was with the owner. Just her and the two of us. I know plenty of wealthy people due to Drew's career, but it isn't often you get to sit down at an intimate dinner with a successful female billionaire.

Dinner was fabulous. The conversation was more valuable than I can explain. She is a wealth of knowledge for me since her background is in interior design and has renovated more properties than I can ever dream of.

She also had plenty of ghost stories to pass along and gave me a few numbers of contractors she fully trusts.

"Is Leighton meeting us there?" Noah asks on our drive from dinner to 'the world's most famous shithole karaoke bar.' His words.

"Yep, she's probably already there. She's very excited."

"Right. Watered down whiskey out of plastic cups and your feet sticking to the floor is definitely something to be enthusiastic about," he snarks.

"Come on, Noah, loosen up just this once. I'll even let you sing a duet with me," I singsong to him.

"No."

I laugh at his stern expression.

"I'll find a way to get you out of that tie and up on that stage if it's the last thing I do."

"No."

This line of discussion continues until we reach our destination in the French Quarter. As expected, when we enter the bar, Leighton is already up on stage.

She's belting out "Ex's and Oh's" by Elle King as if the song was written just for her.

"Damn, she's good," Noah says.

"Oh, honey, this is nothing." I make a path to a table where Sally is waving at us. Mark and Phil, our two cameramen, are with her. Phil has a smaller handheld camera and is filming the stage as I sit.

"Thought I'd catch some shots for social media," he says with a smile. "Your friend is fantastic. She's going to give our Sally a run for the crown."

"Bite your tongue, Phil." Sally laughs good-naturedly.

"Get that girl on a stage and she'll be there all night. I'm glad it's not too crowded in here tonight. Otherwise, she'd be pouting until she got another chance at the mic."

"Oh, she's a lady after my own heart," Sally says.

A waitress comes by, and I order a Hurricane, not caring that it comes in a garishly large and colorful plastic cup.

"Beer. In a fucking glass bottle," Noah grunts to her.

She looks taken aback, so I clarify that he likes IPAs and she scurries off to grab our drinks just as Leighton makes it back to the table.

"Love," she chimes, giving me a hug. "Why are you dressed like Noah?"

Noah looks affronted by the question, but she's not wrong. I strip off the blazer and button-up. The shoes were switched out in the car.

"Better?" I ask.

"God, so much better, you sexy beast." She gives me a hug. "I've already put us down for you know what."

"Which song?"

"The selection is limited, but they had Larry's favorite."

"Perfect."

The others at the table look confused.

"ABBA," I inform them.

"Why?" Noah asks in his disgruntled tone and with a raised eyebrow.

Phil, the oldest of our group, grins widely. "Solid choice, ladies."

"Why, thank you, good sir," Leighton says, giving him a quick curtsy.

"Leighton's dad has a soft spot for the Swedish foursome. We always sing at least one of their songs in tribute."

"Why?" Noah asks again.

"Good grief, Dapper Dan, you're an awful grump tonight," Leighton tells him.

"Who's ABBA?" Mark asks. He's the youngest in the group, barely over the legal age for drinking. I'm guessing he didn't have older family members that exposed him to the same array of music that Leighton and I did. He'll be getting an education tonight.

Sally gets called to the stage as our drinks arrive. Noah downs most of his bottle in one long swig and waves to the waitress for another.

Good, maybe he'll loosen up if he gets drunk.

"Fat Bottomed Girls" starts playing as Sally takes the stage. Queen was a favorite of my grandfather's. My mom played them often during my youth, anytime she was feeling particularly nostalgic about her childhood. This song always makes me happy, and I sing along gleefully while I drink my too sweet hurricane.

Phil's the next of our group to get called. His choice is "Save a Horse, Ride a Cowboy" with incredibly infectious enthusiasm. The growing crowd loves him. By the time Love and I are up for ABBA, we're all on our way to tipsy. Even Noah has eased the stick in his ass out an inch or two. A few times, I've even spied him smirking. He turns it back into a frown when he sees I've caught him, but he winks each time, too.

I'm coming to learn Noah likes his harmless games. I indulge them, as I kind of like them as well. He keeps it entertaining.

Leighton is on to Noah too, so when we head toward the stage, she grabs his hand and leads him along.

"I'm not singing ABBA with you two," he protests.

"Eww, Noah. You are not on ABBA karaoke friendship level with us yet. You're just the prop," she coos back at him.

I just shrug and smile.

On stage, she pulls a chair to the center and none too gently pushes Noah down in it as "Take a Chance on Me" begins.

We sing as we play up our attention to Noah, who keeps up his cantankerous pageant for the first half of the song. He shows his playful side for the rest of it, though, smiling, singing along here and there, even holding our hands as we dance around his seated form.

By the time we leave the stage, he's having as good of a time as the rest of us and he walks us back to the table with his arms around Leighton's and my shoulders.

"I'm not leaving here tonight until you sing a duet with me," I demand of him.

"Don't push your luck," he says, but the smirk tells me I have a decent chance.

The more alcohol we consume, the more fun the song selections. Us three ladies give a rendition of Beastie Boys' "She's Crafty." We hack it, but the crowd participation made up for it. Phil trades his country songs for rock the likes of Bon Jovi and Journey.

Leighton and Sally keep a constant one-up of each other with R&B and rap. Leighton's rendition of Warren G's "Regulate" was such a hit that a handful of strangers from the crowd rushed up to finish the song with her. They then joined our table after buying us all a round of Jell-O shots.

Mark sticks to Bruno Mars and The Weekend. He's horrible at each, but nobody cares.

I never do get Noah to agree to a duet, the rat bastard. There's always next week.

CHAPTER 22

June

"Good morning," I mumble when I answer Drew's call the following morning.

"You don't sound as if it's a good morning." He keeps his laughter soft, and my throbbing temples mentally thank him for it.

"Just a wee hungover. Not too awful." I sit up to be sure that's not exactly a lie.

"Looks like you had a good time."

"Looks? Did I send you videos?" I wasn't that drunk. I'd think I would remember if I'd sent those. We did text back and forth all night, since we were missing our evening call.

"No, baby, you didn't send me any." He chuckles. "It was livestreamed by many spectators, however."

"Oh, fuck. How bad is it?"

"Not bad. Leighton's rendition of 'Baby Got Back' is going viral. Helps when it gets retweeted by the artist himself and he scores you a perfect ten for white girl twerking…his words."

"Oh, God. She's going to love that."

"She'll never shut up about it." He laughs. "You singing 'I'm Not The Only One' is getting a fair amount of attention as well."

Oof.

"You know I love that song. It wasn't meant as any sort of attack on you." That's the honest truth. Of course, the general public will read more into it than that. Whatever. Fair play and all that nonsense.

"Don't even worry about it. I'm getting raked over the coals, which I fully deserve. You, on the other hand, look amazing. A fiercely gorgeous warrior. Everyone agrees."

"I doubt that."

"Most everyone, anyway. You're headed to a high school today, right?"

"Mmhm, one of the best around, apparently. Catholic, in Baton Rouge. Sounds like they have several starters coming up that they expect to garner attention from the biggest schools. It's Noah's thing. I'm just there for window dressing."

"You say that, but I know you. You'll be in tears by how excited they are to meet a former NFL star," he says. He's right. I'm a sucker for that sappy shit.

"Truth. I can't help it. It's heartbreaking how many of these kids have so little in their lives outside of football. You know exactly how that is." I sigh.

"I do, sort of. I at least had food on the table, and I had your family."

"I'm glad you and Reed found each other when you did. When do you get here?" I ask.

"Miss me, do you?"

"I just like to know your schedule."

It's a lie, of course. He knows it as well as I do.

I miss waking up to his arm draped over me. The feel of his fingers play-ing in my hair when he's sitting next to me. I miss being there when he walks through the door at the end of his day, a smile brightening his face when he sees me. The lazy conversations about nothing at all important while tangled together on the couch, streaming creepy documentaries. More than any-thing, I miss having meals with him. As busy as my schedule has become, I still end up eating alone more than I ever have before. I'm comfortable with my own company usually. Though, there is something lonely about eating most of your meals by yourself.

"Soon, Junie."

I ride with Noah to Baton Rouge. The drive takes longer than it should due to traffic.

"How are things, my sweet June?"

"I think they're going pretty okay," I answer.

"What does pretty okay mean, exactly?" Amusement tickles his voice. He likes to tease me by saying I speak like I'm uneducated. He's lucky I like him.

"It means I'm content with where I'm at in the moment, even if I'm still feeling the afterburn of betrayal and am insecure about the direction my marriage may be heading. Is that a better answer for you, Dr. Anders?"

"That's much better than pretty okay. You know I only press because I care about you for some ungodly reason, right?"

Noah has quickly become a close confidant, an invaluable friend. He's tender with me when I don't know I need it and pushes me when I need it the most. He would have made a great therapist. Selfishly, I'm glad he didn't go that route because I would've probably never met him.

"Of course you do. I'm fabulous."

"You have a fabulously large ego," he deadpans.

I mock gasp at him.

"It's nice to see. You were a fractured thing that night we had dinner at Brennan's. You've come a long way, lady."

"In large part, thanks to you. I owe you, Noah." Sincerity bleeds out with the words.

"You owe me nothing. You accomplished it on your own."

He may not think he's been a part of my growth, and maybe he's right. I'll always feel it, no matter what. Noah could ask me for nearly anything and I'd find it hard to deny him.

By the time we get to the school, the special afternoon practice is in full swing. They're putting on a show just for us. It's cute. They're amped by the idea that they'll be featured during half time of the AFC championship game. It's a big deal. Based on the production they're putting on... they know it.

The field is a sea of black helmets and orange jerseys as the boys all run drills. On the sidelines, the cheerleaders surreptitiously eye Noah. Their giggles reach our ears even as they try to stifle them behind their hands.

He's handsome as hell. I can't fault them. Turning to tease Noah, I spy a slight pink painting his cheeks.

"Noah Anders, are you blushing?" I whisper-shout.

"Shut up, June. It's embarrassing," he responds flatly.

My laughter mixes in the air with the girls wearing high ponytails and oversized bows, as we draw closer to the field.

"Jesus, what do they feed kids these days? Drew's a giant and even he wasn't this big in high school," I say, eyeing the forms that are getting larger the closer we get.

"You think by the time we're on death's door, teenage boys will be averaging closer to seven feet tall?" Noah asks. He's only half joking.

"At this rate, I wouldn't be surprised. I feel like Tinkerbell walking into the Lost Boys camp," I answer. "Oh, will you be my Slightly?"

"I don't know what the fuck that is, but I assure you, nothing about me is slight," he replies in a hushed voice, his face stern, which only makes my grin wider.

The crew arrives and gets set up. Phil starts filming various players on the field, while Mark sets up on the side where Noah and I cycle through players one by one. As predicted, many of them get starstruck when they meet Noah, and I do my best to ease them into a casual conversation about themselves. Coaxing them with questions about their favorite music or food, things that aren't college or career orientated, helps them relax. That way, when Noah starts asking about football, they can form words to answer.

The star quarterback is next up. As he approaches, I can see we're not going to need any ice breakers with him. Chance Waters oozes confidence. Or maybe it's cockiness. That QB big dick energy… he has it.

"Hi, Chance, I'm June McKenna," I say as he takes his spot in front of the camera.

"Hey, yeah, I know who you are. I saw that video of you roasting your husband last night at karaoke."

Oh, God.

"You saw that, huh?"

He nods. "Yeah, it was brutal. He deserved it. You're too hot for him."

Chance's eyes roam me up and down. Suddenly, I'm no longer entertained by the attention given to Noah by the cheer squad. This kid is bold and I sure as hell hope he's not this cringy with every female he knows. Because eww…

"Uh, thank you, I guess," I stammer, wondering how on Earth I'm being hit on by a seventeen-year-old. "This is Noah Anders." I gesture to Noah, who's quietly smiling at my dismay.

"Hey, man," Chance greets him.

"Hello, Chance. It's my absolute pleasure to meet you," Noah says, amusement lacing his voice.

I step away while they chat, deciding to go chat up a few of the cheer-leaders. I'll be the first to admit that I spent a good portion of years looking at cheerleaders as vapid attention seekers. Partly because Drew dated, aka fucked, so many of them. That fact alone jaded me. But also, I had a hard time seeing what it could get you in life. I mean, there aren't lifelong careers as a professional cheerleader.

A documentary changed my mind, at least somewhat. The athleticism alone is impressive. The discipline and the dedication are also something to regard with respect. I may not fully understand it, but I no longer turn my nose up to it, and I enjoy watching some of their spectacular routines.

One of the girls sees me headed their way and makes a beeline for me. A couple others notice and follow her lead.

"Hi, Mrs. McKenna!" She bounces on the ball of her feet.

"Hi, you can call me June. What's your name?"

"I'm Noel Etienne. It's nice to meet you, June," she says shyly.

"That might just be the most beautiful name I've ever heard, Noel Etienne."

She whispers a bashful thank you before the two other girls catch up, and I introduce myself.

"Can y'all give us a cheer or two for the camera?" I ask, waving down Phil.

"Really?" Noel asks.

"Of course, we're not here just for the boys on the field."

Noel perks up once we're in range of the rest of the squad. Her entire demeanor changes. Her spine grows straighter, her shoulders dropping down and back. With a chin held high, she announces to the other members what routines they'll be running through.

She's so commanding, even I want to do what she says. Noel was so reserved a moment ago, and now she's ordering kids around like a drill sergeant.

They run through two routines, nothing at all like the basic cheers I expected. Nothing at all like what my high school cheerleaders performed. There are lifts, tosses, pyramids, and other things I don't know the words for. I hold my breath through some of it because, holy shit, are they high.

Thankfully, it's all pulled off with no mishaps and Phil says he's got the shots. The squad disperses, but I pull Noel aside.

"Do you want to hang out with me for a bit? It'd be nice to have a wing-woman while Noah's occupied with football things."

"I'd like that," she says like a quiet little mouse, no longer the take charge young woman who led a squad of twenty to perform death defying acts.

She follows me to a bench where we sit side by side.

"Have you always lived in Baton Rouge?"

"It's all I remember, but I was born in New Orleans." Her body folds in on itself, making her look smaller. "I was a few months old when Katrina hit. My dad, brother, and I evacuated. My mom was going to follow when work allowed."

Her words hang in the silence between us. The result of her mother staying is clear and my heart breaks for the poor thing.

"I'm sorry that happened to you, Noel," I tell her as I wrap an arm around her. "Is it just you three, or do you have other family in the area?"

"It's just us. We have family there still, but Dad never wanted to move back."

"I bet your dad's very proud of you. Your squad is amazing."

"He is." She beams. "He comes to watch me as often as he can. Dad says it's his favorite thing in the whole world. I'm not sure I believe—holy crap, is that Drew McKenna?"

What?

My sight bounces to where Noel's is trained and sure enough, it is Drew. He's not alone, however. A half-dozen other ridiculously enormous men stomp toward the field with him. Seems he's recruited some of his football buddies for this outing, their arms laden with pizza boxes and sports drinks.

"What the hell?"

"You didn't know he was coming?" she asks.

"Complete surprise," I answer, awed by the sight of him as he introduces himself to the coaches.

"He's so pretty," Noel says on a sigh. "Oh, sorry!"

"It's fine, he is," I agree on a laugh. "Do you want to meet him?"

"Yes! But don't let me make a fool of myself, okay?"

"Pinky swear." I hold my hand up for her to shake my little finger with hers.

Drew excuses himself from the crowd of players gathering around the newcomers when he sees me and Noel. Long, confident strides bring him straight to me. He doesn't slow until he's just inches away.

"Hi."

"How are you here?" I ask, still awed by it all. He didn't give any indication this morning that he'd be here today.

"I had just landed in New Orleans when I called you this morning. Asked the guys to come help me surprise you. And the team here." He takes a small step toward me. Without warning, I leap into his arms, knowing he'll catch me.

"Hi," I say to the soft, sensitive skin just below his ear.

"Missed you, Junie."

"Missed you, too."

Drew's face turns into mine, lips finding lips, tongues tangling. It's a steamy kiss and catcalls erupt all around us. He doesn't stop immediately, though. He waits a few more seconds before easing the intensity. I give an ultra-quick tug of his bottom lip, then let go so he can drop me to my feet.

"To be continued?" he asks. I nod in answer.

"Drew McKenna, this is Noel Etienne. Head tenacious cheerleader extraordinaire," I say, as I reach back to pull a shell-shocked Noel into our small huddle.

"Hey, Noel. It's nice to meet you."

"Hi. Hello." She's back to bouncing on her feet, her voice an octave higher.

"Do your girls want some pizza? There should be plenty. Why don't you go grab them? We'll introduce them to my crew." He tilts his head to where the rest of the squad is back to wide-eyed giggling.

Noel smiles widely and runs off at the same time Noah approaches.

"You trying to one-up me, McKenna?"

"Nah, Anders. Just couldn't wait any longer to see my wife," Drew answers, wrapping his arm around me. There's no animosity in either man's words, more teasing, if anything. As if they've come to some silent truce.

I look between them, back and forth, back and forth. Looking for an answer, something that explains. Neither gives me anything.

The hell?

My curiosity is interrupted when Noel and Chance come up beside me.

"Chance, this is Drew McKenna. Drew, this is Chance Waters. He's QB1." All her confidence is back. It makes me smile to see the strange bouts of bashfulness vanish once again.

"Hey, Chance. Nice to meet you. Maybe after lunch you can show me that arm," Drew says.

"I'd like that," Chance replies to Drew. To me, he says, "May I get you a plate, Ms. McKenna?"

Noah doesn't miss that the kid purposely didn't call me misses and chokes on a laugh, quickly walking away, while Drew's eyebrow rises in surprised amusement.

"Thank you, Chance, that would be nice. Maybe you could grab one for my new friend Noel as well."

Chance nods and runs off. I lower to the turf, crossing my legs, and pat the ground next to me in invitation for Noel to join. She and Drew both do. Her sitting directly in front of me, him sitting behind me and lifting me into his lap.

"Does QB1 have a crush on my wife?" He poses the question to Noel, resting his chin on my shoulder.

She smiles and nods, reaching down to adjust her knee socks as she gets comfortable. That's when I notice the scar she keeps hidden there. Just below the striped knitting is a puckered silver patch of skin. Her reaction to me makes more sense now.

I reach out, gently stilling her hand. Her eyes meet mine.

"If you ever want to talk about it, I'm here. I'll give you my number before I leave today. Okay?"

Tears pool in her dark eyes, but she smiles and nods slightly. Drew shifts my hair out of the way so he can place a gentle kiss on the scar decorating my neck. Noel's lips twitch, a hint of a smile playing on them.

"I hid mine for a long time, too. But you don't have to hide them from me. Not ever."

"Okay," she says after a big gulp of air. Once again, she sits up taller.

Chance plops down on the turf next to her, balancing three plates piled high with pizza. He hands the first to Noel, smart child, then the second to me. Drew immediately grabs a slice, taking a huge bite as he gives Chance a wink.

"Thanks, QB1," he says to the kid.

Males are stupid peacocks.

Conversation turns back to football. The younger players pepper the professionals with questions from every direction. Drew brought a well-rounded crew with him, covering both defense and offense. He even has Seattle's assistant coach in tow, a highlight for the school's staff.

"I can't believe you got them to come all the way here."

"It wasn't hard. Just said I needed help impressing my wife." His warm hand slides from my hip where it's been resting, to my belly. He pulls me back into him. "Did it work?"

"It worked. They seem awfully happy to have you all here."

"We're going around to a handful of other schools tomorrow. Ones with less resources," he tells me quietly.

I shouldn't be surprised. It's such a Drew thing to do. Yet, I am, because I know he's doing it as much for me as he is for the kids he hopes to help.

"Later, I'll show you how impressed I am by that."

Noel lets out a squeaky snicker, letting me know that I didn't say it as quietly as I thought I did. Chance's eyes widen, and Noah is once again fighting back laughter.

Oops.

Drew drives me back to New Orleans in the car he's rented, me in the passenger seat, dazedly happy with how the day turned out. I gave my number to Noel, as promised. Also getting hers in case she can't muster the nerve to contact me. I'll hit her up. Embracing my own skin took me far too long. Maybe we could help each other learn to be comfortable with our scars.

Drew and Noah both worked with Chance for a spell, as well as with the two backup quarterbacks. Drew, for his part, did not take it easy on the poor kid. He'll come out of it a better quarterback, sure, and he may have also learned to muzzle his charm on married women.

"What's on your schedule tomorrow?" His arm stretches between us so that his fingers can play with my hair. It's a familiar move, one he's done for the entirety of our 'romance.' It's always been comforting to me. There's doubt in it now because I still feel like my rush to take him back is only out of desire for that familiarity.

"Nothing. It's an off day for us. I plan on relaxing, maybe curling up and finishing the book I'm reading."

"You're welcome to come with us to the schools, if you want."

"No, you go do your thing," I say as casually as I can make it sound. In truth, I'm purposely putting that distance there, not wanting to get wrapped up in all things Drew. I need time for me, to just be June.

Decisions have been made. I said I wanted to give it another chance and I meant it. But, fuck, I'm scared. Terrified of falling into the same space we occupied before he started cheating on me.

Drew has to work on all the things that lead him to his choices. I need to work on being a strong enough person, a happy person, on my own. If I lose Drew, for any reason, I need to be able to stand on my own.

"Okay. Do you want to go on a date with me tomorrow night?"

"That would be nice," I answer as he pulls up to my condo building. "Are... are you staying here?"

"I didn't want to make any assumptions. It's your question to answer," he replies, turning to me. Looking for an indication of how I'm feeling.

"Total honesty?" I ask.

"We need that more than anything else." Grabbing my hand, he rubs his thumb back and forth, trying to ease my building tension.

"I want you to stay. I am ready to try again. Only, I'm so scared we'll fall back to how we were. I can't, Drew. I can't ever..." My throat closes on the words.

"Hey, hey, no. I won't let us ever go backward, okay? I promise," he pleads. His brow furrows in concern and my fingers reach to run over it, trying to smooth the worry away. His and mine both. I take a minute to examine him just as he is me. Hopeful anxiety bleeds out of his stare. Drew is just as scared as I am, only for different reasons.

As always, I want to take that stress away. Carry it on my own shoulders so his worries are less heavy. The boy with the rough home life, so out of his control. The man with all the turmoil buried away deeply. Our current situation is all his fault. That fact doesn't lessen my desire to help him deal with any of it.

I love him. Faults and all. I love him, forever.

"Stay."

Drew's reaction could have been anything. A smile may have taken over the full bottom half of his face, lighting up the dim cab like he was the sun. Or, he might have grabbed my face and kissed me like his life depended on it.

Instead, every muscle relaxes. His tension melts away, and the concern vanishes as his body slumps in relief.

"Fuck, June," he says as his head drops back. "I've never wanted to hear a word so much in my life."

"I can tell," I say, my mouth pulling into a small smile.

Drew shifts to look at me again, and after a quick scan of my face, his gaze stops at my lips. The attention makes them twitch.

"Don't move," he says, voice gruff as he exits the car.

The hatch at the back opens as he grabs his suitcase. Soft, excited curses float my way. It slams shut again and within seconds my door is open. Drew reaches over me, unbuckling my seat belt and pulling me into his arms.

Much like the last time he was here, I wrap myself around him, my face snuggled into his nape. Drew braces me with one arm, not that he needs to. I'm not letting go. He hauls me up to my condominium, pausing only for me to punch the entry code in, or to dig into my handbag to find my keys.

The door is kicked closed behind us, his baggage dropped haphazardly as he moves us to the kitchen. I'm placed on the countertop, bringing me more to eye level with my tall partner.

"I need to say something." He brushes a lock of my hair out of my face, removing the last barrier between his face and mine. His thumb lingers, stroking back and forth along my jaw. "I lost sight for a while. I let old voices in and made so many stupid choices that hurt you, the most important person in my whole life. More than that, I put too much burden on you. The heavy lifting of our relationship was all on you. I didn't give my fair share."

"I didn't do a very good job," I try to say, but his fingers move, softly pinching my lips to shut me up.

"Shh, I'm not done. I've got your back, June. Now and forever. I have you. I have us. I spent our whole lives seeing you as something I needed to protect. After Jonas, I would have burned the world down to keep you from harm. But that's never what you needed. You're strong enough to take care of yourself. All you needed was my support, and I failed you. Nothing like this will ever happen again, baby. I love you," he repeats the words as he assaults my face with little kisses.

"Drew, I did a bad job, too. I held on so tightly to my insecurities and didn't put forth the effort I should have." I shut my eyes, taking a moment to force back the dew growing in them.

"You did, June. The best way you knew how. So many of your insecurities are my fault. I never treated you how I should have. I exposed you to all the worst parts of the football lifestyle. You sat on the sidelines, always supporting me, while I treated you like a backup plan instead of my only plan, my happy ever after. I hope you can someday forgive me for all of it. I'll understand if you can't."

"I could still do better," I quietly argue.

"We'll do better together."

Drew stays attentive the rest of the night. Stripping us both down to nothing, leading me to the shower where he bathes me with tenderness and care. Like I'm fragile. As if I'm the most precious thing he's ever touched.

Afterward, he cocoons us naked in bed. Face to face, skin to skin. He just holds me, surveys me, touches me, gazes into my fucking soul. It's strange how close it makes me feel to him.

"Is it okay if we don't have sex tonight?" he asks. Hesitancy tinges his voice, the apprehension back on his brow.

"Why?" I wonder aloud.

"I don't want you to think that's all I'm about. Or that it's all I want from you. It's not. I want it all." His nose brushes mine. I tilt my face up to press a small kiss on the tip.

"I know you're more than a man who needs a particular type of sex. It wasn't me who reduced you to that." The implication of what I'm saying contorts his features. He was the one who did that, and Lorelai, too.

Instead of responding, he snuggles closer, one hand pressing into my ass so it shifts me closer to his hard length. Bodily instinct wants to grind into it, only my head stops me. If he wants a night without sex, I'll give it to him. I understand what he's trying to do, even if I don't find it necessary. It's not all about me. Any more than it's all about him, anyway. We're a team and we need to start acting like it again.

"Have you gone to the house yet?" he asks, changing the subject.

"No."

"Why not, baby?" Concern takes over his darkened eyes.

"We'll go together. I didn't want to enter it wondering if it was going to be just for me."

"We'll go together," he agrees and kisses my forehead. "Then I'll take you to all the others."

This is how we fall asleep. Wrapped up in each other, talking about everything and nothing. Enjoying being us for the first time in far too long.

CHAPTER 23
Drew

I wasn't expecting a naked June when I walked through the door. Well, naked except for that hot as hell harness Noah bought for her.

I hold my hand up, gesturing for my guest to wait at the door before pacing toward my wife. She's perfectly perched on a cushion, that juicy ass of hers snuggled between her feet. She's a quick learner.

Her pale skin shimmers just slightly, as if she took time to clean and polish herself. For me. I'm half hard at the idea of her primping to please me.

As I step in front of her, she doesn't raise her chin to look at me. Instead, she keeps it demurely cast down. I kneel and lift her face with a single finger.

"What is all this, baby?" She's not only prepared herself but also laden the coffee table with an array of finger foods. Charcuterie and a fruit tray with chocolate and cream—something she's always managed easily since it doesn't require cooking.

"Our date," she says with a sly smile. "Get naked and feed me."

I laugh, the sound low and wicked even to my own ears. Amused that she wants to control the situation, even when she doesn't know what it truly is.

"I had my own ideas for our date tonight. I was going to speak to you about it, but you've caught us by surprise."

"Us?" Her eyes widen in surprise and her chest rises and falls more rapidly.

Glancing over her shoulder, I nod. He comes to mimic my position behind June, kneeling to whisper in her ear. I watch her skin pebble under his words.

"Good evening, my sweet June."

A small gasp escapes her, her mouth parting so her tongue can come out and try to lick away the surprise.

In a million years you wouldn't have been able to convince me that I'd ever invite another man into my relationship with June. But, then again, when I finally manned up to my love for her and made her my wife, I would've never believed the idea that I'd be a lecherous cheater either.

Noah asked me yesterday if he could tag along to the school visits today, saying he misses being on the field, throwing the ball. I agreed because Noah and I need to be friends, for June's sake.

We've spoken every day since June flew back to New Orleans. At first, it was because I looked at him as an enemy for so long, it was best to keep him close.

Only, he's not an enemy. Our conversations have proved that. We spoke at length about June, about his time with her. I believe him when he says he loves her but is not in love with her. And when he says he's only had her best interests in mind since shortly after they met.

He admitted that their first meeting was planned with some ulterior motives in mind. That he would have fucked her out of pure spite if she hadn't been the type of person she is. If she'd had even one unkind bone inside of her.

It was him telling me about the night they spent together that truly let me see him as something more like an ally. Which, yeah, that's weird as fuck to say. But, while I wanted to kill him for having his hands on her, for being wrapped around her all night, he explained his motives.

He told me that she asked to be taken to a sex club. She's adorably naïve to that part of the kink world. She had no idea what she was asking. Not really. By that time, Noah knew her well enough to understand her intentions, perhaps better than she did since I've had her in such a state of confusion.

Then, we talked about June's fantasies and how I can give her a version without breaking our still fragile second chance, but maybe even strengthening it. Nothing about our marriage has been very conventional, after all.

While I've been actively working through all my bullshit, and I've given June a taste of what I like, I have not given her wants big enough importance. I've dismissed them, even. And that's a habit I need to break. I need to trust her as much as I need her to trust me.

So here I am. Trusting her to know what she wants and trusting her to know what our marriage can survive.

"Drew?" she asks breathlessly, looking up at me with hooded eyes.

"He'll leave right now, if you tell him to. Or we can discuss some ground rules. The ball is in your court, June," I say, but I reach forward and gently tweak one hard nipple. "I can see what your body is saying. Tell us what your head and heart are saying."

"I…" She exhales hard. "I don't want to have sex with Noah."

"I'll leave you to your night," Noah says, beginning to rise.

"No," June says. "I want you to stay." Her sight hasn't left mine. There is a flash of panic there. But I don't think she's afraid of what will happen if he stays. I think she's afraid if he leaves, she won't get another chance. I raise an eyebrow at her.

"So, he stays, but he doesn't get to fuck you."

She nods.

"Baby, that was never on the table. But I'm glad you agree," I say. I want to give her what she wants, hard as that is going to be. But come the fuck on. I am not able to watch anyone else fuck her.

Besides, this was a subject Noah and I touched on today. Even though June went to his place with the intention of fucking Noah, turned out she was nowhere near ready for it. He recognized it in her and when he brought it up, she broke down in tears, saying how much she'd wished he were me.

It broke my fucking heart as much as it made me happy to hear. I'll never fuck her over again, but I'd like to think that if she did ever decide to be done with my stupid ass, she'd have a shot at happiness again.

We're both so hopelessly entwined, neither of us can ever give up on the other.

"It wasn't?" She pouts a little and though that brings a smile to my face, it also makes me want to swat that ass of hers.

"No, June. Because we both know that once he sinks into your pretty pussy, he'll never want to leave. And I'm not having that," I tell her. Her tongue darts out again. "Does that make you wet? Knowing how much he wants to fuck you?"

"Yes," she whispers.

I reach over to the tray of fruit, artfully arranged in a rainbow of color, and pick up a slice of orange. Running a thumb down her bottom lip, I pull her mouth open slightly more and squeeze the citrus juice into her mouth. Then I rub the masticated fruit down her throat and over one pert nipple.

"I'm going to go clean up. Noah can feed you while I do that. Okay?" I ask, and she nods again. "Get her messy for me, man."

"My pleasure," Noah purrs as I walk down the hall to the bedroom, trying not to freak out that I just left my naked wife with another dude.

I trust her. I do. But this is a first on so many levels. The one bothering me the most is my lack of control over what is happening in the other room while I take the quickest shower in my life. I don't have a problem with Noah touching her. In fact, it excites me. It's just that I want to be there directing the action. Telling them both what to do.

Fuck, that makes me hard as hell.

Once done with the shower, I don't bother dressing. I've grown up in locker rooms with men; I'm not threatened by anybody's dick. Instead, I rummage through the room until I find her stash of toys. I owe Leighton another damned house for the stellar array of props she's set Junie up with. Grabbing the items I want, I walk back out to the living room.

Low voices waft down from the living room. I slow my pace to listen.

"I just don't want him to do anything he doesn't want to do."

"He wants this. He thinks this will make you stronger as a couple, June. I tend to agree. You need to experience some of the things you dream of. Drew needs to be the one who hands them to you."

He's not wrong. There are so many things, sexually, I've kept from her. So many I can fulfill for her on my own, and I will. This one needs assistance and I don't want her to ever wonder about it, to think that if she'd divorced me or delayed getting back together, that she could have explored her fantasies.

Plus, if ever there was a test of our trust, it's this.

Noah sits on the sofa, June still perched on the floor at his feet, as he feeds her bite-sized pieces of food with his fingers. Her tits are shiny from trails of fruit juice.

Perfect.

"Rules," I state as I walk up behind her. "Do you have any, June?"

"Just the one I said."

"Right, that was a vague answer. Care to elaborate?"

"What do you mean?" she asks, tilting her head all the way up to me as I loom over her.

"Noah. Remind her of all the ways she can be fucked."

He moves to squat in front of her, but she keeps looking at me.

"I can fuck your delicate hand or your heavy breasts," he says as he swipes a bit of chocolate on the underside of one tit. Her eyes flicker closed for a long second.

"That sassy mouth," he continues when I reach down to frame her chin and run my thumb over her lips, feeling her desperate little gasps for more air as her body heats up. "That wet pussy, or your tight little ass."

"Oh my God," she breathes out on a shiver.

"No fucking any of those things?" I ask her with a smirk, knowing she doesn't know how to answer the question and enjoying watching her squirm.

"Um, no penetration below the waist. I'll defer the rest to you," she says before sucking my thumb into her mouth.

"That's your only stipulation?"

She nods.

"Say the words, June."

"That's my only stipulation."

"You're agreeing to anything else I ask him to do to you?"

"Yes, but if at any time I don't like something, I'll tell you to stop."

"Good girl," I praise. "You understand Noah is here to help enhance your pleasure, and you have nothing to be afraid of, right?"

"I do," she says without hesitancy. "You have to agree to the same thing, Drew. If you don't like anything that's happening, you say stop."

"Trust me, baby, I fucking will," I agree as I drop the items I brought out with me to the floor next to her.

"On your hands and knees now, June. Stick that sweet ass up in the air."

She scrambles into the position while Noah rises and strips down to nothing but his pants. He's fit. I'm more fit. My ego likes that.

I gently push June's legs apart with my foot, then I grab the bottle of lubricant and drip a few drops down the seam of her ass.

"What is that?"

"Preparation," I answer her, working the gel down and rimming that virgin hole of hers. Noah grabs the plug, eyeing me. "Open your mouth for Noah."

"Suck on it, get it nice and wet," he tells her. When he's satisfied, he removes it and hands it to me.

"Relax," I tell her as I slowly start to insert it. It's small, a starter, another thing I'll thank Leighton for, as weird as that conversation may be. "Okay, now bear down. Good, good. Okay, clench. Good girl, June," I say when it's fully seated. I flick it a couple of times and a little whimper escapes her.

"You like how it feels?" I ask, giving one ass cheek a soft swat.

"Yes."

"Thank Noah for his help."

"Thank you, Noah," she says in a weak voice. I slide my hand down, feeling how wet she is. She's practically shaking with a needy desire, and my fingers come back up sopped with it.

"You're very wet, June. It's practically leaking out of your cunt," I tell her. "Is that because of me or Noah?"

"You. It's always for you."

"I know. But maybe we can share, just a little, tonight. Noah, have a seat." I nod to the sofa next to us and gently use the harness to bring June back up to her knees before moving to stand in front of her.

Being the perfect creature she is, June wiggles her ass down to cradle between her feet, getting to the height she's already learned I like. There's a brief wince as the plug shifts, sending sensations she's not yet used to. A smile teases my lips as I watch her discomfort rapidly change into pleasure.

"Let Noah have a taste of you. Coat your fingers with yourself," I say and wait while she does. Her movements are tentative at first, still unused to playing with herself, especially with an audience. After a few seconds, though, she finds a stride. "Fingers out now, June. You don't give yourself pleasure tonight. That's our job. Now hold your hand up for Noah."

She stares back at me while her trembling hand rises up to Noah. He's relaxed in his seat, as if he has no care in the world. As if he's not watching a naked, married couple play at sex games. Leaning far enough forward, he doesn't touch her with anything but his tongue at first. He takes a long lick from the base of her palm all the way up to the tip of her middle finger before he sucks it in.

"Ask him if he likes it," I say.

"Do you like it?"

I almost don't hear her over the sounds wafting up from the street outside.

"It was barely a taste. I'd need more to decide for sure," Noah says, his darkened eyes betraying his calm demeanor.

"Climb up on Noah's lap, face to him, and straddle his thighs." Once she's in position, I pause to evaluate my feelings. I promised myself I wouldn't rush through tonight. No acting on just feeling, passion, and desire. Needing to be in tune with Junie's reactions is the highest priority, of course. Yet, I can't deny that I don't mind Noah's nearness. Instead of being enraged by her pussy hovering less than inches away from his dick, I'm turned on by it. His hands going to her waist to help steady her into position has more blood rushing to my aching cock.

I want his pants gone, so he feels her wetness drip onto his cock that will never have the chance to know how incredibly amazing it feels to sink inside her.

"Up on your knees, nice and tall," I instruct. "Push that ass back so I can fuck you while you offer up those sticky tits for Noah." She takes position as I draw closer, adjusting so that both her legs and his are in between my wide stance.

Cock in hand, I tease her opening, making sure to move the anal plug enough to keep her balance off. Noah guides her legs wider, then keeping a hand on one of her thighs, he loops the other in her harness and pulls her forward. His mouth latches onto a nipple at the same time I thrust forward.

"Oh, fuck," she cries at the same time I think it, the small phallus in her ass making it a snugger fit than usual. My head falls back, and I let myself just feel... her wetness, her heat, her walls clenching in time with my movements.

"You have the best breasts, June. Drew's a lucky man."

Right, Noah is here.

I reach around to knead the one his mouth isn't on. The harder my thrusts, the harder it is for her to keep those tits in his reach, and by the noises he's making, he's enjoying his mouth on her.

"Scoot closer to him," I say, pulling out and moving her to where I want her so I can climb up on the sofa behind her. Skin to skin, her tight against my chest, I can feel how warm she is. The air is thick with all three of our sexual tension.

I grasp the low back of the couch, one hand on either side of Noah's wide shoulders, and start fucking June again. Pushing her heaving chest into his face where he can easily latch on. One of June's hands tangles in the back of his hair, keeping him where she wants him as the other comes up to tangle in my curls as well.

"June."

Tilting her head up and to the side, her eyes flick between mine, searching for a sign of distress, I think. But I'm not distressed. Not at all. No, I don't want less of this.

I want more.

"Drew," she begins, but I steal whatever words she was about to say, tangling our mouths together. Her moan sounds as her body takes over all the work. She writhes between us, pushing herself up and down my dick.

"Keep looking at me," I say after releasing her mouth. "Do you want to come?"

"Yes, please." I thrust harder at her politeness.

"Noah, help her out." June's eyes glaze over slightly when Noah's fingers find her clit, brushing my dick with each forward push. I don't hate it. His touch doesn't carry the same rough, calloused tips as my fingers do. They're soft, like an extension of the tender folds of June's cunt.

"Focus on Drew's cock filling you up, June," Noah says against the sensitive skin at the base of her neck. "Feel it in your ass every time he grinds against you. Imagine what it's going to feel like when he shoves that big dick in there next time, instead of that tiny little plug." His fingers vee down on either side of her opening, framing my cock as he thumbs her clit.

Fuck.

June explodes in an orgasm, her body losing all rhythm as she shudders through it with a hoarse cry. I don't stop fucking, and Noah doesn't stop the voodoo magic he's currently performing with his fingers on both of us. He's taken up residency there, cupping her, rubbing along my length, and fingering my balls.

God damn, I'm too close to coming. Thankfully, June's made it through her first climax, collapsing on Noah and allowing me to find my composure outside of her.

"Come here," I call as I fall back into the chair next to the sofa. I watch her make her way on weak legs, moving as quickly as she can manage, appreciating the expression on her face. The one that she always wears when she needs something from me, but I'm too far away. It eases as soon as she clasps the hand I reach out to her, pulling her onto my lap. "You okay, baby?"

"I am," she says quietly, cupping my scruffy cheeks. "Are you okay?"

It's so like her, to check in with me when she was the one who was just flooded with sensation. I'm so fucking in love with this woman. Sometimes, like now, it overwhelms me just how much. There isn't anything I wouldn't do for her. I'd forgive her for anything. I'll love her through Hell and back. I hate that I lost sight of that for as long as I did. Her walking into that hotel room, as horrible as it was, was the best thing that could have happened to me at that point in my lowly life.

June is my savior. My light. My soul's other half. She's the blood once again beating through my battered heart.

"I'm perfect, June."

"Do you mean it? Truly?"

"Junie, yes. You coming for us like that was the hottest thing I've ever seen, and we only just got started."

"We did?"

"Mhm," I hum, giving her a quick, reassuring kiss. "Right now, behind you, Noah's getting naked. No, no, eyes on me, baby," I say when she tries to turn around.

"Sorry, sorry."

"Be patient. I'll let you see his dick," I say, laughing lightly. "First, you need to hop back on mine. Turn around, one leg hanging over each arm of the chair. Spread wide for Noah to see."

Her eyes hood like she might be close to passing out, but she obeys as Noah comes to stand in front of us. He's close, so close I can smell his after-shave. I've never had an attraction to men. I still don't. It's not that I want to fuck Noah Anders. Yet, something about this situation and all our smells swirling in the air… well, it's fucking hot.

Squatting down in between my spread legs, Noah runs his hands up my thighs until they reach the apex. His touch is foreign, different from women. Yes, his hands are soft, but they're firm, confident in ways no woman has ever touched me.

"I'm going to touch you now, Drew, then I'm going to taste your beautiful wife while you fuck her silly."

"I was hoping for raw," June teases.

Damn minx.

"Both," Noah and I say in unison.

Then his hand is on my cock, guiding me to where June is open and ready. But before we get there, his thumb circles and swipes at the precum, causing a stuttering jerk from me.

"Lower down, June. Ride your husband's thick cock."

"Fuck, that's hot," she says as she stares down her own body, watching Noah's ministrations. I can barely see Noah over June's shoulder, but I don't miss when he shoves his thumb, that thumb, into his mouth and sucks it clean.

The fuck?

"Are you bisexual?" I ask.

"I fuck people I want to fuck. I couldn't care less which parts they're working with."

"You want to fuck me, Anders?" I wink at him.

"Only your mouth, so I don't have to hear you speak anymore." He laughs.

"Oh, God," June groans, "somebody needs to fuck me if you two are going to keep talking like this."

"Ride, baby," I tell her in between kisses on her neck as I gather her hair up and out of her face. I pull it tight and wrap it around my fist so I can move her head where I want it, which right now is in the perfect spot for me to whisper in her ear. "Open your eyes, June. Watch Noah."

"How is that so hot?"

I laugh again, because fuck if I know why women get off on guys stroking their own dicks.

"You like Noah's dick, honey?"

"I like yours best," she says as she grinds down on me.

"Correct answer," I say to her. "Put your hands on him, June, and give him a sweet kiss."

She wastes no time, batting Noah's hands away so hers can take their place. I watch as she mimics the strokes he used until his hips begin moving with her. I'm sure she's glad now that we didn't take this off the table, as he thoroughly fucks her hands.

I guide her head forward as Noah leans over to kiss her. His moan brings my eyes up, only to find he's watching me. He's fucking her, kissing her, but keeping watch over me. Making sure I'm not freaking out. By the way she's working him, he knows she's not.

It's all I need to know about who Noah Anders is as a man, and it's nothing like the asshole I always believed him to be.

I wink and the slight tension at the corners of his eyes eases away. He deepens the kiss for a moment before pulling away.

"I'm close, Drew. Tell me where."

"Tits. Junie, stick them out for him and don't you dare stop bouncing on me." I hold her hips, helping her keep the pace I like.

"Okay," she says, leaning forward and pushing her chest out as Noah takes control by wrapping his hand around hers, guiding her just how he needs. "Come for us, Noah."

Her words are all the gentle coaxing he needs.

"Fuck. Fucking hell," he growls as he rises on his toes to rain cum down between their entwined fingers. Spurting it out over her nipples. "God, fuck."

Moving one hand from her hip to her breast, I run my fingers through the mess he just made. Rubbing it in, kneading and pulling as I do. Noah's head vanishes from view, dropping down to his knees. His mouth, his lips, his tongue all join in the fun where June and I are joined. He alternates attention between her clit and the base of my dick, until we're both writhing like animals in heat.

So close, so close. We're both so damned close. Her cunt squeezes me like a vice, my balls heavy with such desire to release.

"Come. Come now," Noah bellows, hot breath fueling the friction of me fucking up into June.

We both shatter in a storm of moans and curses. Her hands reach above her to pull at my hair as her back bows up like she's fucking possessed. To my surprise, I find one of my hands is twisted in her harness, the other holding Noah's head to us, practically forcing him to continue playing us through our last note.

"Holy fucking shit," I say when I remember how to form words. We both watch as Noah rises and dresses. He's done by the time our heaving chests have calmed, June snuggled down in my lap, completely spent.

"How do you feel?" he asks June, standing in front of us and petting her head at a slow, steady pace.

"Fucking fantastic," she says, still a little out of breath. I wrap my arms around her more tightly. Noah bends down and gives her a quick, deep kiss.

"And you? How do you feel?"

I think there is deeper meaning in his question to me, but there needn't be.

"Fucking fantastic," I parrot with a grin.

"Good, take care of each other."

Before he leaves, he presses a slow peck on my lips, leaving me again without words.

CHAPTER 24

June

I startle awake to my phone buzzing beside my bed. Pulling my body into a full stretch that has me rubbing against Drew's sleeping form, I feel every tight muscle. After Noah left last night, we showered together silently. Drew washed me tenderly, kissed me gently, and held me tightly as we both passed out wrapped in each other's arms.

I'm sure we both meant to talk about the turn the night took, but sleep took us before we could. A tickle of apprehension plays at the back of my head, fear that maybe he regrets it. Conversation needs to happen first thing this morning, for sure.

My phone starts vibrating again. Picking it up, I see it's too early for anyone to be calling, including Leighton.

I answer it quietly, hoping not to wake the giant beside me just yet.

"Hey, Love. Everything okay?"

"No. That bitch tried to sell you out."

"What do you mean?"

"Billy, that guy I worked with at the station in California, works for a gossip rag now. Lorelai contacted them, trying to sell them an exposé as Drew's mistress. He said they didn't bite because she didn't seem to know much more about you than what was public record and she wasn't willing to talk about her relationship with Drew."

"Probably afraid to break his non-disclosure," I say.

"Likely. Anyway, I wanted you to know that she's working that angle. Didn't want you to be blindsided if someone does pick up her story. It's unlikely, though. Billy works for the worst. If they won't touch it, nobody will."

"Thanks, Love. I'll be fine, whatever happens there," I reassure her.

"Okay, love you."

"Love you, too."

Months ago, this news would have been harder for me to absorb. A bigger pill to swallow. It's one thing to publish your own life story, but what a cruel betrayal for anyone else to think they have that right. Especially someone who was not even part of the tale to begin with.

We weren't friends then. She was one of Drew's clingers. His biggest, taking everything I know now into account. She'd only know whatever he told her. Which wouldn't be much. He's not a sharer.

Starting the pot of coffee, I try to come up with all the things she hopes to get out of this. Assuming her biggest prize would be Drew… she'd never win him by attacking me or going public with anything about us. Or him. She'd know that unless she's completely unhinged. Strong possibility, that.

I let the coffee brew and walk back to the bedroom. Drew is still fast asleep, his body sprawled out and taking up three-quarters of the bed. He sleeps hot, the blankets pushed off and the sheet barely covering his morning stiffy.

Taking a few moments more to myself, I take him in. A dark curl falls over one eye. Scruff covers his jaw and upper lip; he forgoes daily shaving in the off season, and I've always loved it. The feel of it scratching my skin.

The sheet barely covers any of him, just a portion below his waist, as if it's desperately trying to keep some sense of modesty while he slumbers. I've never known Drew not to be in top shape. He's a fine-honed machine. Yet, since I moved to New Orleans, his physique has changed. Most probably wouldn't recognize the subtle differences, but I do. I noticed that night back home in Seattle. Even since then he's become more toned.

I still don't forgive him. I still want him to suffer in little ways that don't cause real harm but torment him all the same. Someday that want will fade. But not today.

Opening the side table drawer that is full of Leighton gifts, the same drawer Drew dug through yesterday to find the anal plug and lube, I grab the item I'm looking for. Then I crawl onto the bed and onto Drew. I curl my fingers into his and stretch our arms above his head.

"Mmm, good morning," he mumbles with a one-sided smile.

"Good morning, husband," I reply as I snap the ridiculous pink fuzzy handcuffs onto his wrist, then quickly attach them to one of the slats of the headboard.

"The fuck?" he asks, trying to sit up.

"Shh, don't move. Just listen," I whisper right above his lips.

"June?"

"Last night was amazing and I don't regret it happening. I appreciate that you sacrificed a part of who you are to give that to me. But it doesn't have to happen again. I don't need every fantasy I have fulfilled. Do you understand?"

"Yes, but—"

"No," I say, kissing him. "I'm not done. I need you to tell me how you feel about last night. Are you okay? Are we okay?"

There's still a sleepy look on his face as he brushes hair out of my face with his free hand.

"We're better than okay, June. I knew going into it that it would be hard letting him, anybody, touch you. And you him. But I gotta say, that bastard has some magical fuckery that calms me down. Makes him non-threatening, you know?"

"I know. I swear he's a wizard," I say, smiling.

"Besides he, I don't know how to explain it. I guess he was good about keeping the attention on you but making sure I was never left out of what was happening between you two. Did you know he was pansexual?" he asks, his eyes a little clearer now.

"Nope, the subject never came up. Did you like it?" I don't think Drew is into guys, but he didn't seem to hate any of the things Noah did to him. Personally, I loved it. That, too, is probably because it was Noah and I trust him. If Drew had walked through the door with another woman and she touched him the way Noah did, I would have had a breakdown. But Noah enjoying Drew's body along with me didn't give me any anxiety.

The flip side of this is why I'm worried about Drew now. Because if a woman touched me, kissed me, helped get me off—that likely wouldn't feel weird to him. Me jacking off another guy… well, that needs to be discussed.

"I didn't hate it. It's not something I'd seek out. I'm not attracted to Noah. I don't want to fuck him or anything. But it felt good, so I'm not going to question it."

"You don't want him to suck your cock, Drew?" I tease him with a kiss under his chin.

"Mmm, no, I want you to."

"I have other plans," I whisper in his ear after trailing kisses along his jaw. "First, I want to tell you something."

I sit up, still straddling his waist, his hardening cock nestled between my ass cheeks as he wiggles to get comfortable.

"I see the work you've been putting in, both physically and mentally. I see you, baby. And I'm proud of you."

"Junie." His voice comes out a little pained and my heart breaks for him. He didn't grow up with that type of praise. It's difficult for him to hear it still. "You don't have to say that. I get that I'm beyond redemption, no matter how much work I put in."

"Drew, no," I say, placing my hands on his chest. "I don't believe anyone is beyond redemption. It's not like you killed a man. You fucked up. You broke my heart. That doesn't mean that I don't see how hard you're trying to piece it back together. Forgiveness hasn't come yet, but I love you enough to keep working on that, while we keep working on us."

His eyes close and his body sinks down into the mattress.

"You haven't said," he mouths quietly.

"What?"

"You haven't said you love me in so long, I started to believe I'd never hear it again." He doesn't open his eyes. Instead, he shuts them tighter, as if afraid I'll snatch my words back away from him.

I've said so many times these past months that I hate him. Hell, I did in those moments. Though, I wouldn't have been able to feel such strong emotions if I didn't also feel the love. I would have just been indifferent.

I was anything but that.

"Drew, look at me." It takes a moment for him to work himself up to it. "I love you. I never stopped. I never will. I'll love you forever. I'll love you through it all."

"Fuck, Junie. Fuck," he says, relief and tears flooding his eyes. One leaks out to trail down the side of his beautiful face. I lean down and kiss it away. "Uncuff me so I can hold you."

"No. One more thing."

He raises an eyebrow in question.

"Lorelai is shopping the tabloids, trying to sell a story."

"Are you fucking kidding me?" he yells as he wraps his free arm around me and once again, tries to sit up. "Fuck, June. Uncuff me. I'm going to fucking murder her."

"Baby, no." I curl my body around his as best as I can while he struggles. "This is why you're cuffed. Calm down and listen to me."

His body deflates, but his eyes are a swirling mass of wanton anger.

"Why are you so calm?"

"Because Leighton said it's unlikely anyone will buy it. She doesn't have anything juicy to say. That's not my problem this morning," I tell him calmly.

His eyes narrow on me, but he doesn't ask any questions.

"My issue is with you and your poor choice of friends." Fear flashes across his features. I ignore it and continue, "I thought you had better judgment than to spend any time, let alone intimate time, with someone so vile. Honestly, it drops your sex appeal way, way down."

"Are you telling me you don't find me sexy anymore?"

"I'm saying…" I pause to crawl up his body and rise to my knees. Only continuing to speak when my cunt is lined up with his frown as I stare down my body at him. "That you would be best served by finding a way to prove you're still as hot as you were before I had this knowledge."

A relieved laugh spills out of him.

"Fuck, Junie. I'm the dumbest motherfucker on the planet and I give you full permission to remind me of that every day for the rest of our lives," he says before he shows me just how talented that mouth of his can be.

Super Bowl weekend comes upon us quickly. My schedule has been a whirlwind with filming various events. I'm gone all day and exhausted every night I walk into the condo. But Drew is always there, waiting for me. Usually with a warm bath run, a glass of wine poured, and dinner ready.

He's enjoying pampering me just as much as I'm enjoying being pampered. We have made time to talk to Dr. Fillmore once a week. We've discussed keeping that a priority until all my fragile little holes are neatly darned. We're getting there, but we both know it's a slow process.

That's okay, we've got the rest of our lives.

Tonight, the night before the big game, we have a party to attend. Noah and some of the Saints are hosting a big to-do for all NFL stars and celebrities in town. I'm excited for it, instead of being a ball of anxiety over it, a first for me. I feel like a bigger part of Drew's world now. I'm not just his quiet, proper wife.

I'm June Fucking McKenna, and I'm no longer sitting on the sidelines of my own life.

Reed came to town a few days back, finally. He and Leighton played thumb wars to decide who got which side of their house. I wish that were a joke. Regardless, he's behind door A, furnishing away. Now that Drew and I are in a better place, one with a strong commitment for a future, Reed's changed his tune about spending time here. We've discussed making this our off-season home. Permanently.

Reed and Leighton are both on the guest list tonight. Which will be interesting, to say the least, because Connor Anders will be in attendance, too. And he and Leighton are still whatever it is they are.

"You can text Noel that her tickets will be at will-call tomorrow," Drew says from the other side of the bathroom door as I apply my final coat of lipstick.

He pulled a favor to get my favorite cheerleader and her family tickets in the suite we'll be watching from. Noel and I have gotten closer, thanks to our regular chats. Her father reached out to me and thanked me. He said she'd been more confident since meeting me. She even went without her knee socks a time or two.

Much to my disbelief, I've garnered quite a fair amount of positive attention since deciding to show my scars. My inboxes are flooded daily with messages from other people in similar situations to mine. Jared, as well as Drew's PR people, have both pressed for me to continue to showcase my scars.

I don't want to do it for publicity, but if it helps others, I'll do what I can. Whatever I'm comfortable with, at least.

"Thank you, I appreciate that," I say as I exit the bathroom. Drew is bent over, tying his shoe. He hasn't seen the dress I am wearing tonight. Leighton and I had stumbled across a tiny boutique owned by a local designer. Her clothes were all amazing, lots of lace with bits of leather delicately worked in.

She recognized me and asked if she could customize one of her pieces for me. What was a deep emerald green dress is now a two-piece ensemble. The top is cropped and strappy, barely there. All vegan leather with lace inserts in strategically placed areas. The skirt is the same, made from the same imitation leather, and fits me like it's my own skin down to my mid-calf, with one extremely high slit all the way to my upper thigh.

"No problem, baby," he says and looks up. "Fucking hell, Junie. You're going to get me arrested looking that gorgeous tonight."

I laugh, but my ego likes the warped compliment.

"You going to fight over me tonight, Mr. McKenna?"

"I might have to, you minx."

"Doubtful, but I like that you would." I press a light kiss on the crown of his head so that I don't muss him or my lips.

"Anything for you."

It only takes minutes to get to our destination, but the place is a madhouse of camera flashes and paparazzi. Drew would normally bundle me up close to him for situations like these. Tonight, I stride hand in hand with him, feeling comfortable in my own skin. Confident next to his side.

Noah's inside and greets us as soon as we walk in, giving me a kiss on the cheek and Drew some strange bro-shake I don't understand. The two have bonded even more since that night. They work out together several times a week, dragging me along with them when I feel I need it. I'm loving my fatter ass, as does Drew, so I go enough to feel healthy, is all. They still pretend they're enemies because men are strange like that.

There haven't been any more playdates with Noah, by mutual agreement of all. There also hasn't been any awkwardness.

"If you head upstairs, you'll find Leighton on the karaoke stage that was set up especially for you two," Noah says to me.

"You didn't?"

"I did, and your husband gave them the list of songs."

"Oh my God, you two are the best!" I jump up to give Noah a hug, but Drew's hands immediately latch onto my hips and pull me back down.

"You heard him. The full ABBA catalog is because of me. He doesn't need you to throw yourself at him, Mrs. McKenna," the grumpy bear growls into my ear, making me shiver and Noah laugh.

I tilt my head back nice and far so I can see Drew and thank him properly with a kiss. "Thank you, Drew."

"You're welcome. Let's head up. Anders has other things to do."

"We'll catch up later, Noah. Text me if you need any help."

"Thank you, my sweet June. I'll find you all a little later," he says, smirking.

"Fuck off, Anders," Drew says, taking my hand and leading me away.

As promised, Leighton is on the stage already, singing a duet with Connor. My brother broods in the corner, eyes trained on my best friend.

We saunter to him, and I encase him in a big hug. "Hi, big brother."

"Hey," he says, returning the hug, but his eyes don't leave the stage.

"You could just kiss her, like she wants."

Reed gives me a sharp look. It has its intended effect and I drop the subject.

I don't let him damper my high, though. Leighton and I sing our hearts out in between other guests. There are a few professionals here tonight and they give a great show to the sports crowd. One hot R&B singer even dragged Leighton up on stage to perform with him. She's never been so giddy in her life. Even Reed is infected by her happy contagion, just briefly.

The hit of the night, though, is when five former NFL All Stars take the stage for a rendition of Spice Girls' "Wannabe." Karaoke may be low brow entertainment in this circle, but they're all embracing it tonight.

As various acquaintances come and go from our table, I find none of it makes me uncomfortable at all. I don't feel the need to hide away or find safety in Drew's arms. Drew notices and instead of how he'd typically hover, he lets me shine.

It's like I'm June 2.0. The reasons for my upgrade are horribly depressing, but I'll embrace how I feel now. Stronger, more confident, more self-reliant, and far less needy for validation from anyone.

That all changes when I walk off the stage after singing "Mama Mia" and my eyes dart to an ice-blonde woman slinking her arms around my husband from behind him.

"Oh, fuck," Leighton says beside me, her hand taking mine. She guides me through the crowded room so that my eyes only leave the scene at our table when another body blocks it from my view. It happens more times than I'd like.

It takes seconds but of course in my distressed state it feels like an eternity.

Why the hell is she here? How is she here? Noah would've never invited her, nor would he have knowingly let her in. I quickly dart my eyes around the room, looking for him. I don't see him, and I stop looking when we're close enough to our table to hear the conversation happening.

"What the fuck are you thinking?"

"You wouldn't answer my calls. What was I supposed to do, Drew?"

"You were supposed to fuck all the way off. I'm sure I've told you this already," I say when I step up next to my, clearly irate, husband.

"I'm not here to talk to you, June." Her spine straightens as she tries to compose herself.

"Oh, honey, I don't care what your intentions are. You need to leave."

"Lorelai, go," Drew drawls through terse lips.

"Not until you let me explain. Please?"

"Nobody wants to hear it. Leave."

Her eyes flash back to me, changing instantly from the sad, pleading ones she used to look at Drew, to white hot rage for me.

"Fuck you, June," she yells, inches from my face. Drew tries to step between us, but my hand automatically pushes him back. This is my fight. And I want it. Badly. "You have everything. Everything! You don't even deserve it."

She laughs as I stare her down. It's tinged with hysteria and mockery. It's the latter that makes me seethe. It's the direction I know her thoughts are going that makes my fists clench with anger, with all my past pent-up insecurities.

I'm ready when she says it.

"He's only with you because he feels sorry for you," she spits.

I swing.

Damn, it feels good. And, yeah, it hurts, too. I've never punched anyone in my life, not even Reed when we were kids and he'd torment me relentlessly over the stupidest shit.

Lifting me up in restraint, Drew takes a big step back at the same time Noah appears.

"What is she doing here?" He gestures to Lorelai, who is picking herself up off the ground. Blood trickles from her lip, which is already swelling. Nobody offers help, though we have the entire room's attention. The karaoke music plays on, but the only voices are the ones giving me different forms of congratulations and the ones barely stifling laughter.

It's hard to watch. Hard to bear witness to such a low point in any human's life. I'd be ashamed of the part I play in it if she hadn't brought it on herself. Being the bigger person isn't always easy. I'm only human, too.

She doesn't make it easier by keeping her mouth shut. Instead, she keeps pleading.

"I needed the money," she says in a watery voice, though her eyes are dry. "I… I need the money."

I want to look away, to be done with this pathetic creature that I once believed was so beautiful I could never compare. I don't. I just stare instead.

"Enough, Lorelai," Noah snaps, and she instantly quiets. Her face turns down and her shoulders slump. "Apologize."

"No," she whimpers as her hands begin to tremble.

"Noah." I sigh. I don't want this spectacle. I don't feel sorry for her, but this isn't what the night should be about and it's not the sort of attention Drew or I crave. He's still holding me, not that he needs to. But holding sentry, just in case.

"Apologize. Now," he speaks to her, but he gives me a warning look to keep out of it. He's not charming Noah right now. He's bossy, dominant Noah. He's taking control of the situation. And maybe something more. The look in his eyes speaks of vengeance or retribution.

"I'm s-sorry." It's barely loud enough to hear and she makes no attempt to look at us as she says it. I nod all the same.

Noah gives me a sad smile before he picks Lorelai up as if he's a firefighter fleeing a burning building with deadweight on his shoulder. I watch him go, her platinum locks covering his back, nearly sweeping the floor behind them.

"That was so fucking hot, Junie. I'm going to make you come harder than you've ever come in your life, tonight."

"You fucking better." I laugh, letting some of the awkward tension rinse away. "And tomorrow morning, before the game, I want you to take me to see our house."

EPILOGUE

Drew

A year later, June still finds new ways to push my buttons in that acute way that makes me want to fuck her silly. Tonight, we'll be doing it in our newly refurbished New Orleans haunted house. Because my season officially ended two days ago when I led the team to a Super Bowl win.

For a long time, I was convinced nothing could feel as good as sex.

For a long time, I was a dumb son of a bitch.

Winning the Super Bowl is better. Better yet is being loved by June. Nothing feels as good as that.

My mind is clear now. My priorities straight. I'm not the selfish twat my father raised me to be by instilling the attitude that I should take whatever I want before it's taken away from me. And the only voice in my head guiding the direction my life takes… is mine. It's getting damn good at telling me to make the best decisions to keep my family together. It also reminds me to stay focused on the field. Listening to my own voice is paying off.

Therapy is still a part of life. Worth every penny, if you ask me. While I don't chat with Dr. Fillmore on a weekly basis, we keep in touch via regular monthly appointments. June still has Rebecca, but occasionally, if life is extra heavy, she'll pop in on one of my sessions. Or vice versa. Neither of us minds the two extra people in our relationship. They've helped us become the couple we always wanted to be. We're healthier and happier with their help. More importantly, we're stronger. A team.

The most important team in my life.

There's a nightly routine now. We crawl in bed, I tell her I love her, and then I thank her for loving a wretch like me enough to help me heal in ways I wasn't strong enough to do for her when I should have.

Often, it's followed by me shoving my cock into her. But those stories aren't anyone's fucking business, so I'll keep them to myself. I'm not as careless with her as I used to be. I won't be that way ever again.

Some men could learn a lot from me. They wouldn't listen. I surely never did.

I wish I had. I wish I never saw the pain I caused in Junie's eyes. It's still there, sometimes. Maybe it will never leave fully, and that's okay. It's no less than I deserve.

Hearts are mighty, resilient machines. They're also fickle, fragile creatures. Either way you look at them, they need proper care and tending. Not just of your own, but of those that are given into your care. I fucked that up real good.

I never will again.

Because I love my strong, capable, kind, gracious, beautiful wife the way she loves me. Without condition. Through all our faults. For better or worse.

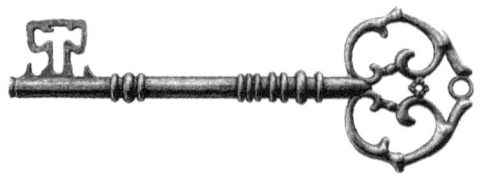

ACKNOWLEDGEMENTS

I almost dedicated this book to my younger self. To the girl who still believed dreams could come true. The one who once thought she would be an astronaut, then a fashion designer, then a pop star even though she's tone deaf. The child that knew nothing could stop her if she really put her mind to it.

She was lost somewhere along the way. In between bills and parenting, if I had to guess. But she's found her way to the surface again. Because it's never too late, and sometimes it's just not the right time.

This time feels right.

So, thank you to that tenacious girl who didn't give up or give in.

Thank you to my husband for giving me the time I needed. To my daughter for being my constant cheerleader. To my ride or die friends who never second guessed me, instead encouraged me every step of the way.

I want to give a very special thank you to Chanpreet who took time away from her life to read my first messy draft. And then my second. Not only was your feedback invaluable, but I firmly believe you are the best of humanity, and I am blessed to have you in my life.

Mylene, your messages gave me the courage boost I needed when I needed it most. You get dibs on Noah as payment. I hope you're ready for him.

To all the members of the Cheating Romance Readers group, thank you for getting me through the past two years.

Zainab... Woman, you will forever be the infectious little voice in the back of my mind egging me on by throwing your panties at the heroes I write. Thank you.

And Autumn, thank you for being someone I never doubted I could trust to hold my hand through every step. Drinks are on me when I see you next.

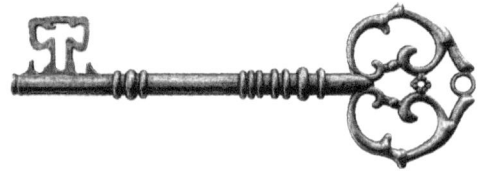

ABOUT THE AUTHOR

Alison lives somewhere in the shadow of a Pacific Northwest Mountain, bordered by the Puget Sound, and not too far from the country roads she grew up on. When she's not writing, she can be found avidly reading, traveling with a youthful wanderlust, or slowly turning the inside of her home into her own personal houseplant jungle.

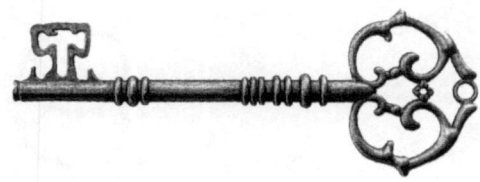

MORE FROM ALISON RHYMES

BRUTAL PLAY

Mistress.

Whore.

Lorelai has been called every name in the book. Except for the ones she's always dreamed of.

My love.

Mine.

Noah Anders is the only man to have ever owned her heart. But it's her soul he wants.

Theirs is a battle of wills, tempers, ego, friendship, and loyalty.

He wants retribution.

She just wants to survive.

BITTER PLAY

Reed Turner has loved his sister's best friend, Leighton, for damn near a decade. He's given her space to grow in her career and her life. Now he's ready to claim the woman he's always believed was his. It's too bad another man in her life keeps getting in the way.

Leighton Ward has never been in love. Now, just as so many things are changing in her life, she finds two men vying for her heart. Both hold strong ties to her future and making the wrong decision comes with heavy consequences.

He knows what he wants.

She's as confused as ever.

DECONSTRUCTING DELILAH

A modern-day retelling of Samson and Delilah…

As the son of a preacher, Pope Blackwell believed he learned the difference between good and evil early in life. After all, it was beaten into him regularly. Now as an adult, he's traded in his life of abuse for one where he holds all the power.

When a young woman strolls into his life full of more bravery than she should possess, he becomes consumed by her fire.

Delilah believed escaping her family's abusive ways would be the hardest challenge of her life. Then she met Pope Blackwell.

One sinner and one saint. A world of differences between them.

Faith. Experience. Age.

His obsession only grows as she challenges him until he's ready to topple any pillar that stands in her way, and she'll fight every demon to be by his side.

RAINFALL

I met the love of my life at ten years old.

At sixteen, I gave him my heart.

Three years later he was drafted to the NHL and moved across the country.

Five years after, he's back. And he's meeting his daughter for the first time.

I still hate him.

Even if my heart says that's a lie.

At ten years old, she changed my life.

At sixteen, I told her I loved her.

Three years after, I left and broke her heart.

Five years later, I'm coming back home to the surprise of my life.

I hate her for it.

Even though my brain says this is all my fault.

FLURRY

Willa

I've been in love with him for years, despite knowing he could never be mine.

Now his charming new boyfriend is determined to include me in all their plans.

Zander

I've been infatuated with him for years, despite us being in different states.

Now we're living in the same city with the only woman who's come close to holding my heart.

Damian

I've been intrigued by her for years, despite us never knowing each other.

Now I just need to convince the two people I care most about that three is better than two.

Flurry is an MMF Hockey Romance

TEMPEST

You can fall in love in a matter of days.

It can take years to recover from the loss of it. I know that all too well. When I fell for Gavin Vaughn, I never expected to watch him marry someone else. The experience changed me, shaped the woman I became.

Now he's divorced and wanting to reconnect after twenty years. As if that same shattered heart doesn't still beat inside me.

He's as charming as he ever was, better looking, too. And a star player for the NHL team in the city I just relocated to.

I'm not that same girl who loved him and watched him leave. I'm a woman who built her own empire from scraps. I'm also the woman who will be mentoring his daughter to do the same.

I'm the woman who can still be brought to her knees by the only man she ever cared about. But it's going to take more than sly smiles and bouquets of flowers to convince me he's worth my time. Or my heart.

WHIRLWIND

Data. Numbers. Facts.

That's what I know.

I'm not great with relationships or men. I don't even date. My entire sexual experience can be reduced to three nights of trauma.

Imagine my surprise when one of hockey's best players with the worst reputation takes interest in geeky old me.

Tyson Murphy isn't what I need in my life. He's hung up on his ex-girlfriend and runs through women like he runs down opponents on the ice. The last thing he needs is a woman who is terrified of intimacy.

The last thing I want is to be is just another puck in his net.

We're oil and water. Order and chaos. Logic and emotion. We shouldn't mix.

So why won't he stop pursuing me?
And why do I suddenly crave the one thing I've avoided my whole adult life?
Love.

www.ingramcontent.com/pod-product-compliance
Lightning Source LLC
Chambersburg PA
CBHW050021120726
47903CB00006B/1864